One Quick Obsession

CARRIE ANN RYAN

NEW YORK TIMES BESTSELLING AUTHOR

One Quick Obsession

One Quick Obsession

The Cage Family
Book Four

Carrie Ann Ryan

One Quick Obsession
By: Carrie Ann Ryan
© 2022 Carrie Ann Ryan

Cover Art by Sweet N Spicy Designs & Wildfire Designs

This book is a work of fiction. Names, characters, places, and incidents either are products of the author's imagination or are used fictitiously. Any resemblance to actual events, locales or persons, living or dead, is entirely coincidental.
No part of this book can be reproduced in any form or by electronic or mechanical means including information storage and retrieval systems, without the express written permission of the author. The only exception is by a reviewer who may quote short excerpts in a review.

All content warnings are listed on the book page for this book on my website.

NO AI TRAINING: Without in any way limiting the author's [and publisher's] exclusive rights under copyright, any use of this publication to "train" generative artificial intelligence (AI) technologies to generate text is expressly prohibited. The author reserves all rights to license uses of this work for generative AI training and development of machine learning language models.

Praise for Carrie Ann Ryan

"Count on Carrie Ann Ryan for emotional, sexy, character driven stories that capture your heart!" – Carly Phillips, NY Times bestselling author

"Carrie Ann Ryan's romances are my newest addiction! The emotion in her books captures me from the very beginning. The hope and healing hold me close until the end. These love stories will simply sweep you away." ~ NYT Bestselling Author Deveny Perry

"Carrie Ann Ryan writes the perfect balance of sweet and heat ensuring every story feeds the soul." - Audrey Carlan, #1 New York Times Bestselling Author

"Carrie Ann Ryan never fails to draw readers in with passion, raw sensuality, and characters that pop off the page. Any book by Carrie Ann is an absolute treat." – New York Times Bestselling Author J. Kenner

"Carrie Ann Ryan knows how to pull your heartstrings and make your pulse pound! Her wonderful Redwood Pack series will draw you in and keep you reading long into the night. I can't wait to see what comes next with the new generation, the Talons. Keep them coming, Carrie Ann!" –Lara Adrian, New York Times bestselling author of CRAVE THE NIGHT

"With snarky humor, sizzling love scenes, and brilliant, imaginative worldbuilding, The Dante's Circle series reads as if Carrie Ann Ryan peeked at my personal wish list!" – NYT Bestselling Author, Larissa Ione

"Carrie Ann Ryan writes sexy shifters in a world full of passionate happily-ever-afters." – *New York Times* Bestselling Author Vivian Arend

"Carrie Ann's books are sexy with characters you can't help but love from page one. They are heat and heart blended to perfection." *New York Times* Bestselling Author Jayne Rylon

Carrie Ann Ryan's books are wickedly funny and deliciously hot, with plenty of twists to keep you guessing. They'll keep you up all night!" USA Today Bestselling Author Cari Quinn

"Once again, Carrie Ann Ryan knocks the Dante's Circle series out of the park. The queen of hot, sexy, enthralling paranormal romance, Carrie Ann is an author not to miss!" *New York Times* bestselling Author Marie Harte

For the ones who look in the mirror and think they aren't enough.
You are.
I promise you.
Those voices lie.
You are powerful.

The Cages

The Denver Cages:
- Aston
- Flynn (t)
- Hudson (t)
- Dorian
- James
- Theo
- Ford

The Colorado Springs Cages:
- Isabella
- Sophia

THE CAGES

    Kyler
    Emily
    Phoebe

The Cages in Age Order
    Aston
    Flynn (t)
    Hudson (t)
    Dorian
    Isabella
    James
    Theo
    Sophia
    Kyler
    Ford
    Emily
    Phoebe

Chapter One
Hudson

When I moved back to Cage Lake, I hadn't thought much of it. In fact, it wasn't technically moving back as I had never lived there permanently. I'd only been there during the summers and some other vacation times with the family. I'd lived all over the country after high school, because I had enlisted rather than dealing with certain parts of my family. Not my brothers, those I could handle. No, it was the rest of them.

Being overseas hadn't been a picnic. I held back a shudder trying not to go too far down that path. And yet here I was, in a town that was not my own, but I had nowhere else to go. I didn't want to live in a big city, didn't want to live in a place where I had to truly start over again. I just wanted to live in the woods and not deal with people. I was never allowed to do that because apparently when you lived in a small town, all you did was deal with people. That was not in the terms of service when I decided to move here.

Because of course my family owned the damn town. Maybe not the title of each property, but enough of them that they named the freaking thing after us. There was really no going back to normalcy and anonymity after that.

In retrospect, moving to a town that held my last name probably wasn't the best place to hide, but I hadn't been thinking clearly when I had come here.

So now I had to deal with people. Daily.

Because once my dad died, may he rest somewhat in peace, somebody had to take care of all the properties. And it wasn't like he had been doing a good job of it. So Aston, James, and Flynn had been doing a decent go of it—with Flynn being the one who dealt with things in the majority once Dad had walked away from the company. Flynn rarely came to Cage Lake with his full-time job at Cage Enterprises in Denver.

So when I had decided to move back permanently, they'd all been so happy. Not that I was back in the country, well, maybe. But no, because now somebody could do their dirty work. And that of course made it sound like we were part of the mob or something. And I wasn't sure we weren't. I mean, I'd been away for a while, and who knew what some of my brothers got up to, but I was pretty sure we were clean on that front. Dad, however? Dad I wasn't quite sure about.

We owned multiple businesses, residential properties, and land, which we knew we would never develop so we could keep the town looking how it needed to. Like it wasn't some overrun piece of land in the Colorado mountains. Which, these days, was hard to find. The number of developers who came after my family, including stomping up to my fucking house, was ridiculous. Once they got to know me though, nobody came by my house. They knew better than that. And I hadn't even shot at one of them. I was growing.

I held back a snort at that. Okay, maybe not growing, but I was too tired to deal with that bullshit. And now they knew it.

So while the Cages owned many of the businesses in town, our biggest source of income was right on the edge of town.

And the source of my annoyance. And possibly my nemesis.

I hated the resort. Full of uppity rich people who did not care about anybody else. They paid for their overpriced hot toddies, cocoa, bourbon, and rental skis. Because while most people brought their own, some people wanted to rent something from the Cages. Because apparently that meant something to them.

If they only knew all of our family secrets. Of

course I didn't even know all of our family secrets, and the media had given most of them away.

But when Isabella had met Weston and decided to spend half of her time in Cage Lake, I was thrilled. Yes, because I liked my sister—not that I would ever tell her that. But also, because she, a brilliant forensic accountant, was also going to take on the responsibility of dealing with the business side of the resort.

While I didn't go through books or anything, not unless they needed me to, I was the guy that all of the business owners spoke to if they needed something.

It was my worst nightmare.

I just wanted to do my art in peace and pretend everyone else didn't exist.

It was kind of hard to do that when you had eleven siblings. Many of which were starting to find their significant others so therefore adding more people to my circle.

And since Isabella was out of town, doing something with Weston's siblings, I really hadn't paid attention, I had to deal with the resort.

I was just not okay with that.

I rubbed my temples as I made my way inside the back entrance. The place was closing down, although just the public areas. There was twenty-four-hour room service, a full-time concierge, and people would be milling about throughout their rooms, but the main lobby would be quiet.

The daytime staff would be gone, and the nighttime staff would come in.

I didn't need to speak to any of them. Instead I just needed to fix a couple things. I wasn't a damn handyman, and I wasn't in the mood to be alone at home.

And how was that for irony. Because I was the dumbass who pushed people away so I could stay at home alone, and now I didn't want to deal with it.

And it had nothing to do with that phone call. Or that nightmare.

I walked inside and nodded at a guest who happened to be going to their room. They were decked out in their finery, weaving a bit from their alcohol consumption, but she just smiled before leaning into her husband. Or at least who I thought was her husband. I wasn't going to judge.

The guy scowled at me, and I scowled right back. I didn't really fit in with this crowd with my worn jeans, flannel, and beard that I needed to trim. They could just deal with it. My hair was too long at this point too, and I was starting to match my twin's look of roughness, but then again, he was usually a little cleaner cut than I was.

He just cursed more than me.

At least that's what I told myself.

I didn't know why we kept this resort open. Yes, it was great for the town, yes it was good income for the company. Why did we have to do something in which we had to make rich people happy?

And now I was just being an idiot.

I moved down the hall towards the back offices. After I slid my key card to get through security, I tried to think about all the things I needed to get done tonight. I wanted to work on my art piece, but it was turning out to be far more difficult than I thought. Maybe I would head down to Harper's later and work on another mural. That would clear my head. And I liked my brother's girlfriend. She might seem sweet and innocent, but she could kick anybody's ass if they ever decided to come and hurt her family. And the Cages were now her family.

I liked her.

I could be doing art. I could be working on my house. I could be doing anything else. Instead I was at this damn resort trying to fix a doorknob that kept getting stuck.

Again, not my job, but if I kept my hands busy, I wouldn't have nightmares. And that sounded a lot better to me.

When I got to the manager's office though, I frowned. The door was open, not locked in place like it usually was. Scarlett was damn good with security. She was damn good at most things, which was why we always butted heads. Because I didn't like her knowing that I thought she did a damn good job. She got all uppity and looked down at me. And I wasn't in the mood to deal with that.

But she never left the door open.

I slid my hand in my pocket, gripping my knife, as I slowly opened the door fully. She stood there, alone, as I scanned the room, but it took me a moment to let go of the knife.

Because while she was alone, she wasn't sitting at her desk working.

Instead the image in front of me made my jaw tense, and anger surged to the surface.

Scarlett, in all her beauty, with her light blonde hair flowing down her back, and that icy way she could put down anybody who tried to hurt her, stood in front of her mirror, her main shirt off and over the chair, in only her pants and tank top.

And there were bruises all over her. She pulled up part of her shirt since I knew she hadn't seen me yet, and the dark bruises turning blue and green there put a metallic taste in my mouth.

"Who. Hurt. You?"

She met my gaze in the mirror, her eyes widening. Her face went deathly pale, before her jaw tensed, and that familiar snarl covered her face. She whirled, sliding down her top.

"Get out!" she yelled as she scrambled for her shirt.

I moved forward, hands at my sides. I was a good foot taller than her, and could scare the shit out of her, but it wasn't like I could look any smaller than I was. I'd be damned if she didn't tell me what the hell happened.

"I repeat. Who hurt you?"

She quickly buttoned up her blouse, her hands shaking.

"I'm fine," she lied. Because it was a damn lie. "I went skiing and hurt myself. I was just checking the bruises."

I leaned forward and reached out to grip her chin. My breath caught as the bruise on the side of her jaw had only just now revealed itself to me when she turned.

And she flinched. *Fucking flinched.*

I let my hand drop, and I told myself to breathe. "Don't fucking lie to me."

"And maybe you should just get over yourself. I don't owe you any answers. Get out. You may own this place, but you don't own me. Get out, get out, get out, get out."

She repeated the words over and over again, before her knees went weak, and tears slid down her face.

I had never once seen Scarlett Blair crack. Not in all the times that we'd yelled at each other, fought, or poked at each other just because we knew we could handle it.

And that scared me more than anything.

I reached out and caught her before she hit the ground and held her to my chest.

Because I knew exactly who had done this.

And I tried not to let the memories slam into me. Because this was all too familiar, and I had failed the first time.

I would kill him. I didn't tell her that, I just let her break down in my arms. I vowed to myself right then and there, I would kill him.

Just like before.

Chapter Two
Hudson

1 Year Later

Fire licked up the side of the building, radiating heat through the wood and stone, scorching my skin. I winced, taking a step back, and bumped into Fox.

"Duck and cover!" Hernandez shouted. I hit the deck, covering my head as debris flew over our bodies and the sound of screaming echoed throughout the now shattered room.

Then we were on our feet, crouched down, moving swiftly, and yet not swiftly enough.

"Cage! Behind you!"

I turned, but not quick enough. Light flashed in my eyes, and sound followed—a cacophony of shouts, screams, and silence.

Then I blinked and looked down at the blood coating my hands, the sickly sweet smell muted for some reason. Only the blood wasn't merely my own.

The bodies piled at my feet pressed against my shins, the blood from my fingertips dripping on their torn flesh. Faces of people I knew—who I called friends—stared up at me with empty eyes and gaping mouths.

Fox. Hernandez. Smith. Williams. Martin. Robinson. Lewis. King. Scott.

So many and yet blood trickled down my chest, coating my skin.

And then it was *her*. *Her* face.

She wasn't supposed to be here. She was all the way back over in the States. She was supposed to be safe. Not with me. But safe.

Michelle's eyes changed once again, and Scarlett blinked at me, her mouth barely moving as she whispered a single word.

"Help."

I opened my eyes and realized that my dreams had taken a turn. I sat up, chest heaving, and sweat coating my body. The sheet pooled around my waist, and I ran my hand over my face and through my beard, pissed off.

I didn't have nightmares every night. I honestly had come back from my tours overseas relatively unscathed. I might have earned a purple heart but so did many of my friends. It was the ones who hadn't come back that had done far more than me.

But it wasn't as if I thought about that every day. It had been years since I'd returned home. Years since my life had changed, and I joined the family instead.

I hated the fact that even after all these years, I couldn't get the sight of their blood on my hands out of my dreams. And real life had been far worse than my dreams—though I hadn't held each of their lifeless bodies in my hands. I had been sent home before a few of them had died.

And wasn't *that* a pleasant thought to think of in the morning.

My alarm went off at that moment and I cursed. I hated waking up right before my alarm. Though it wasn't as if I was going to go back to bed anytime soon. Not when Michelle and Scarlett once again decided to pop into my dreams.

With a grunt, I slid out of bed and padded my way to my bathroom.

I stared into the mirror, annoyed that no matter what I did, getting a full night's sleep wasn't going to work. With a sigh, I brushed my teeth, knowing that today was going to be a long fucking day. Thankfully I didn't have to go to the resort. I shuddered, remembering the last time I had truly been there.

Scarlett had shoved me out of that room and refused to tell me a damn thing about why she carried those bruises. That it wasn't my problem, and I wasn't going to be her protector. I spit into the sink, before washing my face and turning on the shower. Of course it wasn't my problem. I'd wanted to fix it.

Scarlett had wanted nothing to do with me. Which was fine. It wasn't as if we liked each other. We yelled at each other more often than not. She was just so *perfect*. She snapped at me with her orders, as if I were some flunky who was supposed to do what she said. She always thought she knew better and ignored anything I had to say. Except of course when she wanted to counter it. That was just Scarlett for you, and I couldn't stand it.

Why she couldn't be as nice as her twin, I'd never know. Because Luna might not be soft-spoken or unopinionated—neither of which were things that I needed or cared about—but she didn't butt her way into everything that you were doing at all times.

I ran my hand over my beard and figured I should probably trim it eventually. This Cabin Man look might work for some, but at this point, it was turning into a recluse look. That was going to have to change.

I smirked, imagining my family's faces if I went to our family dinner tonight clean shaven. I rolled my eyes and washed my hair and beard. There was no way I was getting rid of it.

Flynn, my twin, had shaved recently, showing his baby face skin and firm square jaw, and that was enough for me. I knew what I would look like without a beard, and while we weren't ugly, I liked the beard.

I ran my hands down my body and let them linger over the puckered scars on my shoulder, and down below on my rib cage. Two edged pieces of skin that reminded me of why I had come home. I swallowed hard, pushing away those thoughts. The deeper I shoved them, the further they would stay away. That was how things worked.

I turned off the shower and reached for my towel before wrapping it around my waist. I had a few projects to work on around my house, and then the old Ackerson place, before family dinner tonight.

My siblings Isabella and Dorian were handling everything with the resort these days, and for that I was grateful. I was tired of Scarlett either glaring at me or skedaddling as soon as she saw me. And it *was* a skedaddle. Even in those stilettos that she loved to wear, she took her little steps and practically hid behind a fucking pillar if I walked by. Well, that was just fine for her. She could handle everything on her own. That's what she claimed after all.

My phone buzzed and then buzzed again. And again. And again.

I groaned, knowing what was to come.

The family group chat.

My family wasn't what some would call normal. Nobody would call them normal. My father, the bastard that he was, had not one family, but two. I had grown up with six siblings—all brothers. We had been loud, rambunctious, and probably annoying as fuck. But our nannies had done their best. It wasn't as if our father had been around often to have a hand in raising us, other than to scream at us. Rather, scream at me. I was always Dad's least favorite. Though I never quite knew why.

Our mother, a shrew of a woman if there ever was one, had once been a little softer. But now all she did was try to barge into our lives, as if she hadn't spewed terrible words at us, and those who had married into the family.

Our loving father had been around when he could, running Cage Enterprises, a real estate firm that gained in financing, worked in development, small businesses, environmental research, and God knew what else. I wasn't part of it. Yes, technically I was on the board because all of our siblings were, but I had nothing to do with the family business. Joining the military at age eighteen and running away from home had ensured that.

Dad wasn't around enough to care at first.

In retrospect it made sense. He was traveling for work or traveling down south to Colorado Springs where he not only had a secret second wife, but I had five more siblings.

That meant twelve. Loren Cage had *twelve* kids.

And somehow, we were all becoming friends. A family.

I shook my head, wondering if my father would've ever imagined that. No, not even a little.

We were forced to have a dinner once a month where at least five people had to be in attendance, three from one side, two from another. Lately we'd ended up with more than five at a function because we liked hanging out with each other. And I usually attended if it was up in Cage Lake.

But with eleven siblings, there came one caveat: The Family Group Chat.

It wasn't just *one* family group chat. There was the mega family group chat that had all twelve of us. Then there was the ultra family group chat that had all twelve of us plus any spouses that had been added in over time. Considering Phoebe, Ford, Aston, Isabella, and Sophia were all married, that included a lot of spouses. And Dorian had his fiancée Harper in the group as well.

And from each of those were subsets of family group chats. The original seven had a group chat, just like the Colorado Springs five did. And then there was a mix and match. There was a one of just the women vs the men. There was the one of people who lived in Cage Lake.

Because of course our family, not wanting to just take over part of Colorado, had its own small town set in the mountains of Colorado. Just off I-70, with a beautiful mountain to the west, and a large lake at the north, Cage Lake was everything you could want in a small town. Complete with flower beds at each street that changed with the seasons, and what once was a simple stop sign, had turned into multiple stoplights. The town halls that made those happen apparently had been slightly dramatic.

The main income for the town was tourism, and the resort that the Cages owned to the east of it. A resort that I wasn't going to step in to anytime soon.

As my phone buzzed again, it pulled me back to the present.

Family.

And their group chat.

I was in at least seven of them, maybe more. Though I didn't initiate. I tried to leave them often, but Dorian always found a way to pull me back.

If it wasn't Dorian, it was Flynn.

My damn twin loved reminding me that I was part of this family, and I needed to participate. He had my face. He could just participate for the both of us. But that didn't quite work when it came to reality.

Today's group chat was the group chat of all group chats. The ultra. All twelve of us and spouses.

If I had my sound on, my phone would probably be constantly making that ding sound with the number of texts going through.

I sighed and scrolled back to the beginning of the current conversation, trying to see where it had started and if I needed to be part of this at all. The answer was usually no. Thankfully.

Aston: Dinner tonight. Isabella at Weston's Place. I'm sorry Blakley and I won't be there.

Blakely: Morning sickness is a twenty-four-hour thing and I hate it.

Sophia: I'm sending you some of the drinks that helped me through. Rest, Blakely.

Blakely: Thank you, Sophia. Everything is just, ugh.

Dorian: And now that I'm done thinking of Blakely puking. Aston. Look at you handing over the reins by having the dinner at someone else's place.

Isabella: We had it at your place in Denver last time. It's my turn.

Flynn: Don't forget the pigs in a blanket. Dorian loves the pigs in a blanket.

Dorian: This is true. They are the best. I don't care if it's processed food. They make me happy.

Harper: Are you kidding me right now? Pigs in a blanket. I'm a baker. I could make you anything you'd like, and that's the appetizer you go with?

Dorian: Why are you texting the group chat when you're sitting right next to me?

Harper: So that way everybody else can see what I'm saying.

Weston: Is there a way for me to be removed from the group chat?

Isabella: You're lucky I love you, husband of mine.

Phoebe: You guys, we were sleeping. You do realize that we're visiting friends in Seattle, so we're not in the same time zone as you?

Ford: Sadly, *we* were up, we do have a nine-month-old at home. Why are we starting group chat so early?

Isabella: Kiss Micah's little cheeks for me.

Sophia: At least the girls are still sleeping. But yes, kiss Micah's cheeks.

Aston: I don't know why everybody has their phone not on silent while sleeping. All I was doing was reminding you of the dinner. We're almost done with these. Thank God.

Flynn: I feel like you should throw salt over your shoulder as you text that.

Aston: Who says I didn't?

Dorian: Marrying Blakely really has made you a lot calmer. I like it.

Aston: I would flip you off, but there might be children watching.

Weston: Again. Can I please leave this group chat?

Isabella: No.

Flynn: No.

Dorian: You can. I'll just add you right back in.

My lips twitched as they continued to text about what

they were doing for the rest of the day, and I set my phone down, knowing that I didn't really have to respond. I would be there at dinner, and that was going to be enough.

When my phone buzzed in a way that told me it wasn't a text message, I groaned before answering the video call. My face filled the screen, although there was a brightness in Flynn's eyes that hadn't always been there, a little shinier than mine. At least if you asked our parents.

"Are you naked right now?" Flynn asked as he put his hands over his eyes.

"Maybe. Hold on, let me put on some clothes."

"Why the hell did you answer the phone if you're naked?"

"Because we look the exact same? I don't give a fuck. Why are you calling?" I slid on my boxer briefs, and jeans, and slid on a T-shirt. Flynn had moved his hand from his face, and I watched his eyes narrow at the scars on my body. I hadn't covered them all with ink yet, so he could still see them. So we weren't quite identical anymore. I ignored the twinge.

"Why are you calling? I thought you were enjoying yourself in the group chat."

Flynn's brows rose as he adjusted his tie. He was the vice president of Cage Enterprises and looked the part. We were exact opposites in most ways, but I didn't mind. Just the idea of wearing a suit gave me hives. "Ah. I'm surprised you're reading any part of the group chat."

"You just hate the fact that I turned off the read status on my phone so you can never tell."

"That is true." Flynn ran his hands over his hair. It was getting longer than usual and nearly matched mine. When I cut mine next, Flynn would probably do the same. Only we wouldn't tell each other about it first and it would just happen. Sometimes the twin thing really was a twin thing. "And I don't know why I'm calling…my heart raced earlier when I was in the shower."

I snorted. "Is there something you want me to know? Wait, don't tell me what you were doing in the shower."

Flynn rolled his eyes. "Oh, shut up. But really, I don't know, I just felt like I needed to call you. A twin intuition thing."

I sighed and brought my phone and brother into the kitchen so I could get a cup of coffee. The house was far too quiet and reminded me that I kept putting off getting a dog. There wasn't a storm raging outside, and the heat wasn't currently running, so the silence seemed amplified. Considering it was April, most places didn't need their heat on, yet we were in the mountains. The weather was going to oscillate wildly for the next month or so—even into June.

"I had a nightmare," I finally answered as I pulled out my mug, the coffee brewing.

"Are you okay? Wait. That's a stupid question. Of course you aren't okay." Flynn's tone left little to the imagination when it came to his annoyance at my lack of communication.

I knew he wanted me to open up, but what was there to tell him? People I cared about were dead and there was nothing I could do about it. The one time I'd thought I'd make amends, someone had already taken care of it for me. "I'm fine, Flynn. Just a normal nightmare." That had ended with Scarlett's face. That wasn't *quite* so normal.

While the coffee brewed, I leaned against my counter, looking at Flynn on my phone that I had set on the kitchen island, resting against a fruit bowl that Isabella had brought over that currently held apples for some reason.

Flynn studied me for a moment before giving me a slight nod. "That's good. I don't really like this whole twin thing sometimes."

"You say that, and yet you're the one who mentions it most often."

"You need a dog," Flynn blurted.

My eyes widened. "What?"

"Your house. It's so quiet. You need a dog."

I sighed. "I was just thinking my house was too

quiet. Damn you. But I don't know if I really want a dog."

"Or a cat. Maybe a goat." Flynn snapped his fingers. "Get a goat!"

I couldn't help the groan that escaped. "I'm not getting a goat. Because then Harper and everyone else is going to want to dress that goat in pajamas so it won't get cold."

"Please for the love of God get a goat in pajamas. I'm asking one thing of you." Flynn held up his hands, and I couldn't help but laugh. My chest shook, and Flynn grinned, his shoulders releasing some of that tension.

My brother had made me laugh. He had done exactly what he had been going for.

Flynn looked down at his watch, wincing. "Anyway, I'll see you at dinner tonight?"

"Yes. Since it's in Cage Lake, I'm going. Isabella would probably drag me up the mountain if I didn't."

"Oh, good. I worry about things like that."

I shook my head, pouring my coffee. "You'll be there?"

Flynn nodded. "Aston won't, which I know is killing him."

"He loves organizing all of us."

"Isabella takes over for him when he can't." Flynn grabbed his keys, taking me and the phone to his garage.

"Get to work, brother. I'll see you tonight."

"And don't forget to smile." Flynn winked and hung up before he could see my middle finger.

Dinner, I had a feeling, was going to be a long one.

"Wait. So you're not getting a goat in pajamas?" Emily asked.

I let out a long sigh before glaring at Flynn. "Stop telling everybody I'm getting a goat."

"Oops?" Emily batted her lashes before grinning. "You don't think you should tell your baby sister about a precious baby goat?"

"I'm not getting a goat. I'm not getting any animal. Harper and Dorian have their dog. I don't need one."

"You can't just borrow another person's dog," Dorian said dryly.

Was that a migraine? Yes, I do believe so. "Yes, I can."

"You guys fight about the weirdest things," Emily said as she shook her head. Flynn wrapped his arm around her shoulder and beamed down at her. "Welcome to the Cages. You don't come to enough of these dinners, so you don't really know how insane we are."

That was true enough. As one of the youngest Cages, Emily tended to have the most fixed schedule. She had just been finishing college when everything had changed in our lives, and I knew she was trying to figure out what she wanted in life. After all, her path had varied widely, a little bit like mine had. She and Kyler, my other half-brother, rarely came to these things. She couldn't get out of work as much, and as Kyler was currently touring the world because my brother was a damn rock star, he barely had time to make these things.

Of course, I only showed up when it was in my small town because I rarely ventured into Denver, so I didn't have much leg to stand on there.

"Okay, the girls are down," Sophia said, as she walked inside, and wiped her hands. "I love Violet and Hazel with every ounce of my being, but I wish bedtime was easier." Sophia rubbed her temples, and Isabella came forward and wrapped her arm over her shoulders.

"Where's Cale?" I asked, looking around the room.

We were at Weston and Isabella's house, so of course those two were here, and Dorian and Harper had showed since they lived in Cage Lake part time, and Flynn had come up mostly to annoy me, same with Emily it seemed. Sophia was staying with Isabella, and had brought her kids, and husband Cale. But I hadn't seen him since dinner.

Sophia's smile widened. "He got a promotion at work and is now on a call." She rolled her eyes. "He ignores some of those calls, thankfully. But between his promotion, the twins, and my dance studio, I don't know what sleep is."

"Is there anything I can do to help?" Emily asked.

Sophia reached out and patted Emily's cheek. "No, I've got it. You need to focus on your job. I know getting time off is difficult."

The light seemed to die out of Emily's eyes slightly, but she smiled anyway. "If you ever need perfect toddler clothes, I will do my best to design them for you."

"They're growing so quickly, I would need an entire wardrobe full."

"How are they liking their beds up there?" I asked, taking the attention off Emily. She gave me a thankful look even though I'd rather be anywhere else but here at the moment. Even with family, too many people made me itchy.

Sophia smiled softly at me. "They're beautiful. Thank you for painting them."

I shrugged, ignoring everybody's stares.

While Sophia could have any one of the homes around Cage Lake that our family owns, or part of the land and build something for herself, she usually opted to stay with one of us. Isabella mostly. Isabella had bought two sets of cribs that could turn into big girl beds, as they called them. They had come with just plain wood, and were ornate, but I had wanted to add a little bit more to them. Call me sentimental.

I'd also painted the murals in that room and had done my best to ignore Sophia's quiet, thankful sobs.

"I seriously don't know how you do it," Cale said as he came forward and slid his phone into his pocket. He wrapped his arm around Sophia's shoulder and kissed her temple. "I can barely draw a stick figure."

I shrugged. "It's something I do. And since Weston's sisters said that they would give up one of their rooms for Sophia's twins, it all worked out."

Weston had two younger sisters and a younger brother, who were now adults and living outside the home. When they visited, they all piled together, or stayed in one of the various guest rooms, or in one of our homes. When you happen to own a town, we had a lot of real estate where we could stuff your family and friends when they needed to find a bed.

Conversation turned to the next family dinner, and I frowned, realizing that we were running out of them. In order for the family to keep Cage Enterprises, Cage Lake, and all of the estate business whole, our father had put certain things in his will. We weren't even sure of all of the rules and stipulations yet, but the main thing was we had to have these family dinners.

I didn't know what we would do when we reached the last one. Maybe I wouldn't be dragged out so often. That would be a relief.

By the time everybody was ready to wind down, I was bouncing on the balls of my feet, ready to get home. I loved my family. I really did. But I needed time alone more than anything.

"Hey, Hudson, I wanted to ask you a question," Harper called out as she came forward.

I turned, holding back a frown. "Everything okay?"

"Yes. I think. It's about Scarlett—"

I held up my hand, cutting her off. "No."

Harper's smile dimmed. "Hudson."

"She's your friend. She works for the family business. She doesn't work for me or with me. And she doesn't want me to have anything to do with her." I ignored the annoyance at that last part. *None of my business.*

"But seriously. Hudson."

"No." Dorian gave me a warning look from across the room and I tried to soften my voice. "Harper. I love you like a sister I know you're going to be soon. But no."

"Okay then. Fine." She lifted her chin, the look digging in.

Scarlett wanted nothing to do with me. And I did not want to know anything about her. All she did was get under my skin, and all I did was annoy the fuck out of her. It was better when I didn't have to deal with her. With a sigh, I didn't even bother to say goodbye to anyone before getting in my car and driving around the lake to my place.

I passed the smaller house near mine and let out a

breath as I realized the lights were on. The fact that Scarlett was my neighbor irked me to no end, but the driveway was long enough that technically I didn't *have* neighbors. Yet I could see the lights were on. Scarlett was home and safe.

Unlike Michelle.

And that was just another reminder that I wasn't the hero. And I never would be.

Chapter Three
Scarlett

"How is Mom?" I asked as I poured each of us a glass of the spinach, apple, and other assorted fruits smoothie I had made earlier. I'd been trying different recipes the past month and finally found one that I liked that didn't taste like kale. I hated kale and never put it in my smoothies and yet no matter what I did, I could sometimes taste the evil plant if I mixed too many greens together.

Luna eyed the concoction warily but took the glass from me anyway. The ingredients may sound a little off, but I made a good smoothie. Plus I could add all of my protein and fiber powders to it and call it a day. No, it didn't make up for the fact that I sometimes missed lunch while working at the Cage Resort, but that was just life. When you needed to work hard, and prove yourself, sometimes you skipped a meal or two.

"Mom is Mom." She stared into her green smoothie, frowning as she answered.

There was so much in those words of hers I wasn't sure I wanted to dive deeper. After all, I knew what "Mom is Mom" meant. Because it could mean nothing and everything all at once. I reached over the kitchen island to tap her glass. "Drink it. You'll like this one. I added extra honey for you."

She perked up and took a sip. "Tasty. Surprisingly."

"For somebody who spends her days out in the wilderness most of the time, you would think you wouldn't mind eating something with greens in it. It's healthy."

Luna rolled her eyes. "Excuse me. I think you're confusing me with Ivy. Our bestie. She likes to take pictures of green things. And probably eats them as well. Me? Not so much."

"You do your studies out in the real world. All of your research grants force you into that forest to actually hike and gather specimens. You might be a general science and chemistry professor down in Denver, but you're still somewhat outdoorsy."

"You're just lying to yourself because you don't even go out to the slopes anymore."

"Jerk."

"Dork."

We giggled, the same pitch, the same laugh, the same expression on our faces.

Whenever somebody asked me what it felt like to be a twin, I wasn't quite sure what I was supposed to say. I had always been a twin. Luna and I had shared a womb and hadn't been separated until after college. We were in the same classes, did the same sports, we had the same group of friends, we never dated the same guy thankfully, and we had similar interests.

While my Type A went into managing and organizing, her Type A went into the sciences.

I couldn't read her mind, and she couldn't read mine, much to each of our consternations. But she was my best friend. She had seen me at my worst.

But so had he.

I quickly pushed that thought out of my mind and went back to my original question. "Thanks for stopping by Mom's house. I couldn't make it yesterday because I had a late delivery that I wanted to check on with the resort, as there's an event coming up that I'm really excited about."

I pushed my white-blonde hair behind my ear and knew I would just put it up in its usual bun later. While Luna tended to have hers flowing around her face unless she was in the lab, I needed mine back. I looked far more professional that way.

"I don't mind. She's my mom too. And it was nice coming up for the weekend to hang out with you both. It would've been nicer if we could have gotten her to go to Harper's bakery, or to the Cage Free diner. The diner has the best pancakes, but Mom makes good ones too."

I winced. "We've both been trying to get Mom out of the house for years now. We're just lucky that our doctor makes house calls for certain things."

I shuddered to think what would happen if Mom needed something more than just a checkup. Yes, we got her out of the house for certain appointments, but we practically had to drag her to our doctor. He helped where he could, but it wasn't enough.

Slowly over the years, our mother had lost herself to her own demons, becoming an agoraphobe in a way that I hadn't ever thought possible. My mother with her bright smile that had dimmed over the years, and a laugh that I hadn't heard with such sincerity in far too long, was afraid of the outside world.

I didn't blame her. Not when our father was still around. He might not be in Cage Lake anymore, but he could show up at any minute, and all of us knew it. Mom felt she was safer behind the four walls of her house and locked doors.

I ran my hand over my shoulder, remembering the bruise that had darkened there, and swallowed hard. I didn't blame my mother for wanting to hide. Wasn't I doing the same?

"Scarlett," Luna whispered. "Have you talked to anybody about it?"

My gaze shot to hers, and the glass slipped from my

hand. It shattered on the counter, leaving its green contents and glass shards spraying over the granite. "Shit," I whispered as I reached forward to clean it up with my hand.

Luna gripped my wrist. "Scarlett. You'll cut yourself."

I froze at her touch, bile coating my tongue, and immediately felt ashamed. This was my twin sister. Not our father.

Not Ronin.

My ex.

Luna didn't miss the motion and let out a soft sigh before relaxing her grip. "Let me clean it up. Okay? I won't talk about it again. Not today."

I hated the worry in her tone, but I knew there wasn't much I could say to make it better when it came to this particular subject. "I'm fine, Luna. I'm leaving the house, even though Ronin still comes into Cage Lake."

"If you would talk to the authorities, you could get a restraining order."

I snorted. "Oh yes, because restraining orders worked just fine and dandy with Dad. He routinely pushed past that to beat our mother. Don't you remember?"

Luna rang out a towel underneath the faucet and glared at me. "I was there too you know. I remember it all. I know what our father did, and I know Mom is healing in her own way. But you have to stop blaming yourself for all of this."

I rolled my eyes, even though my hands shook. "I'm not blaming myself. Thank you very much. It's done. Ronin hasn't come by again. If he sees me across the street, he goes the other way. And our breakup was just a breakup. Nobody has to know that I fell into the common trap of becoming a statistic."

"I never want to hear you say that again," Luna warned, her voice harsher than I'd ever heard it.

Tears pricked my eyes, and I pressed my lips together.

"Scarlett. I love you. But we both know that you are not a statistic. You are a woman whose boyfriend hit her."

"Luna. I thought you weren't going to talk about it anymore."

My twin held up her hands. "Just because our father was an abuser, doesn't mean we're both destined to fall for abusers. It's not how it works."

"And yet I did." A single teardrop slid down my cheek, and I angrily brushed it off. "I thought I knew better. I thought I could see the signs. And I didn't. But it's done with. And Mom's being taken care of, and we'll figure out something whenever she needs to leave the house again."

"Maybe I should just move back up to Cage Lake."

"No, you don't. You have a job you love at a prestigious university in Denver. You are going to stick it out, because you've earned this. I can take care of Mom."

"You don't have to do it yourself. And Mom should also take care of Mom."

"I'm going to be late for work. And I know you have to head back down to Denver soon. So I need to go and gather my things." I turned on my heel and did my best not to react to my sister's sigh.

If we wanted to, we would continue going in circles, and there would be no coming out of it. I ignored the little voice in my head telling me that my sister was right. That I probably should talk about it more. But it wasn't going to happen anytime soon.

I quickly gathered my things, slid my feet into my heels that I knew Hudson hated, then made my way back into the kitchen. Everything was cleaned up, the lone glass in the dishwasher, and the kitchen looked sparkling. A note lay on the counter, and I swallowed hard, heart thudding.

S—

Love you. I'll see you soon.

Remember, you are the light as well.

You deserve happiness.

L

I closed my eyes tightly, willing myself not to cry, before setting the note back on the counter. I patted the paper with two fingers, feeling lighter , and left any worries that I probably should focus on behind.

Luna hadn't left for good—she'd probably only left the house to give me a moment. She would be back to gather her things and then head to Denver for work.

She didn't teach on Mondays, at least not this semester, so she had been flexible in her down time. I was grateful for it because even though The Pantry, our local grocery store, and other places delivered, our mother still needed help.

I pulled out onto the road that surrounded the lake, passing the small houses of local residents that I had known for years. Airbnbs and other types of short-term rentals weren't allowed inside town limits. There were town homes, cabins, and the resort for vacationers.

In order to stay in one of the homes in Cage Lake proper, you had to be a resident. Or call it a vacation home and use it as a vacation home personally. There were rentals within the community, but those were long-term rentals. For those Cage Lake residents just starting out or not wanting to own a home and all the issues that came with that responsibility.

I didn't have many neighbors, however. Unlike some. I lived around the lake, where most of the Cages had homes of their own.

I also ignored my *actual* neighbor. Because it wasn't as if I ever saw him these days. We had both made our stance firm. There was no need to be near one another or acknowledge each other's existence. It was much better that way.

While I could have driven through town, down Main Street, or even to Aspen Creek and Champagne Peak, I went east, towards the resort.

Whenever the original Cages had founded the place, not that I wanted to know too much about that family history, they had taken the environment into consideration. Much like the current Cages, to be fair. The resort was off to the east and was the main draw of tourists to the area. There were homes along the resort where many of our employees lived, and it was surrounded by forests, and the large mountain of Champagne Peak. The place was known for its rolling hills and great skiing and snowboarding. I didn't do either one of those often anymore. Mostly because I didn't think my knees could handle it.

But there was a spa, and enough conference space that people could have weddings, events, and other types of conferences. And if I had my way, the Cages would allow me to do even more with it.

Hikers could go through any one of the numerous trails that began and ended at the resort, and we worked with the local authorities and rangers to keep everybody safe. I loved my job. I loved the views, the history, and working with countless little pieces to ensure that everything did what it was supposed to do.

Life didn't work out the way it needed to. And my

personal life clearly didn't. So having my professional life succeed was the only thing that mattered, which meant I needed to get the Cages on board.

As manager, I wanted to upgrade Cage Resort. People loved the place already and came out in droves. However, I thought we could do better. There were a few upgrades that I wanted to do on the structure itself, a few housekeeping items, and I wanted to do a decent social media push for weddings and other high class events.

I had been working on a plan for months, and I knew if I just asked, they would probably let me. The Cages were nice, at least some of them, and they wanted the place to succeed.

I just knew that the family was going through its own issues recently, with the whole secret family thing, so asking them before hadn't seen prudent.

I pulled into my parking space and made my way into the resort offices, speaking with my night crew team members one by one, as I said the goodbyes for the day. I was usually the first one there for my shift, and the last one to leave. But I was the boss, at least right below the Cages, so that was what I was supposed to do.

While I was the manager of the resort, I didn't have the final say in things. That was Cage Enterprises. Flynn used to be the one who would come to town to work on any businesses that the Cages owned, which happened to be the majority of them.

Hence why they even had their name in most of the businesses.

The coffee place was named The Cage Bean. The bakery, Rise and Cage. The diner, Cage Free. And my favorite, the Italian restaurant, Cage Italiano. The latter made zero sense, and the recent crop of Cages hadn't named any of them, but it still made my eyes roll to the back of my head.

When Hudson had moved to town after getting out of the military, or whatever else he had done, everybody thought he would be the one to take over for Flynn so they wouldn't have to continually drive through the mountain pass.

Only that hadn't happened.

Hudson wanted nothing to do with us. Fine by me. Dealing with that bearded growly man near my home and around town was enough. But then he'd stepped in a few times for Flynn, until Isabella had taken over. She had married Weston, a local, and now lived here half of the year. Meaning when Isabella was down in Denver, and Flynn couldn't make it up, we still had to deal with Hudson.

That was fine. I'm an adult. And I didn't need to think of him. I hated the fact that I kept thinking of him however. I refused to be weak. I refused to let anyone see that I could be.

He had seen me at my weakest.

Just like my mother.

I pushed those thoughts from my head and went to work. Cage Lake and its resort was going to shine, and I was going to make it happen.

By the time I was done for the day, I was exhausted, and my feet hurt. I probably should be wearing more sensible shoes, and I did so when I was outside, but I liked my heels. I liked the way they made me feel, the way they made me look.

I liked that Hudson hated them. Not that I had seen him today and I wasn't going to be too relieved about that.

I drove the winding road home, darkness settling in, and pulled into my garage. I loved my home, as small as it was. I didn't live where the majority of people did in town, but I had my silence, and my alone time. I had three locks on each door, because being a woman alone wasn't easy. I needed to be safe.

I changed into comfortable clothes, reheated my dinner from leftovers thanks to Luna, and settled onto the back deck, letting the sound of nature sink into my pores.

Off in the distance I saw a light, and smiled, knowing that Hudson was probably in his studio back there.

I wiped the smile from my face. Why did I have to know that? And why did he have to be my neighbor.

I sighed, and took another bite, before the sound of footsteps echoed through my backyard. I froze and reached for my dinner knife.

"I wouldn't do that. Hello, Scarlett."

I whirled, knife in hand, my plate shattering to the ground. Another dish in one day. I was going for a record. But as my ex stepped into the light, I couldn't care.

I swallowed hard, my hand surprisingly steady as I held it out in front of me. "What are you doing here?"

"Is there a reason that you're holding a knife at me?" Ronin asked.

My pulse raced—just the idea of him nearly sending me into a pure panic. I hated the fact that he could do this to me. "Get off my property."

"I just want to talk, Scarlett. We ended things on bad terms. And I need you to get my side of the story."

Of course that's what Ronin wanted. Or at least said he wanted. Because he would never be the villain, only the victim in his own story. "There is no your side of the story. You hit me."

He sighed, giving me those sweet puppy dog eyes that I might have fallen for once, but now could only see the lies beneath. "It was an accident. I was angry. I didn't mean to take it out on you."

"You hit me. And it's never happening again. Now go away."

"And you think threatening me with a little steak knife is going to help you?"

"I don't care. Just go." Bile coated my tongue, and my hand began to shake.

His gaze caught the movement and his lips twitched. "Do you even know what to do with that, Scarlett?"

Lifting my chin, I tried for the strength I knew I needed to maintain even if it were only veneer. "Just come closer and see."

"Okay then." I should have stayed silent. I should have done anything. But instead he took a step forward, and I swiped out, knowing it was no use. Ronin used to box and then went into MMA. Not the legal stuff. Not the things that were about passion and strength and showing your humanity.

No, it was about beating someone brutally because you could.

He knocked the knife out of my hands and shoved at my shoulder. "I just wanted to talk. Why do you make things so hard?"

Heart beating rapidly in my chest, I lifted my knee and slammed it into his balls. He staggered back, cupping himself, even as he shouted. I ran inside, closed the door, and locked all three locks, tears sliding down my cheeks.

"I just wanted to talk, Scarlett," he shouted through the door.

And I stood there, my head pressed against the door, waiting for him to leave. And when he finally did, I sank onto my welcome mat, wondering why he wouldn't leave me alone.

My phone buzzed on the counter where I had left it in a fog of exhaustion, and I reached up for it, hand shaking. I nearly knocked it to the ground before I caught it.

Hudson: Are you okay? I heard a shout.

I squeezed my eyes shut, blowing out my breath.

He had heard. I wasn't alone.

I wasn't alone.

Me: I'm fine. I just dropped a plate.

Hudson: Open your back door then.

Alarmed, I stood up, nearly fell down again, and looked out my kitchen window. Hudson stood there, staring at the mess I had left behind, and I wanted to curl into a ball and hide.

"I'm fine!" I called through the window.

Hudson turned to me and shook his head. "Are you sure?"

"Just go, okay?" He didn't miss the crack in my voice.

He let out a breath and met my gaze through the window. "I need to see you. Just see you. Then I'll go. Promise."

I let out a breath, knowing he wouldn't leave. He would sit there and wait. Or worse, maybe he thought somebody was inside with me and wanted to help. I didn't want him to see me, but I was fine. Ronin hadn't pushed me hard enough to bruise. At least I didn't think so. And it wasn't like the bruises would show up yet.

And doing something I knew I probably shouldn't, but was the only thing I could do, I unlocked the door and slowly opened it. Hands fisted at his sides, he studied my face, before his gaze roamed over my body, as if checking for wounds. It wasn't as if he was going to see them.

"Was he here?"

"He's gone now," I blurted. I hadn't meant to say that. Hadn't meant to think it.

"Do you want me to check the house?"

I froze, as I hadn't thought of that or the full ramifications of Ronin being here, before I finally relaxed. "I'm fine. He's not in the house. He was out on the deck, and I heard him leave."

"Are you sure about that? I can check the property."

"I can check my security cameras." I cursed. "Which I should have done to begin with. Just like I should have called somebody when he first walked onto my porch. I should have had my phone near me. I didn't think. I never think when it comes to him. And I hate it."

"Scarlett. Don't blame yourself. It'll just piss me off."

"People keep telling me not to put the blame on my shoulders, and yet, here we are." I sighed. "And yes, pissing you off is something I never want to do." Even I didn't believe the sarcasm at that point and the look on Hudson's face proved he didn't either.

"If you're sure you're okay, I'm going to check around the property. And you should check the security cameras." He paused, studied my face again. "And put ice on your shoulder."

"How did you know?" I whispered, my voice breaking.

"He tore your shirt, Scar," he whispered, before he leaned down and began to pick up the broken plate.

"Why are you doing this?" I asked, incredulous, ignoring the fact that Ronin had indeed torn my shirt and I hadn't even noticed.

"Because somebody should. And I know you've got this on your own, but, as my family continues to tell me, you don't have to."

And with that, I knew I didn't understand Hudson at all. But then again, I didn't understand myself.

So I picked up my phone, went through the security cameras, and then went to get a broom.

I couldn't sweep this away, couldn't push it away, but I could at least help him clean up this mess.

Because it wasn't as if he was going to let me do it on my own. At least not tonight.

Chapter Four
Hudson

I had moved to Cage Lake to escape and to get out from underneath the eyes of my family. I had thought living in the mountains would mean I would be able to avoid many of the commitments that came with being around people. It wasn't that I *hated* people, it was more that I didn't like them all the time. They could be greedy, loud, rude, and intrusive. They could break you, take everything that you thought you could want, and shatter the lives of those you care about.

I did better on my own and *liked* being on my own.

Then I realized that moving to a small mountain town wasn't exactly like I thought it would be. Because living in Cage Lake didn't mean I could escape my problems or avoid the rest of the world—it somehow made it worse.

"Why the hell did you drag me down here again?" I rumbled, my voice as low as possible. But with how deep it was, it still carried. Hence the glare on a couple of faces.

I watched Isabella's grin twitch ever so slightly and resented it. "I asked if you would like to join us. You're the one who decided to follow through and join."

I looked over at Weston, who just shrugged. "Hey. I'm only here because I fell in love with her. I didn't have a choice."

My friend grunted and rubbed his stomach from where Isabella's elbow had just gone. My sister merely raised a brow at his look. "Really? You're going to make that type of comment? You're the one who's *from* Cage Lake. Not to mention you're the one who told us that there was an event today."

Weston sighed. "It's St. Patrick's Day. And we're Cage Lake. I assumed you knew there would be some form of ridiculous parade and event, with pies and whatever else they find. It's what we do. We just didn't help organize it this time because we were down in Denver, so I didn't think about it."

"I mean really, how dare you," I said, my own lips twitching.

"Seriously, you should know by now that it's Cage Lake, and we really do just go overboard," my friend finally said, no longer hiding behind his smile.

I ignored both Weston and my sister. "This still doesn't help me realize exactly why I'm here."

I had been safe and happy in my own house, without having to deal with people, or this event, and yet here I was. With no escape because a few people had already seen me. Now running away was no longer an option.

"You're so cute when you're grumpy."

I flipped off Weston and ignored the glare on one of the passersby's face. I didn't know what the lady was expecting. I was Hudson Cage, the town recluse and asshole. They should be used to my inability to act like a citizen of a polite society by now.

"If you really want to leave, we can make excuses for you," Isabella whispered, worry in her tone.

I let out a sigh, my shoulders dropping. And that right there was why I couldn't leave. Because of course Isabella would be kind to me in the end. Sure, she had just as much of an attitude and ability to put all of our siblings in place as Aston could—it had to be an older sibling thing—but, just like Aston, she actually cared about us too.

"No, it's fine. I'll stay."

"Because if you stay now, then you don't have to do the next couple of holiday things? I see how it is." Weston smirked, and this time avoided Isabella's elbow.

He wrapped his arm around her shoulder, tilted her

head back, and took her lips in a kiss that was mildly inappropriate for the public area, however, people just clapped and looked ecstatic that the town mechanic and one of the new Cages were happy and in love.

I rolled my eyes and watched as yet another parade float with green shamrocks and fake gold coins slowly meandered past.

"It's still been snowing," I said after a moment. "We have a fresh powder on the mountain, and I know that the resort has been busy as hell, and yet we're out here in the cold, dealing with this. Why?" I asked.

Isabella gave me a look. "Because that's when St. Patrick's Day occurs during the year. I mean, it always happens on March 17th, so it's not that big of a surprise. And you sure know a lot about the resort."

This time I full-on glared at her, and she held up her hands, conceding. At least I hoped she was conceding. "Touchy subject."

"I know about the business, thank you." Because that was a decent excuse, right?

My sister slid her fingers through Weston's as she spoke. "Okay. Though I know you haven't been around lately. And Weston and I are heading back down to Denver soon. You think you can handle the resort? Or shall we send Flynn up?"

I tried to hear any worry or pity in her tone, maybe even a little disappointment, but there was nothing beyond a question. She was honestly asking and would move her plans or force my twin to town so I wouldn't have to deal with the resort. I was still getting to know my new siblings, figuring out their tics, and Isabella surprised me daily.

"No, I'll handle it."

The smile on her face brightened, and she squeezed my shoulder through my light jacket and Henley. It might be winter, but I was used to the cold.

"Good. I mean, Scarlett has everything down by now. She really doesn't need our oversight. It's more of us being there to make sure she knows she doesn't have to do everything alone. You know?"

I mumbled, once again not wanting to think about Isabella. Because if I thought about Isabella, I thought about Ronin. And I thought about those bruises. And the fact that I hadn't been able to do a single fucking thing about them.

"Hudson? Are you okay?"

I grunted and pushed thoughts of Scarlett from my head, or at least I tried to. Because of course there she was, the sun bouncing off her hair like it always did so she stood out like a beacon.

"I got it, don't worry," I finally answered, not knowing if it was an actual answer to what Isabella had asked. After all no one was paying attention at this point. Isabella didn't say a damn thing, but then her attention moved to Scarlett, and she let out an odd noise that I couldn't decipher. It couldn't be good for me either way.

"Scarlett! Over here," Isabella called out.

I wanted to curse. Why the hell would she ask Scarlett to be here? Why couldn't she just leave well enough alone. And why was my sister doing this to me? Of course, that was just selfish thinking. After all, the two were friends. That had nothing to do with me. For once I just wanted to be self-centered enough to think it like that.

"Hello Weston and Cages. I didn't realize you would be here." Scarlett reached out and hugged Isabella tightly, then did the same to Weston. When she made it to me, she just raised her brow, but her cheeks flushed. At least we could both be awkward in this. Isabella didn't miss the interaction, but it wasn't what my sister probably thought it was about. No, there was nothing going on between the two of us. Instead there were only memories that we both wanted to forget.

"Hudson."

I lifted my chin. "Scarlett. Surprised to see you here. You're usually chained to a desk at work."

Her gaze narrowed, and I was only marginally annoyed at myself for even saying something like that. I was an asshole, but I didn't need to be constantly rude.

"My bosses sometimes give me the day off." She turned away from me, giving me her back as she spoke to Isabella. "I figured it's time that I tried to get more involved in the town, rather than working nearby with mostly tourists. Perhaps I should take a break and not work too hard."

"You know, I don't quite believe you," Isabella said with a laugh.

"Oh?" Scarlett said, eyes wide.

"I mean about the whole not-working-too-hard thing. Scarlett, you work far too many hours, even though we yell at you constantly to take a break."

The pretty flush on Scarlett's cheeks deepened, and I held back a groan, hating the fact that I was even thinking about her skin. What the hell was wrong with me? Oh yeah, *she* was what was wrong with me.

Another parade float passed by, but this time, when they began tossing chocolate coins, everyone around us began to move closer, laughing and reaching for the chocolate. I cursed, not wanting to move as they shoved by, but as a super-sized chocolate coin the size of my fist flew in an arc in the air, I moved without letting myself think about it. Two steps forward, and then my hand was over Scarlett's head, catching the damn coin before it smashed into the side of her face.

Somebody cheered, ignoring us, as I looked down at Scarlett who was now so close to me I could feel the heat of her against my chest.

Eyes wide, she blinked. "Thank you. Though I could have caught it myself."

I clenched my jaw and dropped the chocolate into

her open palm. "Sure, Scar. Unless you mean catching it with your face."

"I was moving. But thank you."

"Not fast enough," I grumbled.

The cannon on the side of the float sputtered, sending a large burst of sound directly towards us. Without thinking, I threw my arms over Scarlett, pulling her close, as sweat slicked my brow and my entire body threatened to shake. Nobody seemed to pay us much attention, but I tried to catch my breath, my chest seizing.

Then I realized what I was doing and quickly dropped my arms, embarrassment crawling up my skin.

"Hudson?" Isabella asked, worry etched on her face.

I held up both hands and shook my head. "Fine. Just startled me." An understatement. I tried to turn on my heel and walk away, but then Scarlett's hand was on my shoulder, and I froze.

"Hudson?" she asked, the thousand questions I knew she had buried deep within that one word.

"It's nothing," I lied.

I pulled away from her, bumping into a few others as I moved back to the main street. I'd done my duty, shown up as a Cage in a town that our family owned. I nodded at a few townspeople, knowing they would probably gossip about me later. Just another soldier coming home from deployment, jumping at loud noises. A shocking development.

I sighed and turned down an alley so I could take a deep breath.

I wasn't like most of the people who had come home. I could sleep during a thunderstorm, and fireworks didn't bother me. But every so often, a single loud noise would take me right back to a time I didn't want to remember.

But it wasn't what came at me. It wasn't the memory of the burning metal tearing its way through my skin, leaving puckered scars. No, it was those left behind. Every loud sound that slammed into me was a lashing at my brain of those who didn't come home.

And the person I couldn't save.

I ran my hands over my face and knew I needed to get back to my truck. Maybe I did need that dog. Somebody that would be at home waiting for me. Or hanging out with me at something like this. Maybe then Isabella and the rest would get off my back.

I let out a breath and turned, only to run smack into Scarlett. I reached out, grabbing her shoulders to keep her balanced.

"What the hell are you doing here?" I snapped, embarrassed that she had seen me trying to catch my breath.

Her eyes widened. "I was just checking on you. No need to yell at me."

"I'm not yelling," I yelled.

"It sure sounds like it. But if you're just going to shout, I'll go."

"I didn't need you here to begin with, Scarlett. That's what we do, right?"

"What the hell do you mean by that?"

I didn't know what the hell I meant by that. Because if I went down this path, we would talk about the one thing that we didn't ever talk about. "It's nothing."

Her eyes widened. "You're not still mad that I wouldn't let you help me, right? Because I didn't need help."

"Just like I don't need help. Now, if you're done, I'm heading home. I did the small-town thing. I'm out."

"Then go. Isabella's already here, and your family takes turns doing the Cage thing and showing the rest of the town that you're nothing like your father. There's no reason for you to be here."

"What the hell would you know about it? Is that what you think? That we're trying to right wrongs? Everyone knows that we're not our dad. He was a philandering asshole who didn't like his kids. Which is funny because he had so many of them. He didn't like this town. Didn't like anything. He only liked gaining power. So I don't think this entire town thinks we're anything like him."

I couldn't believe I had said those words. Or even

spoken at all. What was it about this woman? And why did she have to ruin everything?

"We don't think that any of you are like your father. Even Aston turned out to be a nice guy."

I snorted. "I love the qualifications on that. Though marrying Blakely did seem to make him a little nicer." My lips twitched.

"That is true. I like Blakely." She let out a breath. "I'm sorry, Hudson. For intruding."

My shoulders stiffened again. "There's no need for an apology. I'm heading home."

"Because you did your duty."

I nodded, feeling the disappointment dripping from her tone. "Because I did my duty." I moved past her, out into the crowd and towards my truck.

I could feel her gaze on me, but I ignored it.

We didn't need each other. And we sure as hell didn't need to help each other. Life would be better off if I just stayed out of the main part of Cage Lake.

And away from Scarlett Blair.

Chapter Five
Scarlett

"Oh, I love this shawl so much, Mom. It feels smooth and airy. It's so light and intricate too. You're getting quicker too because you weren't working on this very long." I held up the cream shawl that my mother had crocheted and let my fingers slide over the smooth and nearly silky wool.

My mom beamed and moved forward, hands outstretched. "It turned out really lovely, didn't it? I want to thank you again for the pattern. You don't have to keep buying me patterns that I say I like when we scroll through them online. But I do appreciate it, daughter of mine." She lifted her hand once more and cupped my cheek. I leaned into the touch, loving the light in my mother's eyes.

I would work constant hours and do paperwork until my fingers bled in order for my mother to smile like that again. I only wish she'd smile outside of her home.

At first, her leaving the house had been a difficult but not nearly impossible thing. Yes, we could still get her out for important appointments that couldn't be done at home, but a few years ago, she would get in the car, take deep breaths, and we would traverse Cage Lake. We would have afternoons where it was girl time, and we would enjoy lunches, coffees, and sunning ourselves on the lake. She would shop for wool in person, knowing the exact dye lot that she wanted.

And yet, with each passing month, as each additional threat of my father would slyly blend into our lives—even from afar—her circle would shrink. Eventually she would only go to the closest shop. And then would only walk to the edge of the street. Now, unless we physically forced her—which would result in crying and sobbing for all parties involved—she didn't leave the house. My mother was the queen of online shopping and finding the best deals to make that happen. She still worked a full-time job but was able to do it from home. The invention of the internet was honestly the best thing that had ever happened to my family, and something that made it easier for my mother to walk away from.

The idea that my father was still out there, lurking, made things even more difficult. There was a restraining order which said that my father couldn't be within a hundred feet of wherever my mother was, nor could he even be in an area where he could set eyes upon her home, but restraining orders had to be enforced. Our sheriff and local officers were wonderful, but they couldn't be around twenty-four hours a day. The worry that had etched itself onto my mother's face years ago would never go away.

Yet this simple shawl that she had made, that wasn't simple at all, lightened those lines ever so much.

"Honestly, it's probably the best shawl you've ever made. It's so intricate."

Mom leaned into me, her smile still shinning. "I'm glad you like it. Because it's yours."

I shook my head, not surprised at her generosity. "No. You should sell it, Mom. Your shop is doing fantastic."

In addition to my mom's full-time job as a copy editor, she also sold a few of her projects in a small online store. I was so proud of everything that she was doing, knowing that while she couldn't always get outside, with those times that she could coming fewer between, she was still living a life.

Perhaps more than I was these days, considering she had a full online community that she spent time with. They had online parties, and even a book club and wine night.

I hung out with the girls when they were all in town, but honestly, I had missed the past two because of work, and well, Ronin. I didn't want to think about him, especially not in my mother's home. She didn't know the truth about Ronin. I'd told her we'd broken up and I didn't want to see him again because it hurt emotionally — not that I was truly afraid of him. I wasn't going to put that stress on her shoulders.

I didn't want to stain her with the shame of my own choice. I would never blame my mother for what my father had done. Never blame her for not leaving when she had tried multiple times for herself and for her girls. I did blame myself for following that path. She might not have paved it for me, but I hadn't listened to the signs that I had learned the hard way through my mother's pain.

I pushed those thoughts from my mind, because they weren't going to help anyone right now, and shook out the shawl once more. "I still have that lovely sage green one you gave me. You should sell this."

Mom pressed her lips together slightly before giving me a shake of her head. "I might, when I make the next one. But this one's for you. And I'm not taking no for an answer." She lifted her chin, that fire in her eyes reminding me of years past.

"Oh, thank you. Seriously. I love you, Mom." I slid the shawl around my shoulders and then wrapped my mom in a hug. She held me close, each of us standing there for a long moment, just breathing one another in.

I stood back as her computer dinged. "That's the

group chat. Carla is going on a date, and we're all helping her choose what to wear."

I didn't know who Carla was, but she had to be one of my mother's friends. "I love that so much, Mom. Does she do a little fashion show for you?"

"Of course. Just like you and your sister used to do for me when you were younger. Never on dates since I know you didn't date until after high school, but for your events and outings with your friends."

Of course Luna and I had gone on dates, just not when our father had been around. We'd hidden so many things from him. So we'd find ways to bring Mom into our lives while trying to hide our happiness because he'd use it to punish Mom. When Dad hadn't been there to judge or to yell. Or to throw Mother down the stairs because Luna and I had to be whores for daring to date a boy. I pushed those thoughts out of my mind, hating the memories that always seemed to creep up.

I grabbed my purse as I followed my mom to her little desk where she'd set up her laptop. She no longer lived in our childhood home. The memories of her screams no longer dug into the patterned walls. This new place was all hers. And had slowly become her self-sustaining prison. "You tell them hi for me, I need to get back to the house. It's my day off, so that means errands, errands, errands."

"That's how it always is. I hope the Cages aren't

working you too hard, dear." She tapped my hand as her attention drifted to the chimes of the active group chat.

My lips lifted into a smile since I knew she was distracted but I couldn't help but defend the job I loved —not that Mom had a problem with the Cages. "They aren't. I just want to show them that I'm the best at what I do. They deserve to have the best."

"So do you, light of my life. And you're allowed to take time for yourself."

"I know. And I'm doing it right now."

"Spending time with your mother," she said dryly.

"You're one of my best friends. You're just going to have to get over it."

She rolled her eyes, laughing, and it made the long nights worth it. Because my mother hadn't left in a long while, until recently. She was doing good, at least in some respects. So when she kissed my cheek and walked me out of the house, careful not to step a toe off the threshold, I held back a small sigh and made my way to my car.

She had an upcoming doctor's visit soon, one that we couldn't do with just a home visit, and she would fight it. She would never yell at us, never push, but she would break down inside, and it would break me. But as the sister left in Cage Lake, it was my responsibility. I would never begrudge Luna for moving to Denver, for finding her passion at a university there, but some part of me wished that life could be different. But that wasn't the case and wishes never came true.

I drove down the side streets of Cage Lake, before turning right on Main Street and going north towards the lake. Soon people would no longer be near the slopes and instead, on the lake for something other than ice fishing. Of course, weather in Cage Lake meant that one could probably do both within the same day and not find it odd.

I nodded at a few people that I knew and waited as tourists jaywalked across the road without paying attention. I rolled my eyes and told myself that tourists were my bread and butter. They were literally why I had a job. Part of me wanted to check in on my staff, to see how they were doing today with a full resort, but I had promised my second-in-command I wouldn't. They would call me if there was an emergency. I apparently needed to just have a day off.

I tapped my finger along the steering wheel and finally pulled into my driveway. The sun shone brightly through the tall trees, and I smiled at my small two-story cabin. It was mine, and no one else's. My little refuge.

With another sigh, I got out of the car and made my way around the back of the house. I looked up at my security cameras, and then down at my watch that buzzed about the movement on my own property. I'd immediately added more security after Ronin had stopped by, and some part of me felt like it wasn't enough. Maybe it would be better if I lived in town, where everyone would be watching me at all times, but I needed this place. I needed my solitude.

I worked with people and strangers for hours a day, and part of me just needed a moment alone. So I would do all that I could to make it safe. I resented that Ronin was trying to take that away from me.

I went through the back door, set my things on the counter, and then went back out to the firewood station. It was nearing April now, so we probably had one or two more snowstorms on the way thanks to living in the mountains, so I would still need my fire going, but at least I didn't have to have so many cords like I did during the heart of winter.

I reached for my gloves and then one earbud in so I could listen to music as I did the heavy lifting that came with owning a home of my own. I left the other one out so I could hear if someone came up behind me. With my favorite pop star scream-singing about men and how we didn't need them, I laughed to myself and got to work.

Even though it was a little chilly out, sweat slicked my brow, and I knew I had to look amazing. Lips twitching, I pushed thoughts of how I looked out of my mind and turned to get the next log. The scream that ripped from my throat was probably heard in the next county, as I dropped the piece of wood on Hudson's foot and ripped out my earbud.

"What the hell are you doing here?" I asked, chest heaving. "You scared the shit out of me."

Hudson blinked at me, then looked down at the wood that had barely missed truly hurting him. "I called your name three times, and you weren't listening. Good to know that you're careful about your surroundings."

I winced at the judgment in his tone, but then again, I hadn't been paying attention at all. That wasn't good. Not with the fact that I had extra security for a reason. Honestly, it wasn't like me to be so lax and I knew I needed to get my head in the game.

That's when I realized Hudson wasn't wearing a shirt.

No, he wore work boots, jeans that rode low on his hips, and a ball cap turned backwards. Sweat slicked those rigid muscles of his, and the man still had at least a six-pack. I'd never actually seen one of those in real life, and I didn't quite believe he was real.

The hoops sliding through his nipples nearly made me want to press my thighs together. I hadn't known Hudson had nipple piercings and now all I wanted to do was lean forward and see what the metal would taste like on my tongue. Of course, it made me think of my own bars through my nipples that was my personal secret, and I knew this line of thought was all trouble.

My gaze went to the rigid scars on his side and shoulder, and then I forced myself to look at his face.

His very handsome, very bearded face. I was *not* just ogling Hudson Cage. I had better taste than that. No, that was cruel. Because there was nothing wrong with Hudson Cage other than his attitude. In fact, from what I could see, there was everything right about him.

And perhaps I was getting heat stroke.

"Everything okay there? You look a little flushed."

I narrowed my gaze at the twitch of his lips. "Is there a reason that you're half naked on my property?"

He gestured towards the tractor trailer that I hadn't noticed. My God, I needed to lower the volume on my music if I wanted to be safe. What the hell was wrong with me? "Didn't mean to startle you, Scar. I was moving a fallen tree on the other side of my property, and I'm already working with firewood. I figured you could use help."

"Why? Because I'm a woman that happens to have her nails done?" I asked. I held up my hands, and then realized they were covered in gloves.

Perfect, Scarlett. Perfect.

Hudson sighed. "You know what, Scar, you annoy the fuck out of me."

"My name is Scarlett. Not Scar. And I'm sorry that I annoy you, but you do the same to me."

"I like calling you Scar. Scarlett sounds like you

need to be in a mansion or something with a hoop dress. Maybe the one with the curtain rod in the back."

I pressed my lips together so I wouldn't laugh. "From *The Carol Burnett Show*? Based on *Gone with the Wind*. Neither one of us was born when that show came out. You know that, right?"

He shrugged and I resisted the urge to watch his muscles move. Barely. "I like the oldies. Plus, that episode's a classic. Don't tell me you've never seen it."

"Of course I've seen it. And it is a classic. And I'm not going to be on some staircase trying to make an entrance."

"You could probably make an entrance in a burlap sack," he muttered.

I blinked, knowing I must have heard incorrectly. "What did you say?"

He glared at me for a moment before turning away. "Nothing. If you don't need my help, I guess I'll go back to my own property."

"Good for you, for finally understanding that," I said, confusion settling in.

"I was just offering to help, *Scarlett*." He drew out my full name, and I rolled my eyes.

"And I don't need your help."

"Oh, look at this, a lover's tiff."

My entire body stiffened, and I tried my best not to hunch my shoulders and hide behind Hudson at that voice.

The voice of a man who wasn't supposed to be in town.

Hudson immediately stepped forward, blocking me, and I resented him for it. But perhaps I resented the fact that I needed it in that moment.

I reached out and gripped Hudson's forearm, grateful for the gloves so I wouldn't feel his skin in that moment, and turned to face the man who had tried to ruin my life from the day I was born.

"What are you doing here?" I asked, embarrassed once again that a man I didn't want to be near me was on my property and I hadn't even known.

That's when I realized that my watch was buzzing, and the cameras had finally picked up on the movement.

"I don't know why you're getting such an attitude when I'm just here to check on my baby girl. I was down in Denver but didn't have a chance to see your sister."

He smiled that perfect smile of his, and dread crawled down my spine.

Had he found Luna? It wasn't as if her work was hidden, but we had done our best to make sure Dad could never find her home. Our father had never laid a hand on her and had only hit me once. It was our mother that he had broken down. It was our mother who had sent him to jail. No, that wasn't right. He had sent himself to jail. But his fists on her body and soul had been what had finally pushed the authorities to take action. Because the old sheriff hadn't cared as much. Probably because he had used his own fists on his wife.

The new sheriff cared. The new sheriff had done his job.

And yet here my father was, looking perfect as always.

Jail hadn't changed him in any way from what I could tell. He still had the perfect coiffed honey-blond hair, that chiseled jawline, and bright white smile. He didn't look like the drunk who used his fists to take out his anger on his wife. But that was the problem, wasn't it?

You couldn't always tell the monster beneath the façade. Sometimes they hid in plain sight. Dirt and grime didn't cover my father, at least not physically. No, his soul was the shadowed part of him. And he hid it damn well.

"You need to get off my property."

"And you need to learn some respect. I'm just here to check on you. Why do you have to be so mean to your father?"

"Maybe because you're an asshole? I don't have time to deal with you. Just go."

I sounded far more confident than I felt, but I needed him gone. I needed Hudson not to be here. Why did he have to witness not one, but two men in my life trying to break me down? Why did the man who wouldn't leave my thoughts have to be my neighbor? I just needed everybody to be away so I could just live my life and not deal with anyone.

But that wasn't my life. And part of me was glad Hudson was here. Because my father would be on his best behavior if another man was around. He couldn't be seen as anything but loving and doting. Even though most of the town already knew he had been in jail for assaulting my mother.

"Hudson, can't you see that I'm just here to visit my daughter? Maybe you could have a word with her, set her right."

I nearly hunched into myself, hating the idea that Hudson was here to witness this, but then Hudson stepped right to my side. He didn't block me, didn't let me block him. Instead, it was as if he was letting me know that he was on my side. He folded his arms over his massive and naked chest and didn't say a damn word for long enough that my dad rocked back on his heels, looking uneasy.

I needed to learn that look. I tore my gaze from my father completely and looked up at Hudson. He just stared at my father, narrowing his gaze.

"I'm pretty sure Scarlett told you to leave. There's a reason you're not allowed on this property, Mr. Blair, and there's a reason that you're not allowed on any Cage property from what I can remember. I mean, didn't you get that cease-and-desist letter from my brother? I can have another brother send it to you. It's what we Cages do. Isn't that what you said the last time that you yelled in my face and practically spit?"

I froze, wondering what the hell he was talking about. What had I missed? And what other secrets was this man keeping from me?

"You Cages. Just because you own a couple of properties you think you own this whole town. But you're wrong. We residents know our rights, and you can't tell me what to do."

"On any property my family owns you bet your ass I can tell you what to do. Now, as for this property, your daughter already told you to leave. And we both know that if I took a step forward, you'd cower back like the little shit that you are. I could force it, or you could leave with your tail tucked between your legs and maybe act like the man you're supposed to be. You don't intimidate me, Blair. You sure as fuck don't intimidate your daughter. Maybe for once in your life you should listen to a woman and go."

My father looked between us, lip curled. "Fucking a Cage, are you? That's one way to raise yourself on that ladder of yours. How many blow jobs did you have to give this one to get your job?"

I moved forward, ready to throttle my dad, but Hudson was already there. With one movement, he had my dad by the back of his neck and lifted enough that my dad's toes dangled against the ground.

My God, I hadn't realized Hudson was that strong. But from the way that his muscles bulged, well, it would make sense.

"You're going to want to watch your mouth."

"Hudson."

"Listen to the little girl," my dad snapped, as if he wasn't dangling along the ground from a man who could probably break him with his pinky.

"Go, before I stop listening to my inner demons and take it out on you."

If possible, my dad paled even more, and when Hudson let him down, he nearly fell down on his knees, but then scrambled away, indeed looking like he had his tail between his legs.

Hudson stood there with his back to me, hands fisted at his sides as his shoulders moved up and down with each deep breath.

"I would say thank you—"

"Don't. Don't say a damn thing," he cut me off.

"He would've left eventually."

"Maybe." Hudson turned then, staring at me with those intense eyes that nearly forced me to take a step back. "Maybe he would have. But I didn't like the fact that he wasn't budging when you told him no."

"My dad never hurt me," I lied.

Hudson just shook his head. "If you see him around, let me know. I'll handle it."

That made me narrow my gaze. "You don't have to handle it, Hudson. You don't have to fix everything."

His jaw tightened, and he gave me a slight nod. "True. That's not in me. I don't fix things. I never did." And with that, he stomped past me and to his tractor.

I watched as he turned on the engine and slowly made his way back to his property, leaving me standing there, alone, wondering what the hell had just happened.

I looked over at my home, my oasis, and it didn't feel like mine anymore.

Why did men have to continually come and try to take something that was mine? Why did they have to try to break me along the way? Why did I resent the idea that Hudson had been there to witness everything?

And why did I finally feel a slight ounce of comfort that he did?

Chapter Six
Hudson

"Hi, Uncle Hudson!"

Another little girl came on the screen, her hair in pigtails as she grinned widely. "Hi, Uncle Hudson!"

I smiled despite myself as Violet and Hazel each waved dramatically at the phone, and continued to repeat the phrase, "Hi, Uncle Hudson," until Sophia finally took the phone from them.

"Okay, girls. It's back for finger painting. Your uncle needs to get off the phone and go back to work."

"Work, work, work, work, work," Hazel sing-songed.

"Work like Daddy!" Violet put in. "Daddy loves work."

Sophia winced and then smiled into the camera. "Sorry about that. Let me just set them up really quick, and I promise I will ask you the question that made me call you in the first place."

I let out a rough chuckle and waved it off. "It's okay. It's good to see my nieces."

If you asked anybody in the family, I was probably the asshole of the group. The grumpy one who didn't speak much. And that was fine with me. I had my reasons, and I had never been like Dorian who could smile and pretty much get what he wanted. Or at least pretend he could. There was just something about my nieces and nephews who could make me do anything.

I still couldn't quite believe we were all old enough to have nieces and nephews. Time flew when we were finally free of our father.

I didn't get to see them often, since I didn't live in Denver, but we were close enough that the girls knew me in person. And since Flynn and I looked different enough these days with our facial hair, the girls could tell us apart. Plus, I wouldn't be caught dead in a suit. Especially not for the upcoming show my agent wanted me to do. I shuddered at the thought. I was already ignoring my agent's calls, because he wanted me to do an entire art show down in Denver. Hell no. He could sell my art, do whatever he wanted with it, as long as I didn't have to deal with the paperwork or talking to people who wanted to judge my work. They didn't know what I was thinking while I did it, and I wasn't doing it for them. I was barely doing it for me some days. I liked painting. It was something I was good at that wasn't shooting things. But I wasn't about to let someone dictate what I was supposed to do or not when it came to my job. And that meant I didn't want to deal with assholes in suits who thought they knew better than me. I didn't know much, and wasn't the expert on any of this, but sometimes I knew my own mind.

I could hear the girls giggling in the background as Sophia set them up with their water-soluble finger paints that I had sent them a couple of weeks ago, and then Sophia made sure the drop cloth was all ready to go. They were going to be a complete mess later, but it would be an easier cleanup than otherwise.

"Thank you again for the paints. They come out of clothes as well. At one point I thought I was just going to have to get the girls naked and let them paint that way." Sophia shuddered.

"That would make quite a spectacle down at the park," I said dryly.

"Oh yes. I can just see it now. Either me or the nanny getting judged by other parents for not letting the kids get dirty enough or getting too dirty."

I grimaced. "Other parents sound exhausting."

Sophia grinned. "Tell me about it. Anyway, I wanted to thank you for agreeing to do the mural at the dance studio."

I waved her off, wanting to duck my head. I loved

what I did, but I didn't like when others mentioned it. Weird artist shit and all that. "It's fine. It's a blank wall and you're letting me do what I want."

"Within reason," she qualified, eyes dancing with laughter. She had dark circles under those eyes, but I knew between work, owning the studio itself, and the girls, she couldn't be getting a lot of sleep. Cale traveled a lot more these days with his promotion, and I knew they had a nanny. But maybe I should talk with some of the other siblings to see what we could do to help. I might not be as physically connected to them as the others, but I wasn't about to let one of us work ourselves to the grave.

"I'll be down next month to work on it. My agent wants to meet with me anyway, so I'm not getting out of it."

"I still think it's wonderful that they want you to do an art show." She held up both hands. "Not that you have to. Please don't do anything that you don't want to. But I'm glad that I'm getting an original Cage mural on my wall. I'll be the talk of the town."

I snorted. "Oh yes. Because everybody knows a Hudson Cage original by sight."

Her lips turned down in a frown. "I don't know, you're more famous than you think."

"I'd rather not be." I rubbed my hand over my chest, that lingering doubt edging its way through the storm. Was it any wonder the voice of that doubt varied between my father and Michelle? It didn't take a therapist to get to that point.

"As in just famous enough to be able to afford two homes?" Sophia raised a brow before looking over her shoulder to check on the girls.

I winced and looked around the nearly bulldozed house I currently stood in. "Without having to use extra Cage money that is."

"With what that you have planned for it, you know that all of us would do what we could to pitch in."

"I know." I ran my hand over my chest, not realizing what I was doing until her gaze went to the gesture. I let my arm drop. "Anyway, once it's done, you and the girls can come and take a look. Just not right now because it's not safe for two-year-olds to toddle around."

"That makes complete sense. And thank you again for everything." She turned and called out, "Say goodbye to your uncle, girls!"

"Goodbye, Uncle Hudson!"

"We love you."

My cheeks heated as I said my goodbyes and hung up. I could always tell the twins apart, even though I knew Sophia sometimes had issues with it when she was tired. It must be a twin thing, but either way, Violet and Hazel had to be some of the cutest human beings out there. And Sophia and Cale were doing a damn good job with them.

I put my phone in my back pocket and looked over the land that was now mine. I'd bought it from Dorian after the mudslide had taken out some of the property. It wasn't pretty, and it was going to take a hell of a lot of work, but once the contractor came in to help, it would be a little bit easier.

The old Ackerson place had been full of secrets long before Dorian had taken over. Our father had used it to hurt our family repeatedly, and I had a feeling our dad hadn't been the first one to use the place for illicit ongoings. But it wouldn't be that way anymore.

Once I was done, it would be something a Cage could be proud of. At least our generation of Cages. Because I was damn lucky that I had had a refuge to come back to after getting back from deployment. I had been broken, mentally and physically, and no amount of therapy would've worked if I hadn't had the lake. I knew that, and so did my therapist. So this place would be a refuge for those who couldn't do it on their own. A place for veterans to breathe once they could, to be with their families, or connect with their friends that they couldn't see otherwise. And they wouldn't be charged a damn penny. I had enough money, despite what I joked about with Sophia. I was a little more famous than I let on, and I used that to hoard as much cash as possible for this place and others like it.

I had things to do in my life that had nothing to do with…

My phone buzzed again, interrupting my thoughts, and I looked down and scowled. Today seemed to be a day for siblings. "Hello, Isabella."

"I hear that tone. But you promised."

I frowned. "What? What did I promise?

The sigh was loud enough to make my lips twitch. "Tonight is the Spring Flower Party. You *promised* you would come. In fact, you were bullied into it because you lost a coin toss, but you still told us you would be here after you lost the bet. I expect you at five o'clock tonight. It's early because there will be children and teenagers there, but you still need to show up. As you know, the Cages need to show their faces at events like this."

I pinched the bridge of my nose and sighed right back. "That damn thing is tonight?"

I ignored the laughter that sounded much more like Weston than it did Isabella. My friend would pay for this. "It is. I sent you a text about it yesterday, and it's on your calendar. You know, the shared calendar that we Cages have? You might not answer back in any of the group chats often, but I know that you know that I know you have a calendar that you use. It's color-coded and everything."

I resisted the audible groan. I was as organized as the next guy, but the connections and over the top Type A of some of my siblings nearly drove me over the edge. "Aston and Flynn color-coded the ridiculous platform. James is the one that adds random shit to it just to annoy me." I paused, remembering a time where a certain person had added timeslots for excessive brooding and labeled it as Grumpy Ass Mother Fuckin' Hudson. "On that note, so does Theo."

"Our brothers do love to annoy us. But that's why we love them. And that's why I love you. But you're coming tonight. You haven't been out of your cabin for like a month."

Because it had been a month since I'd nearly killed a man on Scarlett's property. She'd had no idea how close I had been. With just a few movements, I could have snapped his neck and not felt an ounce of remorse. The fucker had laid his hands on her. Just like the old man had done to her mother. And Scarlett had been scared.

Scarlett Blair *never* got scared. She could stand up to anyone, including Ronin and her father.

But she had broken down in my arms at one point because of those men. And she had nearly done it again. Yes, I would've killed him. I still didn't know why I hadn't. Because of my own restraint or due to Scarlett being right behind me.

Either way, I had stayed on my own property since then, not bothering to come to town. I had promised to go to this damn party after the St. Patrick's Day parade when I had stormed off, and now I regretted every single moment I had ever spoken to Isabella.

"Be there at five and wear something nice. Maybe don't scowl the whole time. You're welcome to scowl most of the time. Weston will because I'm dragging him."

That made me smile. "So he'll be in hell as well?

"It's a dance. There'll be punch. And alcohol. And food."

"And flowers. Because it's April, and we like to plant flowers in the beds at each street corner, as if we're not going to get snow."

"They're the spring flowers that are hardy through bouts of snow. The summer flowers we get in will do just as well. Be part of the community, Hudson."

I heard the worry in her tone and pushed it back. I didn't need a mirror shoved into my face. "I've been part of this community longer than you."

"No, you haven't. And we both know it."

I cursed. "I really don't like that you don't back down."

She laughed into the phone. "Of course I don't. I'm the eldest daughter. It's a thing."

"I wouldn't know. I didn't grow up with you girls."

"All the more reason for you to get annoyed by us now. And if you don't show up, Weston will have to drag you down, and then he'll be grumpy. And while I love my grumpy husband some days, grumpy because you annoy him won't be my favorite thing."

"As long as I don't make Weston grumpy, that's the most important thing," I said dryly.

Isabella chuckled and sounded far too pleased with herself. "At least you've learned. Now go shower, because I know you've been working on the cabin and the old Ackerson place all day."

I paused. "And how do you know that?"

"Because I stopped by your place earlier and you weren't there. I have my ways."

"Well then. Glad to know that if I ever die and am rotting alone on my carpet, I won't be rotting for too long."

My sister clucked her tongue. "This is why you need a pet. That way they can bark and let the neighbors know."

I thought of Scarlett being alone for so many hours in the day. She might be safe at the resort, but at home? Maybe she was the one who needed a dog. Or a cat. Then I couldn't help but think of a cat in my place. I may love animals, but I was always afraid they'd get out in this damn forest since I liked to leave my doors open on the way to the studio, and I'd never see them again. "Sure, let me get a pet and then the cat or whatever can eat my dead body. No, thank you."

"And on that note, I'll see you at five. Don't be late." Then she hung up, always getting the last word.

I let my head fall back as I put my phone in my back pocket. There was no escaping this family, no matter how hard I tried. I let out a breath and got back to work. I could at least get another hour in before I had to shower and get ready. And deal with this dance.

Of course, I couldn't help but remember one of the last dances I had gone to. Michelle had been dressed in blue with glitter, and had smiled up at me, all sweet and happy. I hadn't known that she had been cheating on me with Jefferson at that point. Or that she would marry him by the time I got back from my deployment. We had gone all through high school at each other's sides, and I had been a different person back then.

When I had gotten back from my second deployment, there hadn't been any dancing or smiles.

I push those thoughts from my head, knowing this dance would be different. I wasn't a kid anymore, and I didn't have a date. I would go and make my sister happy and not step foot on the dance floor. I knew the rules.

By the time I was showered and decently ready to go, I already wanted the night to end. However, I didn't really have much of a choice when it came to the rest of my evening. So I parked in front of the old barn that had been renovated a few times over the years and could fit most of the town locals. A few tourists would come as well, since the entry fee would go to helping restore some of the older buildings and the town bridge. And I figured that was a decent reason to have a dance.

After all, the last time the town bridge had gone out, tragedy had struck, and the town would never have that happen again.

I could hear the music from outside, a country tune where people seemed to be line dancing, and I held back a groan. I was officially entering one of my worst nightmares. At least I wouldn't end up covered in blood in this one. Unless this was going to be a recreation of that old Stephen King book. We did have a farm nearby with pigs. You just never knew.

"You're here!" Harper said as she moved forward and wrapped her arms around my waist. I immediately hugged my future sister-in-law back and lifted my chin at Dorian.

"I see you've been forced to come here too."

Dorian just beamed, his eyes bright. It was a damn fine thing to see considering the state he had been in last year. I hadn't blamed him for the darkness and had sat next to him through it since I understood, but being with Harper had truly changed him for the better, and it was good to see.

"Are you kidding me? I get to see my fiancée in a sexy dress as we slow dance? Of course I'm the one who had to come."

"I donated some baked goods, but really this was all Dorian's idea," Harper agreed.

I rolled my eyes. "Well. At least you're consistent."

Isabella and Weston came over next, and I said my

hellos, until I was forced to speak to resident after resident, who were just excited that I was out in public.

I didn't always hermit up in my cabin, but apparently going so far as to not leaving for nearly a month was too much for this town.

Isabella gave me a knowing look, and I nearly flipped her off but thought better of it since the local pastor was speaking to me.

"There you are, darling," Ms. Patty said, and I counted to ten so I wouldn't scream or run away.

"Hello, Ms. Patty." I leaned down and brushed my lips against her cheek. She giggled like a schoolgirl and waved me off.

"It's so good to see you out and about. I know you've been busy up in those woods of yours, and you're taking such good care of the area. You also must be painting up a storm. I can't wait to see more of what you do. Mr. Mayor and I were just talking about the old Johnson place. And how there used to be a mural there years ago before weather took over. We should have you do it. A Cage working on Cage property would just be perfect, don't you think?"

I was pretty sure Ms. Patty didn't take a single breath during that entire speech, and the fact that she squeezed her husband's forearm as she spoke, and called him Mr. Mayor, always made me pause. But the two were in love, you could tell from just the way that he looked down at her, and I couldn't really say a damn thing. Ms. Patty might love her gossip, but she would fight for anybody in this room. She's somebody you wanted on your side, even if I didn't want her in my business.

"We can talk about it in a bit. How about that?" I hedged.

The mayor just grinned at me. "You do know that it's going to happen anyway, don't you, son?" the man said slowly, and I held back a laugh.

Oh yes. Because once Ms. Patty wanted something, she got it. A few other townspeople came over, including a few older residents with their younger and single daughters, and soon I was surrounded.

I glared over their heads at Isabella, who looked at me wide-eyed. When she mouthed the words *I'm sorry*, I figured she hadn't expected this part.

Because I was the only single Cage here. In fact, I was one of the only single men here.

I had been conned. Bamboozled. And I needed to get out of here. However, from the way that Ms. Patty was looking at me, I was going to need to get on the damn dance floor at some point.

"Oh Hudson, you're here. I have a question for you," a familiar voice said, and I immediately turned and grabbed Scarlett's hand.

"I'm all yours," I growled, and her eyes widened.

"Okay, then. Let's talk while we dance."

I found myself on the dance floor, Scarlett fitting in

my arms far too comfortably, as the rest of the town looked on. Others joined us on the dance floor as a slow song began to drift from the speakers, and I let out a groan.

"Should I thank you?

"For saving you? Let's just call it tit for tat." I raised a brow, and her cheeks pinked. "Not in a dirty way, you freak."

"Is there something you really wanted to talk about?" I asked, ignoring the way she felt against me. I could feel her nipples pressing against my chest, and it was all I could do not to lean down and lick her lips. Or inhale the sweet and spicy scent of hers. *There's something wrong with me.*

We swayed back and forth, and I continued to ignore the knowing looks as well as the interested ones.

"I didn't have a question, only wanted to get you out of Ms. Patty's clutches. But now I'm regretting all of this."

I grunted. "Can't be seen dancing with me?"

"You're my boss and everyone will talk."

I shook my head and then twirled her around. She snorted, considering this was a slow dance, and I brought her back to my chest. Where she belonged. *No, I wasn't going to think that last thought.*

"I'm not your boss."

"I work for your family. And this town loves gossip. I was just getting you out of that awkward predicament since it didn't seem that Harper or Isabella was going to do it."

"Traitors," I grumbled.

She laughed against me, and we continued to dance.

I didn't like this feeling, the odd warmth spreading through my chest. I didn't like how she felt right against me. There was something wrong with this, but there was no easy way out of it.

"Thank you," I ground out.

"You sound thankful," she whispered.

"Now that I had this dance though, I can leave. I did my duty."

She looked up at me and studied my face. "So this is all duty?"

"What do you want me to say, Scar?" Because I had no idea what I was supposed to be thinking in that moment.

The song ended, and I took a step back, letting my hands fall.

"Thank you for the rescue."

Then I turned on my heel and practically ran from the building. I was a coward, and we both knew it.

"Hudson!"

I turned as Scarlett ran up to me. She held out my phone, and I frowned. "I dropped my phone? Hell. I'm sorry."

"It must've been hanging out of your pocket earlier,

or maybe Ms. Patty was trying to steal it. You know, to check your schedule."

"I wouldn't put it past her." I slid it in my back pocket, wondering how exactly that had happened, and shook my head. "I guess it's the night I should be thanking you."

She stood in front of me, as I swallowed hard. She was so damn close. What the hell was wrong with me?

I looked down at her, my breath quickening, and I licked my lips. Her gaze went right to the gesture, or maybe I was just seeing things. But I reached out, doing the unthinkable, and pushed a strand of her hair back from her face and tucked it behind her ear.

"I like your dress by the way. I didn't really say that before."

And I did like her dress. She wore red that faded into a pale pink and matched her name perfectly. It was one of those older-type dresses that flared around her knees and had a heart neckline. Or at least that's what I thought it was called. Either way, it made her breasts stand out, and I really needed to stop thinking about her breasts.

"Thanks. I don't get to wear dresses like these often. I'm usually in more business attire."

"You look good then too." I nearly bit off my tongue wondering what the hell I was saying.

"Oh. Well you look good now too. I mean, last time I saw you, you weren't wearing a shirt, so you looked good then as well, but... well, I'm just going to stop thinking or talking. Or whatever."

I let out a curse and lowered my head. "This is a damn mistake."

"Totally."

And then my mouth was on hers, my hand sliding through the back of her hair, and I stepped off that precipice that told me that this was going to end badly.

She tasted of sweetness, and Scarlett, and it was everything I could do not to press her up against the side of the barn and take her right then. Instead, I just deepened the kiss and let my hand fall to her waist. Her hands went to my back, her fingernails digging in, and when I tilted my head, our tongues colliding, I finally tore myself away, trying to catch my breath.

"Mistake," she blurted.

I nodded, not knowing if either one of us was telling the truth. "Mistake."

And with that, I stormed to my truck, grateful that nobody had seen. Out of the corner of my eye, I saw Scarlett join the others, so I knew she was safe.

Safe from anyone who wanted to hurt her, and sure as hell safe from me.

Chapter Seven
Scarlett

After three days, I should have been able to push all thoughts of a certain Cage out of my mind. In fact, I should be able to ignore that he even existed in the first place. I hadn't slept a full night since the moment I'd left him, however.

I could still taste him on my lips, I could still feel his body pressed into mine. Why was it so difficult for me to even breathe when it came to Hudson Cage?

He made no sense. He practically hated me and I wasn't sure what I felt about him. How could I when every time I saw him, our push and pull nearly gave me a migraine? He'd seen me at my worst and yet I'd never seen him close to his. He hid himself so well it was hard to even imagine what that could be. But I could still taste him on my tongue and had to wonder where the hell that had come from because there was no way I was going to ever be able to breathe the same way again when he was around me.

I was losing my sense of reality when it came to him. I paged through my planner on my desk, knowing I had a long day ahead of me. And having Hudson on my mind would only complicate things.

And yet there had been something on his face. Not lust, not need. But something else. Something I couldn't quite put my finger on.

Perhaps I was looking for something that would appear, but it felt as if there was a damage beneath the surface other than him being worried about me. Other than him always being angry that he had to step in to help me. As if I wasn't just as angry that he had to do the same.

I ran my hands over my face and went back to my planner.

Today was a big day at the resort. We had a sizeable and grand wedding, and I wanted to make sure it was perfect. Not only for the bride, groom, and wedding party, but for anyone else who happened to be at the resort. The Cage Resort didn't normally do weddings on a scope such as this. Yes, there were a few smaller ones that fit the atmosphere the elder Cages had envisioned, but the resort was usually for skiing, hiking, and other outdoor activities. Getting your hot toddy while the rest of your party was out on the slopes, or hiking in the spring, was the main event.

I wanted to help bring the resort into a new era. Climate change was affecting the way the timing of the resort worked. This generation of Cages were environmentally and economically responsible and doing their best to combat climate change. They were putting their money, talents, and designs into making sure the resort was self-sustainable on solar and wind energy and were looking into different ways to help increase the population of certain wildlife, as well as aid in water conservation and quality, and even had a science team on property working on different erosion studies. I knew Hudson's father had been staunchly against things like this. In fact, I knew that he would rather burn the place down than worry about any tree-hugging nonsense.

This generation of Cages cared. Truly cared. I was grateful that I could be part of *something*. And as the changes affected more than the environment, it meant that what happened on property would also need to evolve. There needed to be a way to make the Cages money, that way they could put it towards more research and to ensure that they didn't only rely on using what was around them. I was so thankful to be part of this company, and I wanted to show them all that hiring me wasn't a waste.

At first, I had been afraid they had hired me because I was a local and had stood up to their father on more than one occasion. Part of me also had thought that maybe they were using me to get back at their dad, or even just because I was a pretty girl who happened to live in town.

I knew that they trusted me. They believed in what I could do. At least, they used to. Now I was adding more and more to their plate, trying to get them to see that there was so much more that could be done within the Cage name. And considering I wasn't a Cage, sometimes it felt as if I were perhaps taking on something far too big that wasn't mine to begin with.

But I needed to push that from my mind and get back to what I knew would be beneficial for the town, the resort, the Cages, and maybe a little to me.

"Hey, I was just stopping by to check on you. How are you?" Isabella asked as she walked into my office after tapping on the doorframe.

I'd had the door open, and she knew that if the door was closed, I wasn't ready to talk to anyone and was focusing. But I did have an open-door policy. If the door was open, I was free to chat, or to see what anybody needed.

I couldn't help but remember the last time I thought I had closed the door, but had failed.

The bruises had healed, even the bruises within. Perhaps those were more scarred over than anything, but I wasn't the same woman I had been when I had looked into that mirror and realized I had failed. And yet having Hudson there, watching my failure, had been the final pin. I had yelled, screamed, and hated myself for breaking down in front of him.

And it turns out it hadn't been the last time I would do so in front of him.

And that was why I needed to stay away from him. Of course, his sister was here, and I was trying to impress my friend, as well as the rest of her family, when it came to the wedding today.

No pressure.

"Hey there. I'm okay. I didn't know you'd be here this early." I smiled, looked at my watch, and held back a wince. Apparently daydreaming about Hudson had made time move far too quickly. I wasn't behind, but I was no longer ahead either. This man was a menace.

I quickly closed down my computer and moved around the desk to hug Isabella.

Her hold tightened as she let out a sigh. "It's good to be back. I love living in Denver. But I think I'm slowly becoming a Cage Lake resident."

"You *are* a Cage Lake resident, considering you're married to a local. It just happens."

Isabella shook her head. "Weston needs time in the city too though. So this way we're both able to get what we need, and we don't have to choose. And frankly, I enjoy being able to work in the office."

Isabella worked with Cage Enterprises. Everybody in the family had the option of doing so, although they needed to find their niche. Not every sibling did, however. Ford owned his own company with his husband and their family. They ran security for the Cages, but they had a completely different business and focus. Hudson didn't work with Cage Enterprises at all. He was an artist. I held back a smile thinking about that art. He always surprised me, how talented he could be, even beneath the gruff growly exterior.

Isabella hadn't always worked with the Cages, and in fact, I knew had resisted working with them even after she'd found out that they were siblings. She was damn good at her job as a forensic accountant and could do most of her job outside of the offices. Getting to know her family and becoming a cohesive unit was a large part of why she spent so much time in Denver.

"Anyway, I see that your team as well as the wedding planner are running around with such efficiency that I knew it had to be your doing."

I smiled at that, even as nerves began to tense my shoulders. "Oh good. I'm glad that they're on schedule. I was just working on a few things and then I'll get back to it. I promise I'm not leaving them alone."

Isabella frowned at me, and I realized my voice had gone slightly high-pitched.

"They're your team. Of course they're doing what they should. I'm not here to check on you, Scarlett. I just wanted to see how the wedding was going. I trust you. You're the best manager we could ever want. In fact, you could be managing an even bigger establishment. I'm just glad that you're here."

Even as she said the words, I wanted to believe her, yet part of me knew that she was still part-owner of the place that paid my bills. She, more than some of the other Cages. Aston, James, Blakely, Flynn, and Isabella were all part of Cage Enterprises and therefore my bosses. They were the owners of this establishment. Technically everybody else in the family were considered owners, because they were part of the main trust, but they weren't part of the day-to-day ownership. Much of the Cage business and will info had been newsworthy and I couldn't help but pick up on some of it. Hudson didn't work for Cage Enterprises.

Of course that's just reminding me that technically Hudson wasn't my boss, and that was my main excuse for telling myself not to think of him. But that was fine. I had plenty of other reasons not to think about him. Ever. At all. For anything.

I swallowed hard and tried not to let my thoughts show on my face.

"Oh. I know." I paused. "I should still go check on them. It's good to see you. Is there anything you need?" I asked, my voice still slightly high-pitched.

"We are good. Do your thing."

I moved past Isabella and down the corridor. I was stopped by a few of my team members, answered their questions, and kept moving to the beautiful open area where the wedding would take place.

The flowers were set, the chairs in order, and yet, I needed to go by each point with the wedding planner to ensure this went off perfectly. This wedding and event was the first step in ensuring that we grew as a company.

The couple, Mark and Jacob, were fabulous, caring, and had wanted their perfect day. And I was going to make sure that happened.

Denise, their wedding planner, came up to me with a list in hand. "We have a few little snafus, but nothing we can't handle."

I gave her my calmest of smiles. "Give me the list and I've got it."

The other woman's eyes widened. "No it's okay, I can handle this."

"You work on the next steps and let me see what I can do for the resort."

Out of the corner of my eye I saw Isabella frown at me, before another person came into view. Shoulders tense, I told myself that I could handle him. Of course I could. Just because Hudson was here, hovering, didn't mean I needed to fall into a heap.

"Okay fine. I'm going to take you up on that. Thank you," Denise said with a sigh. "You have been doing so much for this wedding, and I know we couldn't have done it without you." She squeezed my hand, and then practically ran towards another person on her staff. I lifted my chin and read through the note. There were only small things, ones that my team members could do, but I would make this happen. I needed to ensure that I wasn't going to fail at this. I had already failed at so much.

"Scarlett. Are you okay?" Isabella's phone rang then, and she cursed. "One second. And then you're going to tell me why you have that look on your face."

"Everything's fine. I'm just working." I moved past her towards the kitchens where I needed to speak with the chef about a minor thing that could turn into a major thing.

"Scarlett, breathe." I moved out of Hudson's reach and glared over my shoulder as I kept going.

"I don't have time for you and your growling. I have to get through this list, and then countless other things. We only have a few more hours until the wedding begins, and it has to be perfect."

I ignored Hudson's curious look, as I went to the chef and went over the minor alterations. He nodded, although I felt like maybe he should be slightly more worried. But he said he could handle it, and therefore it should all be fine.

And yet nothing felt fine. If this wasn't perfect, then all of the extra money and time that went into this would be for nothing. The Cages needed to understand that I could handle this.

And me running around like a chicken with its head cut off wasn't truly showing that.

I moved past Hudson again as I went to the next person, my list feeling heavier and heavier. Why did my chest ache? This made no sense, but it was fine. I could handle this.

By the time I got through my list, I realized that Hudson had been following me, but I continued to ignore him. People moved out of his way, eyes wide, and I hoped to hell he wasn't around when the wedding started or he would scare the guests.

As I turned the corner to get to the next person on my list, I bumped into the solid wall of man that was Hudson Cage.

"Excuse me. You're in my way."

He looked down at me, then gripped my shoulders. He didn't have to say a word and yet every ounce of trepidation, annoyance, and whatever the hell else I refused to feel burst to the surface.

"Get your hands off me," I snapped, my breath quickening.

"Scarlett. Breathe."

As if I didn't want to? As if I wasn't already trying to? Why did my chest hurt? And why did he sound as if he cared?

"I'm working, Hudson. If you want to yell at me or growl or do whatever you like to do, do it later. Okay?

I'm trying to ensure that this wedding goes off without a hitch, and you're in my way."

He let out a grunt I couldn't quite decipher. "You just stressed out the cake decorator, because you tried to guarantee that the mother-in-law gets a certain iced flower on her cake, versus the other mother-in-law, because they fight. Even though the wedding planner had already told them, and the grooms assured everyone that it wouldn't matter. And yet you're panicking."

"Just because it seemed like a little thing to you doesn't mean it's not a huge thing to the person who is worried." Although the idea of an iced flower when there were multiple of them made no sense to me, but it was on the wedding planner's list, and I was going to ensure that everything was perfect.

"It's a wedding. They're going to say their I do's, be happy, dance, someone's going to get too drunk, and someone's going to break something. But in the end, they'll be happy, and it won't matter. You're doing a great job."

"And I can do better," I blurted.

"Scar," he said with a sigh. "What the hell is going on?"

"*Nothing*. I just need to ensure that this goes well. It's the first one of this size that we're doing."

"And they have a wedding planner that's working

with your event coordinator. You manage the entire place. You don't need to be doing these small things."

"Are you saying they're below me? That's rich coming from the owner." I knew I was losing my mind, but whenever Hudson was around, I tended to do that.

"Scar."

"My name's Scarlett."

"You like it when I call you Scar. You smile even as you tell me you hate it."

I blushed and shoved at him softly. "Hudson. Stop."

Though I did like him calling me Scar. There was something wrong with me.

"By the way, I'm not the owner. I just help out my siblings when they can't be here. And I like to make sure you're not running yourself ragged."

"It's not your place to care if I run *myself* ragged."

"Yes it is. Because somebody should fucking care."

"Watch your language. One of the guests might hear you. Some of them stayed overnight."

"And that's great for the bottom line, but I don't care right now. Go get some water, take a break. You're going to end up getting sick of you don't take a break."

"I'm doing my job."

"And you're fucking amazing at it. All of us know it. Stop trying to prove that you're the best at everything. You already are."

Maybe if I hadn't already been having a panic attack, his words would've meant something to me. But instead, I raised my chin, gripped my note in my hand like a lifeline, and pushed past him.

I didn't know what it said about me that his words just then meant everything. That he believed in me.

But maybe I was just hearing what I wanted to hear.

I needed to be the best. Because if I wasn't, that would be one more failure, and I could not let that happen.

Not again.

Before I could move down the corridor, he gripped my arm and pulled me towards him.

"Hudson," I breathed.

"You've got this, Scar. Stop stressing out."

"I'm not stressing."

"Then don't lie." His mouth was so close to mine that all I had to do was go to my tiptoes and let him take me.

No that would be wrong. Oh so wrong. Not only was I working, this was Hudson Cage.

We didn't even like each other. And yet that felt like a lie. Such a damn lie.

"Scarlett?" Denise asked from behind me, and I realized that if she kept moving towards us, she would be able to see. I didn't know what this was, but nobody was allowed to see this. So I pulled back and lifted my chin.

"Thank you for your concern, but I can handle this."

Hudson met my gaze, as if searching for something that wasn't there, before finally letting out a breath and letting me go.

It was for the best. It had to be. Hudson Cage and I were merely neighbors. Nothing more. Nothing less.

And I was going to prove to everyone that I could handle this.

And that I wouldn't fail again.

Chapter Eight
Scarlett

I sank into the soft chair and carefully accepted a glass of wine from Isabella. "Thank you. I think I'm going to name this wine My Best Friend." I winked at the woman across from me. "Other than you, of course."

Isabella just shook her head and lifted her wine glass. "To finally having a moment to relax."

We clinked our glasses together, and I took a sip of the crisp Pinot Grigio.

We didn't usually have time during the week for a girls' night, but since Isabella would be leaving town soon to spend the next couple of weeks in Denver for her job as well as Weston's expansion, it meant that this was the only time that we could make it work. And considering the day I had already been through, I was forever grateful for this moment.

"That bad, huh?" Isabella asked, and I nodded, staring into my wine.

"I nearly caved and called Luna to help me." I looked up at my friend and sighed. "I don't know what to do about Mom. I love her, and respect her, and admire everything she's done. But she had a panic attack today because we had to go to her doctor's office. It broke me, Isabella. I don't know what I was supposed to do. Doc Henry is doing all that he can to help, and if it wasn't for Allie being nearby on a jog, I don't know if I would've been able to lift my mother into the car."

"Allie didn't mention that she was there." Isabella set down her glass. "At least she didn't mention it to Weston, as he would've told me."

"I think she just wanted to keep it quiet. She's a brilliant mechanic, and a wonderful person, and I'm glad that she kept it to herself. Honestly, I was afraid someone else would see and it would become gossip fodder. Mom would hate that. She always despised when people spoke about her whenever Dad went to jail, or when people would whisper about her bruises." My fingers tightened on the stem of the wineglass, and I forced myself to relax slightly. "But if you see Allie before I do, tell her thank you. She's the kindest person."

"Of course I will. And she *is* kind. I didn't mean

that I had expected her to gossip, only that I wish I would've known so I could have helped."

I shook my head. "We got it handled this time. I just don't know what we're going to do next time. Even a simple checkup today was nearly too much. And Sheriff Brothers was walking by on our way out and helped me get her into the car to take her home." I lowered my voice. "They had to use a sedative on her, and I nearly broke down."

"Scarlett. You have so much on your shoulders. I'm glad others were there to help you, but there has to be something we could do to help your mother. Is she seeing a therapist?"

I nodded and took another sip of my wine, this time it was more of a gulp. "Yes, but I don't think it's helping. Not the way that she wants. Or selfishly, not the way I want."

"It's not selfish for you to want your mom to be able to function as a member of society and be happy."

"It sure as hell feels selfish because I don't want to have to be forced to take half a day off work just to get my mother to the doctor and feel like I'm kidnapping her in the process."

Isabella opened her mouth to say something, but the waitress came at that moment.

"Welcome to the Rustic Cage. We're so glad that you're here. I see that you're sharing a bottle of wine, are we waiting on another member of your party?" she asked.

The Rustic Cage was a new restaurant in town that Theo Cage owned along with his business partner that I didn't know. Theo was one of the Cages who rarely came to town, and he owned a high-end restaurant called The Teal Door in Downtown Denver. He was a brilliant chef and had wanted something similar in Cage Lake since so many of his siblings were spending time here and even moving here. Theo didn't cook here often, as he had hired a chef to run his menu, but the place was reasonably priced, and I loved sending resort guests to the restaurant on the days they weren't eating in our restaurant.

Isabella looked up at the waitress and smiled. It was nice to have another person take over answering questions and dealing with organizing. We were both Type A, and yet we took turns in taking over. "Yes, we're waiting on Harper and Ivy. They should be here soon."

"My name is Jackie if you need anything. I'll be back in a moment when they arrive. And honestly, I'm really excited to see Ivy again. She's been out of town for the past couple of weeks."

"That's our friend, constantly leaving Cage Lake for other forests."

Jackie winked. "But she always comes back. I'll get you guys some bread while you're waiting."

"With the amount of wine I'm about to drink, I'm going to need that bread," I said softly, and Jackie gave me a nod, a bright smile, and hurried off presumably to get our bread.

I turned to Isabella and drained the rest of my wine. "I didn't know Ivy was coming."

Isabella, the wonderful friend that she was, immediately filled up my wine glass from the bottle left on the table. "She didn't know she was going to be able to either. But she's on her way. She just needed to finish showering, as she arrived less than an hour ago. Harper should be here soon, though when she called to let me know that she was on her way, Dorian was behind her, and there was giggling." Isabella shuddered. "Things I don't need to know about my brother."

"Knowing the two of them, she could be here any moment, or in an hour," I said dryly.

"I don't need to know details," Isabella said, holding up both hands.

Guilt swept over me when I realized that I hadn't told her that Hudson and I had kissed. Or the fact that we kept bumping into each other, and that heat I wanted to ignore continued to be there.

I shouldn't mention it at all though, because it wasn't going to lead anywhere. Hudson was just as ornery as always, and it wasn't as if he wanted me like that. Maybe for a night, but Hudson wasn't meant for long-term. He had even said as much to me before.

Hudson Cage wasn't for me, and that kiss would never be repeated. Whatever overprotective urge he had within himself would be over soon, and neither one of us would need to think about it again. The fact that he was my neighbor, and his sister sat right across from me, meant nothing. And if I kept telling myself that, it would make sense eventually.

"I'm late, I'm late, sorry!" Harper said as she bounced into the dining room and took one of the empty seats on either side of Isabella and me. "I'm seriously sorry that I'm late."

I smirked as I poured her some of the wine. "What made you late?" I teased.

Harper blushed.

Isabella rolled her eyes. "Seriously? I don't need to know these things."

"What do you mean?" Harper asked far too innocently as she pulled her dark hair from her face.

"I realized I just poured you wine without asking if you wanted it," I said with a laugh, knowing that the wine was already getting to me. I was a lightweight and probably shouldn't have even had two glasses of wine. But I had taken a rideshare here and would do the same back home. Yes, the rideshare was usually one of two older men who were retired and enjoyed talking up a storm with the locals and tourists, but it was safer than me walking home around the lake at night.

"This wine is perfect, although, we're probably going to need at least another bottle," she said with a laugh.

"Already on it," Isabella said as she waved at the waitress.

Of course Isabella would be on it. I might be Type A and could get things done with a list like nobody's business, and yet Isabella could always out-organize me.

I didn't have a complex at all.

Just as the waitress brought a second bottle of wine and two baskets of bread—I was going to marry her—Ivy showed up in a storm of cheeriness and bright smiles.

As a nature photographer, she was outside more than not, and though she wore plenty of sunscreen and hats as well as all sun protection possible, she was currently sporting a golden tan in a time where most people were just starting to see sunlight again after hibernating in the winter.

"I'm so glad I could make it. There's a blizzard happening in the next town, and it's sunny here. I was worried that the bridge would be closed, but there was no storm here. Shocking."

I pulled out my phone and frowned. "Did I know there was a blizzard? I should."

"It's miles away and won't affect the resorts. You're off work tonight," Isabella chided.

I set down my phone and tried not to think about all the little things I might be missing.

"Sorry. Hi, Ivy. So good to see you." I reached out and squeezed her hand, and she beamed at me.

"I love seeing you too. I feel like it's been forever. And not just a few weeks."

"So tell us where you were. Tell us everything." I poured her a glass of wine and then filled mine up as well. I couldn't help it. I needed that drink.

When we were all settled, Jackie came to take our order, and I sank back into the chair, listening as my friends spoke about their weeks.

It was odd to think that the last time we had truly done this, I'd been with Ronin. And each of my talking points would have been about him, and what we would be doing. I had thought I'd found the one. The person who I would spend the rest of my life with and create a future with. I had been oh so wrong. To the point that I could have broken everything. My hands fisted on my fork, and I forced myself to move back and focus on the people in front of me. They were who mattered. They were my future.

Not a man I thought I could trust and had been wrong about.

"When we go down to Denver, I'm going to go and kidnap Ford's son," Isabella said.

I blinked. "What?" I asked, apparently not having fully been paying attention.

The girls laughed, and I set down my fork, wondering perhaps if I'd had *too* much wine.

"My brother Ford? He and his spouses have their nine-month-old son Micah. And I'm going to kidnap him for an auntie day."

Now I was really confused. "An auntie day?"

"It's a day where I can be the aunt and spoil him. He's still a baby, but he has those little biteable cheeks and legs, and I'm going to kidnap him and spoil him to my heart's content."

"That sounds perfect," I said, my heart aching just a bit.

"You'll be able to do that with Luna once she decides if she wants kids," Ivy said with a smile.

I nearly choked on my wine. Was this glass three? Four? It didn't matter. I was feeling good. "I would love to be an aunt, and I hope that Luna provides me that recourse sometime, but I'm not going to pressure her into becoming a mom and starting a family. Of course, she might need to find someone to do that with, but for all I know, she has a secret boyfriend."

What the hell was I saying? I was the one with secrets. Not that Hudson was my boyfriend, or mine in any way. But I had kissed him. Did I say that out loud? No. I was still safe.

"We should totally text her right now and see if she

has a secret boyfriend," Harper said as she clapped her hands. "I know she's coming up soon so we can work on planning the wedding, but I feel like I don't see her enough."

"That's what happens when we all grow up and move to different places," Ivy said with a shrug. "My home is here, and yet I'm rarely in it. So I don't know when I'll have time to start with the whole family and baby-making."

"We'll be perfect aunts when the time comes," Isabella said. "Plus, since Harper's marrying into the family, we'll be co-aunties, and because I have one hundred siblings, there's going to be a glorious number of them."

"So many little nibblings," I teased.

"Exactly," Isabella said with a snap of her fingers. "Aston and Blakely are having a baby soon, and I know Kane and Phoebe are talking about it." She turned to Harper. "I know you guys are waiting."

"Yes. Waiting. Probably a long while."

"And Sophia and Cale had the twins," Isabella continued, smiling so brightly her cheeks looked like they were going to ache.

"Your family's growing. I love it," I said after a moment.

"Me too. After everything that's happened, it's good just to know that we're finding our spaces. And you should know that Weston and I have decided we are not having kids," she blurted and quickly went to her meal, cutting up her steak as if she was worried what we were going to say.

I met Ivy's and then Harper's gazes, before we each turned to Isabella. A pause. "Good for you."

Isabella's gaze shot up. "Really? We had been talking about it, and well, Weston practically raised his siblings, and I don't know, I've always pictured myself being an aunt and helping my siblings and doing all of the fun things that comes with that, but I never really thought of myself as a mom."

"You don't have to be a parent in order to find your happily ever after," Ivy said as she squeezed Isabella's hand. "You and Weston are traveling more, and it's not as if Weston's siblings are completely out of the house since they can come back whenever they need to. So between them, and all of the Cages, you're going to have plenty of family. I'm so glad that you're making a decision for yourself, not for anyone else."

Isabella let out a relieved sigh. "It's not that I was afraid you guys would judge me, more that I didn't know anything. I am so blessed with my family. With all of you, and I like the way that things are."

"That just means you're going to spoil your little nibblings even more," I put in.

"Exactly. They deserve all the spoiling."

"And if Dorian and I ever decide to have kids, I expect all the spoiling. And the babysitting."

Ivy rolled her eyes. "You've already mentioned that you want plenty of kids, and Dorian is one of those men that screams breeder."

I nearly choked on my wine. "Ivy!"

"What? He like gets all growly and protective around her. He's ready to imprint his DNA all over that." She waved her finger around Harper, and all of us burst into laughter.

The conversation turned to the upcoming parade, and yet another Cage-like event, and I sank into my wine, finally feeling relaxed after far too many months of hiding. My mother was safe at home. Luna would be visiting soon. My job was doing exactly what it needed to, and I wasn't failing. At least that's what I kept telling myself. And I was doing just fine. My father would get bored of bothering me soon, and Ronin hadn't been back in a while. I was surviving and figuring out how to thrive. It was enough for now.

"I see you guys loved your filets and sea bass, are we thinking dessert?" Jackie asked as she cleared away our plates.

I put my hand over my stomach and shook my head. "Oh no, I have zero room. But dinner was delightful."

"Yes, please tell the chef." Isabella narrowed her gaze. "It's not Theo, is it? I never see him, and he continues to hide from me. I think he's scared of his sister."

Jackie laughed. "It's not Theo today, but he does like to show up unexpectedly."

"You should ask that group chat of yours and force Theo to let you know when he's here," I said, hoping my words weren't slurring. Maybe it was time to get a little more water into my system.

"I do need to head out soon though, I walked here, and I want to get some fresh air," Luna said as she squeezed my hand. "Do you have a ride home?"

I blinked, feeling warm and happy. "I was going to do a rideshare. I'm okay."

"You can go home with Weston and me. Or at least, we can drop you off," Isabella said with a giggle. She'd had nearly as much as me.

"And then there's Dorian of course. But then, with the way he looks at me, he might be in that breeder mood."

I burst out laughing, as Isabella groaned into her hands.

"It's okay, I'll take her home." That familiar voice slid down my spine, and I froze.

"What?" I burst out, turning in my seat so quickly the chair buckled. Hudson moved forward, wrapped one large hand around the arm of my chair, and the other on my shoulder.

"Easy there, Scar," he mumbled.

The girls might've been speaking, but I couldn't focus. *Why was he here? What did he want?*

"I was just having dinner with my brothers, and they're here to take their women home."

"Did I say that out loud?" I asked, my cheeks heating.

"Yes. You did. Did you have any water?"

"Some," I mumbled.

Hudson sighed and tugged on my arm. "Come on, let's get you home, neighbor." He spoke over my head, but I wasn't paying attention. Instead I leaned my cheek against his chest, feeling that nipple ring slightly, and let out a contented sigh. Maybe I'd had a little bit too much to drink, but in the end it didn't matter. This was all a very odd dream anyway.

"This is interesting," Ivy whispered, or maybe she shouted. I wasn't sure.

Either way, I found myself walking alongside Hudson to his truck.

"In you go," Hudson mumbled.

"I'm fine. I'm going to call someone."

"I'm not letting you get in a stranger's car, Scar."

"You're not the boss of me."

He buckled me into my seat, his breath warm against my cheek. "Maybe you need a little bossing around."

I tried to say something funny, but instead I just closed my eyes, and the next thing I noticed when I opened them, we were parked in his driveway.

"Wait. Where are we? I thought I was going home."

"Can't find your keys," he grumbled, and I reached for my purse, only to realize it felt half empty.

"Oh no," I mumbled.

"Woman, you're going to be the death of me."

Things were moving rapidly, yet felt like I was four steps behind. Maybe I'd had one too many glasses of wine. It wasn't something I did. Ever. I needed to be aware of my surroundings, I knew that, and yet I just wanted a moment where I didn't have to think.

I found myself in Hudson's arms, my cheek resting against his shoulder, as he carried me into his home.

"Your purse fell in my truck, and your keys are somewhere. I'll get them in the morning. Let's get you to sleep."

"I'm fine," I pouted. "I don't want to stay here."

A lie.

He rubbed his beard against the top of my head. "Someone needs to take care of you, Scarlett, even if you don't want it."

"I can do it on my own."

"If you just mumbled that you could do it on your own, we both know that's usually the case but just let me help."

With a sigh I let him carry me up the stairs, and then found myself tucked into soft sheets, and my shoes on the ground next to the bed.

I tried to say something to be clever, but there was nothing.

I merely let Hudson take care of me, with giving me a glass of water, and finally sank into the pillows, wondering what the hell I was doing.

Hudson Cage was a menace, but in this moment, he was *my* menace.

Chapter Nine
Hudson

I wasn't quite sure how I had ended up in this position, but I knew that something was going to have to change. Spending so many hours constantly fighting with Scarlett, even though it felt as if we were always forced in each other's proximity, wasn't going to work anymore.

Although the sun had risen about an hour ago, I had been up for more than two. I had my studio door open, as well as the back door to my home with just the screen door, that way I could hear if Scarlett woke up. I still couldn't quite believe that she was in my guest bedroom, snoring away, hopefully waking up without too bad of a hangover. I didn't know if Scarlett got hangovers.

Since we weren't really friends, it wasn't something I should know. I frowned and dipped my paintbrush into the green. Though it really wasn't a true green, more of a cerulean.

Were Scarlett and I friends? Perhaps we were after all this time. We had just done such a good job of pushing each other away, it didn't feel as if we should consider ourselves friends. I didn't know what we were, but I was damn tired of fighting it. Ms. Perfect didn't want me to protect her? Fine. But I had a feeling keeping away from each other like we were trying wasn't going to work as it should.

From what I knew, Scarlett had the full day off today, so she could either sleep it off, or go with what I had planned. I frowned, trying to get the shade just right for this part of my piece. My head clearly wasn't in the game, if it was taking me this long to find the right green. I sighed, set my supplies down, and stared at the easel.

I didn't always work with such small pieces, but I'd wanted to gift Ford's son something cute-ish for his nursery wall. The kid soon would get a big boy bed, at least that's what I thought, and that meant his decorations would change. Right? I didn't know kids. The idea that my siblings were all having them meant I needed to learn what milestones were. And that wasn't something on my radar. When did they learn to talk? Walk? Were Sophia's twins dating people yet? Were they even two yet?

I ran my hand over my face and cringed before I

realized I didn't have paint on this particular one. The number of times I had slid paint through my hair was astronomical at this point.

Ford's son liked frogs from what I could tell, since he always babbled and smiled when frogs were around, so I figured I'd paint a frog-like picture for the kid. They could throw it away for all I cared, but I could at least give them something.

I had started the tradition with Sophia's kids, and I would continue to do so with Aston and Blakely's once it was born.

I quickly cleaned up my area, and washed my hands, and figured I'd get back to this whenever my head was in the game. My thoughts had been straying towards the woman in my guest room far too much. I knew some things about her, but not enough. And the part of me that I had thought long since dormant wanted to know more.

Like why the hell she had chosen Ronin in first place.

Growling, I shook my head and closed up my studio. I liked being out in the mountains, away from the rest of the world. The idea that Scarlett was so close however, hadn't really bothered me before. Before the huge storm that had taken out part of the Ackerson place, there had been a line of trees separating us. So I hadn't really seen Scarlett that often. But we had lost four large trees in that storm, creating a perfect view between the two places.

My sense of solitude had been disrupted.

And that was what Scarlett Blair was good at.

Destruction.

I checked my watch and realized that she would be waking up soon. She was always an early riser from what I could tell, so sleeping off however much wine that she had, would end soon.

I pulled out bacon and eggs and a couple of potatoes, I figured I'd put up a sort of breakfast for her.

A scramble could work. I added some spinach, peppers, mushrooms, and hoped to hell she liked all of this.

When grapped the serrano, I grinned and remembered the time we'd eaten all of Harper's dinner, because Harper hadn't realized it had been so spicy, and Scarlett could handle it.

If she wanted heat, I'd give her heat.

I frowned in the midst of chopping.

What the hell was that about?

Did she want heat? Well she had sure as fuck kissed me back. But what did I want from that?

I hadn't dated or wanted anybody in a long while. Sure I'd slept with people, but it had been transactional. Each of us had wanted a single night, and that's what we'd had. And I didn't fuck people in Cage Lake. I went to one of the other small towns around the area, like Ashford Creek, or Silver Lake, or even Sunrise Ridge. It was easier to find somebody for a single night there, than deal with the drama of fucking with anybody in Cage Lake.

I didn't know what the hell I was thinking when it came to Scarlett Blair, but she was in my house, and something needed to change, or I was never going to get any sleep.

Footsteps sounded on the stairs, and I quickly tossed everything into the skillet, working on my scramble. "Good morning, sleepyhead. Coffee is made, but if you prefer tea, I have an electric kettle because Isabella dropped it off." It amazed me how quickly our two families had begun to blend. Though I hadn't grown up with any of my sisters, I saw them nearly as much as I did the brothers I *had* grown up with. The only one I didn't see often was Kyler, and that was because he was out on tour. And frankly, he didn't spend much time in Cage Lake. And I did my best to avoid people in Denver. Our father had done his best to split us up, and then forced us together, and somehow in spite of him, we were becoming a family.

"Thank you for the water and ibuprofen," Scarlett said softly as she padded towards the kitchen. She'd unearthed a hair tie somehow and piled her hair on the top of her head. Thankfully she had put on the long sweats and T-shirt I had set on the edge of the bed. I'd put her to sleep in her dress, and while part of me had wanted to undress her so she would be comfortable — and probably other reasons — I hadn't. Being a gentleman wasn't easy. Not that I was actually a gentleman.

"Thank you for the clothes too. And, well, everything." She put her hands over her face and groaned. "I never drink that much." At least that's what I thought she mumbled.

"I don't either, but when I do, I like a hearty breakfast the next morning. You in or is it going to make you queasy?"

I looked over my shoulder at her silence and she just stood there, frowning at me, her hands at her sides. "Why are you being so nice to me? You're never nice to me."

A sliver of guilt slid inside me at that comment, but I did my best to ignore it. "I'm tired of fighting all the time, and I'm hungry. Are you going to eat? I found your keys by the way. They had rolled to the back of the truck, at least inside the cabin. So you can get into your house when you need to. But I did make enough breakfast for two."

She was quiet for so long I was afraid she had left, but then she came to my side and looked down into the skillet.

"Is that a quiche? Or the beginnings of one?"

I snorted. "I'm not Theo, or that fancy. But it's a

scramble. Everything will be cooked, you won't die of salmonella. At least I don't think so."

"That makes me feel safe." She paused, and I knew she was wrestling with similar thoughts to my own. "I would love breakfast. Thank you."

"No problem. Do you want that coffee?"

"I can get it. Are the mugs near the maker?"

"They are."

"Would you like me to top you off as well?"

We met gazes, even though the unintended innuendo lay heavy between us, and I nodded. "Yes please, I don't need cream or sugar."

"I'm in the mood for all of the cream and sugar if that's okay."

"I don't have any of that fancy creamer stuff, but I have half-and-half. I think."

Her lips twitched. "I can make that work." She paused. "Thank you."

"You don't have to keep thanking me."

"Would you rather me yell at you? For old time's sake?"

"It would feel normal, but come on, let's get you fed. And then we can go on a ride."

I had been thinking about that for hours and knew it was probably the best thing to do. I loved riding my bike in the mountains and couldn't for half of the year. But now that the snow had melted in some of the passes, we could wind around a couple of small towns and have lunch. And yes, the idea of her legs wrapped around me as we rode *had* entered my mind, but I wasn't going to mention that.

"Excuse me?" she asked as she poured nearly half of the container of half-and-half into her cup.

"I'm going for a ride and you're coming with me. It's your day off, isn't it?"

"It is. Which I'm glad it is since I slept so late. I haven't slept in ages."

"You needed it," I said with a shrug.

"Maybe, but it makes me feel lazy."

"You are the least lazy person I know, and I have Aston and Isabella and Blakely in my family," I said dryly.

"I suppose that is true." Her lips twitched. "And you want me to ride your motorcycle with you. Like a date?"

I paused in the act of scraping the rest of the scramble onto two plates before letting out a breath.

"Not really. It's just a ride."

"Okay." She blinked as she said it before taking a sip of her coffee. "Good coffee."

"Okay, as in you're fine it's not a date? Or okay, as in you're coming with me."

"You didn't really ask. You told me I was, and though I don't tend to take orders, a bike ride sounds lovely. I've never actually been on the back of a motorcycle before."

That made me smile. It was odd. Ever since losing Michelle, I hadn't smiled often. It wasn't that I still loved her. I had fallen out of love with her long before she died, but there hadn't been much to smile about. Then the Cage kids started to be born, and who wouldn't smile around babies?

And of course there was Scarlett. When she wasn't making me want to rip my beard off, she was making me laugh.

I did not know what was up with that.

I scratched my chin, my beard longer than usual. "I'll make sure you know what you're doing when you're on the back. And I have a helmet that should fit you. Emily used it last."

"I don't know her that well. But she seems really sweet."

"Phoebe don't visit often because they have their own lives in Denver, but they're the youngest of us all. So I feel overprotective."

"Even though Phoebe's happily married," Scarlett added with a snort.

"Hey, they were already together when I found out she existed. I didn't get to do the whole big brother thing."

"And did you do that with Weston when it came to Isabella? Cale, too?"

"Yes, with Weston, no, with Cale. Cale and Sophia were already together as well."

"And you only do that with the sisters?"

"I figured Isabella can take over when it comes to the women. You know, ensuring that whoever my brothers pick is right for them."

"That's a lot of trust in her. But I have the same trust."

"I take it she didn't like Ronin?" I asked and could have kicked myself. Instead of letting her answer, I gestured for her to sit at the kitchen island and put a plate in front of an empty chair. "Ignore me. Eat."

"You didn't like Ronin. Nobody did. I thought it was because they didn't know him. But apparently, I didn't know him. It's over though. I haven't heard from him since that night. Thank you. For your help."

"What did I say about thanking me?"

"I'm going to keep doing it. Especially if you're being nice. It's kind of creepy."

"I'm sure I'll be an asshole soon."

"That would make me feel better."

She smiled then and dug into her breakfast. "I don't exactly have a hangover, but I feel a little off. And this is perfect. I didn't know you could cook."

"I can't really. I'm glad you like the spice though."

"It's not that spicy," she added with a roll of her eyes.

"I'll have to add more peppers next time." I started eating, grunting as I realized that I had said there would be a next time.

And she hadn't countered that.

By the time she went back to her house to change, I assumed she would change her mind. After all, it wasn't like I was forcing her into this. But maybe I sort of was.

I pulled my bike out of the garage, grateful that the sun was shining, and it felt like it was going to be a good ride. I put on my leather jacket, knowing it was still going to be a little chilly while on the bike, and packed the saddlebags with water and snacks. I knew where I was heading and there would be a good lunch there, but it always proved to be safe.

We weren't going for hours, so I wasn't going to add the full biker gear. I'd done Sturgis once, and never again. It wasn't my type of scene. But Theo and Flynn had had a grand old time, at least for a few moments before they decided it was a one and done as well.

Just when I had given up hope that Scarlett would be joining, she came up the drive, wearing boots, jeans, a long sleeve shirt that made her breasts look fucking amazing, and a red leather jacket.

"I don't have the biker babe attire, but I figured this would work."

I let my gaze run down the curve of her body and knew that she had to blush all over, especially with the reddening of the tops of her breasts that I could see. I barely resisted the urge to lick my lips. "I think you're a kick ass biker babe right now."

"Oh. Well. I liked the leather jacket."

I gestured towards the bike and then leaned down to pick up her helmet. "Let's get on our way."

Her teeth worried her lip once more and part of me wanted to reach out and rub the sting. Maybe with my mouth. And that was enough of that. "Do you know where we're going? Or am I about to find out that you're an ax murderer and you're taking me to another part of the forest to bury the body?"

"First, I wouldn't tell you." She laughed. "Second, there's plenty of land on this property for that to happen. Third, after what happened in our family recently? I'm going to flat out say that, no, I'm not going to cut you up into a thousand pieces and bury the body."

Her face paled, and she reached out for my arm. "I'm sorry. I wasn't thinking."

I looked down at where her hand covered my arm over the leather jacket. "It's fine. We all make jokes."

"I know this is an odd segue, but have you heard from your mother?"

I threw my head back and laughed, surprising the hell out of both of us.

"I don't think I've ever heard you laugh like that."

"You just thought of my mother after we talked about serial killers. I think it's apropos."

Her eyes danced. "Look at you with the big words."

"I learned them good while in the service."

She rolled her eyes. "Oh, stop."

"Get on the bike. And I'll show you what we need to do. And no, I haven't heard from my mother. Dorian blocked her, and I'm pretty sure the rest of the family did as well. One day maybe she'll realize that she wants to be a grandma and figure out that maybe she was just as toxic as Dad was. She still has time to figure things out, but I want nothing to do with her."

"Well good. I don't like her."

I laughed again. "I don't like her either. Not the best thing for a son to say but fuck her. Now, let me show you what to do."

I put my hands on her hips, and her eyes widened, but I taught her the few things that she needed to know to ride on the back of a motorcycle.

"I'm not going to speed, and in this area there's not allowed to be any trucks. At least not the eighteen-wheelers. They can't make it on this path, and they have their own highway for that. And we won't be riding that highway."

"Where *are* we going?"

"I thought maybe we could head to Sunrise Ridge or Silver Lake. Silver Lake has a decent place for lunch too."

"I'd like that. I go to Ashford Creek often with Luna and Ivy, but I don't really know the other towns that well. Even though I've lived here all my life other than college."

"They're growing like weeds just like Cage Lake is. But it's nice to get out of town."

"So says the hermit."

I strapped on her bike helmet and tapped the top. "So says the hermit."

I got on the bike first, straddling it as I held it up straight. "Okay, put your one leg there and then swing your leg over like you're getting on a horse."

"You think I've been on a horse?"

"Isabella mentioned it," I mumbled, and she gave me a look, before putting her hands on my shoulders and doing exactly what I had said.

She felt even better against me than I thought possible. I leaned back, and she chuckled, the movement warm against my back, and when I turned on the engine, she let out a squeal.

"Wrap your arms around my waist," I called out, and she snuggled into me, and then we were off.

We went the back way, so we could do the full circle of Cage Lake. However, in order to get out of town, we had to go down Main Street. She'd known that when we had made this plan, so the town would see her on the back of my bike. Tongues would wag, but they always did in Cage Lake.

We made our way past the beginning of the street, and I was grateful that we hit every green light and only had to stop at a few stop signs. But people had still seen. Including Ms. Patty.

"She's going to tell her entire knitting group," Scarlett called out over the engine as we moved towards the main bridge out of town.

"Yep!" I yelled back and then there was no more talking.

Though Scarlett had pulled her hair back in a braid, I knew we'd both end up with messy hair at the end of the day, but that was the fun part of riding. We had sunglasses on to combat the wind and light. It was still slightly colder than when I usually first rode out. I'd wanted to get Scarlett on a bike, even though we knew the cold was probably an issue. She learned quickly, leaning into the curves with me and waving at the kids in cars as they passed by.

I leaned back, feeling far more relaxed than I had in ages. This was going to be a problem, but with Scarlett around, the voices stopped. At least the ones that screamed I was guilty.

I was guilty, but not exactly how she thought.

Not exactly as the world thought. But with Scarlett pressed against me, I could breathe. We pulled through Silver Lake, a town decently close to ours, and I parked in front of a small diner.

"You okay to eat here?" I asked as I turned off the engine.

"If you say it's good, I'm game. Plus, I think I really need to walk."

I reached back and squeezed her thigh, noticing the way she moaned.

"Is that moan because you liked that? Or are you going to be sore later?"

"I plead the fifth," she laughed.

I helped her off the bike first, then slid my legs over. When her knees nearly gave out, I cursed.

"You okay?"

"I've only ridden a horse a few times, and it's been a while."

I ran my gaze over her body before I finally undid the strap underneath her chin. "You'll get better at it."

"You keep saying things like that."

"Things like what?" Though I knew the answer.

"Like this will happen again."

I shrugged. "Maybe." I didn't say anything else, but I gestured towards the diner behind her, and she turned, letting the non-answer slide. When I opened the door for her and pressed my palm to the small of her back, she didn't flinch.

I had no idea what the hell I was doing, but I might as well go full tilt.

Nobody recognized us here, we could have been tourists for all they knew. We sank into a booth, and as the waitress came over and took our drink order, I sat back, knowing I was going to get the same burger I always did.

"Do you come here often?"

I shook my head. "No. I mean, probably as often as I go to any of the places in Cage Lake. I cook for myself, even though I'm not great at it."

"I like to go to all of the places in Cage Lake. It's home." She sighed. "And frankly, I want to make sure that the residents knows that the resort is a huge part of the town, and I want them to be happy with us."

"I get you. Not everybody was excited to have such a large and exclusive resort right at the edge of Cage Lake. It helped with sales tax, but it increased property taxes."

"And it brought in people they didn't know. I know the cabins on the west side and the lake, and the river, all had tons of tourists, but we brought in even more."

My lips twitched. "You said we."

"I know that you Cages own the place, but I think of it as mine."

"I think of it as more yours than mine, Scarlett. We both know that."

Before she could say anything, the waitress came, and we each ordered. She got the club sandwich with French fries and a side of ranch, and I got the burger, also with a side of ranch.

"I love that you got French fries and not a side salad."

"I'm still in that greasy mood after the wine last night."

"Is there a reason you were drinking so much?" I held up my hand. "Not judging. Just wondering."

She stared into her water and pressed her lips together. "Just everything all at once. My dad, Ronin, trying to increase revenue at the resort, you, and my mom having a panic attack."

There was so much in that statement, I didn't know where to begin, so I did the one thing I wasn't good at.

I just spoke.

"You're doing fantastic at the resort. I've already told you that, and the family believes the same. If you weren't, you know Aston, Flynn, and James would say something about it. Hell, Blakely's job is to cut pieces that aren't pulling their weight. And to push money into places that help others. It doesn't matter that you guys are friendly, she'd can you if you weren't doing the job."

"That makes me feel better."

I shrug. "I'm not in the family business, but I get the family business, if that makes sense."

"What would you do with the Cage Enterprises if you had a choice?"

I shuddered. "Me in a suit, having to work around people all day? No thank you."

"I don't know, you would look quite nice in a suit."

"You like the way that I look?" I teased, my voice low.

"You already know that, or I wouldn't be here."

"So you just like me for my looks." I had no idea what the hell I was doing, but it was fun. Different.

"Your personality is a little gruff, so it has to be."

"Touché."

"I like wearing a suit and working at the resort. It is customer service, but it's also a strategic business. It gives me so many things to do."

"And all the better for me because that means I don't have to have any part of it. Unless it's coming to annoy you."

"So you do come into the resort to annoy me?"

I shrugged and changed the subject. "Is your mom okay?"

She sat in silence for a moment, and I wondered if I had said something wrong. The waitress bought our meals, and I waved her off when she asked if we needed anything else and then nudged Scarlett's plate to her.

"Don't answer if you don't want to. Eat your fries before they go cold."

She dipped a fry in ranch and took a bite, moaning.

"That is so good."

"Right? But you're going to need to stop moaning. Just saying."

A pretty blush slid over her cheeks, and she finished the fry. "My mom is an agoraphobe. We've been careful about the word, but her therapist is using it now. So is she. We're trying to figure out what we can do to help her, but it's out of my control, and I hate when things are out of my control."

"There's nothing I can do to help with that, or anything to say to make it better. But if you need me, you let me know. Okay? Even if I'm being an asshole, I'm not going to let your mom feel like she's alone." Scarlett's eyes filled with tears, and I cursed under my breath. "I'm sorry. I'm pushy, ignore me."

"You're only pushy when it comes to putting me where you think I should be, but you stand back and watch every other time. I didn't realize you were so nice." She said nice like it was a bad thing, and frankly it was in this case.

"I'm not nice. I'm just a Cage. And not my dad."

"That reminds me, what are you doing with the Ackerson place again?"

I sighed and dug into my lunch as I told her my plans. My family didn't even know my full plans, but now that Scarlett did, it was like a weight off my shoulders.

And when she smiled and gripped my hand, I thought that maybe I was doing the right thing.

After we finished our lunch and paid, we got on the bike and headed toward Cage Lake, along the winding roads. When I stopped at a park bench so she could stretch and we could walk into the park area where I knew there was a small waterfall, Scarlett slid her hand into mine.

"I think this was a date, Hudson. And I don't date anymore."

I squeezed her hand and pulled her towards the bike.

"I don't date anymore either. I don't know what this is."

"Just don't not date anyone else when you're not dating me. Okay?"

My eyes nearly crossed as I tried to figure out that sentence. "Okay. I can do that." And then my lips were on hers and there was nothing else.

She groaned against me, her hands going up my jacket and shirt to slide over my skin. I cupped her face, deepening the kiss, needing her close.

"We should stop," she whispered, but then kept going.

I continued my exploration of her body with my hands, cupping her breasts underneath her shirt, and then sliding my hands down her sides and up. When my fingers slid over her nipples through her bra, I let out a soft groan.

"I knew these were pierced," I whispered.

"Twins, I guess," she said with a wink.

"You're a twin. I'm a twin. That's a lot of twins."

"Shut up and kiss me," she muttered.

In answer, I crushed my mouth to hers and pressed her back to the bike. With an idea, hoping like hell I didn't break anything, I lifted her up and sat her on the bike.

She let out a moan and continued to kiss me as I explored her body with my hands. I let my palms slide down, my fingers playing with the button of her jeans. When she moaned, arching her back to me, I undid the button and slid down her zipper ever so slightly.

"Hudson!"

"Shh. Just let me."

She kissed me, arching for me as I slid my fingers underneath her panties. She was already soaking wet, and I groaned.

"Scar, baby, you're killing me."

"If we break this bike, I'm not buying it."

I smiled against her lips as I flicked my middle finger over her clit.

"Deal."

She melted in my hand, panting, as I slid two fingers into her wet cunt. The walls of her pussy squeezed around me, and I continued to pierce her, slowly, since her jeans were slightly restricting for my hand.

"You're going to need to rock on my hand. Go slowly so you don't knock over the bike. Is that okay? Can you do that, Scar?"

"Hudson. Please."

I smiled again and continued to slide my fingers in and out of her, using my palm to grind against her clit.

And when she came, her lips parted, her eyes darkened, and she gushed over my palm.

I took her lips in a kiss, continuing to ease her down her orgasm, knowing that I was in for a long ride home.

Riding my bike down the winding roads back to Cage Lake with a raging hard-on might kill me. But she wasn't ready yet, and frankly, anybody could drive by at any moment.

When she finally slowed her breath, I slid my fingers out of her pussy and sucked them into my mouth. Her eyes widened, and I grinned before licking her wetness clean from my skin.

"So fucking good."

"I can't believe you just made me come on the back of your bike."

"It's a first for me too."

She narrowed her gaze at me. "Really?"

"There's been a few firsts for me, Scarlett. And I don't know what the hell I'm doing."

"That makes two of us."

She looked down at the clear evidence of my erection, but I just shook my head and kissed her softly.

"Let's head back before it gets dark."

"Are you sure you're going to be able to ride straight with that third leg of yours?"

I barked out a laugh and maneuvered so I could get

on the bike in front of her. It wasn't easy, but we made it work.

"I'll do my best. Now hang on."

She laughed as I leaned down to get both of our helmets, and we got situated. And then I started the bike, and we were off.

And I knew I was one step closer to my obsession when it came to Scarlett Blair.

And with our luck, we'd both end up hurting in the end. But with her taste on my lips, I truly did not care in that moment.

Chapter Ten
Hudson

"You're not giving me any slack. You're going to end up leaving me splattered on the rocks below," Flynn grumbled from less than twenty feet above me.

I sighed, and then did what all twin brothers should do, I flipped him off. "We've been doing this for how many years? You're fine. Now get up the damn side of the cliff face."

"I see that life in the mountains has really worked well for you," Weston said with a laugh. "I mean, you have the sun shining on your face, at least whatever face is showing considering your hair's long, you're wearing a hat, and your beard is getting bushier by the moment. You're hardly looking like a serial killer anymore." Weston reached out and gripped my shoulder, but I didn't look at him, as I was spotting Flynn.

"Is there a reason that you're trying to speak and discuss my facial hair while we're trying to be out here and relax? You're the one who made me come here to begin with."

"You like hiking and mountain climbing. And also rock climbing. Since I guess that's what we're doing right now." Weston moved forward and held out Cale's water bottle.

"Hey, keep hydrated. I know you're not used to the elevation out here."

My brother-in-law pushed his hair back from his face. "Thanks." He smiled as he took the water bottle from Weston. "I truly appreciate it. I know Denver's the Mile High City, but damn, I guess the elevation change between Cage Lake and my house is just different enough that I'm panting like a dog."

"You should get a dog!" Flynn called out as he reached the top of the relatively small cliff face we were climbing this afternoon.

It was late April, and we'd had a week of full sun with warmer than average temperatures. And that meant we could have a nice hike and not have to worry about a blizzard coming our way. At least not yet. I'm sure there would be a freak storm coming at us at any moment, just because I thought it. The lake was still frozen in some parts but was thawing enough that soon people would be out on their boats, and the places where people would go to swim, and not just off the docks, would be open to the public. The few passes that were off to the east, that were easy to climb over, and Payne Peak would soon open as well. That meant the resort would be changing focus from Winter sports, and into their spring and summer deals. It would be rock climbing like we were doing now, trails, camping, and even tours out through the mountain itself. I knew that my brother, I knew that Flynn had set up some sort of deal with the people who owned the cabins on the river on the west side of town, and while we as a company owned a few, including the rafting and boating section, they were still a different business than the resort itself. That meant Scarlett was the one who worked on the contracts and ensuring that there were deals when it came to any guests in town.

I was just glad I had nothing to do with it. I had finished the painting for Sophia's girls, and would be taking it down soon. I'd also finished the one for Ford's son, and rather than shipping it to him, my brother would finally come to visit.

Each of my brothers had a house on the lake. We'd bought it with our own money from the trust before we had found out that we'd even had additional siblings. We also owned nearly all properties on the lake itself. Scarlett's home was set back so she didn't own the land, but she did own the house. I was the one who technically owned that land, not that I was going to tell her. It didn't matter in the end, because if she wanted to buy it, she could, but it wasn't as if I was going to build on that land. If I'd built something, that meant more people would be out there, and that was one of the last things that I wanted.

A bird cawed overhead, and I looked up for a bare instant, before setting my gaze back to Flynn who was rappelling his way down.

"I could've slipped in that one moment you were distracted by a bird or squirrel."

"You're fine." I growled as Flynn's feet touch the ground. "Did you always whine this much?"

Flynn grinned at me, as he slid his hand over his newly smooth skin. Now we barely looked like twins since he didn't have a beard. But again it was nice to know what I looked like underneath it.

"I think you've just gotten grumpier. Which you shouldn't be so grumpy considering I hear you have a woman finally."

"Oh really?" Cale asked as he got ready to take his turn up the cliff side.

"I have no idea where you're getting your news, but I don't have a woman." I stood back and let Weston and Cale get set up. Cale wasn't as experienced in this as we were, but we were teaching him. He might not have the Cage last name, but we were at least trying to be good brothers-in-law. Hell, I was trying just to be a good brother at this point.

"That's not what I hear. I mean, riding your bike

with Scarlett on the back through town probably wasn't the best thing to do if you're wanting to keep things secret."

"You and the manager of the resort? Wow." Cale's eyes widened.

"It's not like that," I grumbled.

Flynn gave me a look.

I let a sigh. "It's a little like that. I don't know. We're just starting out, and I could really use some time before the Cage family group chat goes insane."

"I have noticed you haven't responded to any texts in the group chats," Flynn pointed out.

"Neither have I. You Cages and your group chats," Weston put in.

"I'm truly afraid of the group chats. There's so many," Cale said with a shake of his head. "Oh, speaking of, thank you for letting me stay at your place on the lake."

"No problem," Flynn said with a grin. "It was fun bunking with Hudson last night and annoying him. Though I am heading home tonight."

"You snore." I grinned as I said it, and Flynn just flipped me off.

"I like how all of you guys have houses. You don't always use them," Cale added. "Do you know if you and Isabella are planning on getting a house out on the lake?"

Weston shook his head. "We like the house that

we're in now. Even though I've always been in it. And if we want to head out to the lake for any recreational things, we have plenty of places to do so. I do know you guys are all talking about making sure that the rest of the Cages have opportunities to buy in, right?" Weston asked.

I looked over at Flynn, and my twin just rolled his eyes at me. "Again, it's in the group chat." He turned to the others. "We all built on our land when we were younger, and everything just made sense with Cage Enterprises. We have a few houses that we rent out right now but they should be coming up soon that we can work on selling slash giving them to our siblings that want a place. I know Kyler's been thinking about building on one of the empty plots, and Emily said that she was fine staying with you and Isabella. But I don't know about Phoebe, or even you guys," Flynn said.

"I don't know. I know we were able to come out this weekend, and while Sophia and the girls are with her sisters shopping downtown or doing whatever, it's hard for me to take off so much time at work. But it would be nice to have a house out here. To feel like a Cage." He winked as he said it, and I shook my head.

"It's not always fun feeling like a Cage. To the point that I don't even know what that means anymore."

"Huh." Cale gave me a puzzled expression, before he turned to the cliff face and began climbing.

"Speaking of not understanding what's going on,

are you going to tell us about the Ackerson place?" Flynn asked. "Because Dorian's being very careful about not talking about it." Considering I'd bought the place from Dorian for a dollar, and all of the negative aspects that came with it, I wasn't surprised. I didn't want to hurt my brother, but I wanted to try to find a way to pay it forward. At least pay for what my father had done.

"The whole place is a gut job, I'm tearing it down."

James's eyes widened. "Seriously? Good on you. You need help?"

I laughed. "Demo is the fun part of the job."

"I'm in too. I thought you were going to refinish things, but with half of it gone, I guess it makes sense."

"I was going to try, but I know my own limits. I have contractors coming and doing most of the work, but I'm going to build some of it."

"What are you putting in its place?" Weston asked, his attention on Cale.

"I'm putting in cabins."

Cale nearly slipped down the rock face and looked over at me. "You? Cabins?"

I barked out a laugh at the three incredulous looks staring at me and let out a breath. "Not for tourists, but for people like me."

"Mountain men with attitudes that like to hide in the forest?" Flynn asked, but I heard the worry in his tone.

Because I remember seeing his face after I'd returned home. All of my siblings had been worried about me when I'd nearly died. The day that I'd lost all of my friends in that explosion and gunfight. The bullets had torn through my shoulder, had nearly taken me, but it had been Flynn's face that nearly sent me into the abyss. He hadn't been able to feel my physical pain, but I swore he could sense everything else.

I knew the jokes and the laughing were to set me at ease, just like he did with everyone else, but he was worried about me.

"I want them to be for veterans, even active duty that are on break. I have a shit ton of money that I don't need, from the family, and from my art, so I'm going to use it for good. I'm not going to charge them, and they can come with their families, and pay it forward in other ways. But this place let me breathe for the first time in too many years." I met Flynn's gaze, knowing that Cale and Weston probably had questions of their own. "I need to do something."

"You're a good man, Hudson," Flynn whispered before he hugged me tightly, and I shoved him off.

"So we're really not going to talk about Scarlett?" Weston asked, and I just shook my head, a smile playing on my face.

"No. Because I don't know what the fuck I'm doing."

"Michelle was really the last person that I know

you talked about, so I don't know if I've ever really seen you date"

Cale rappelled down the cliff face again and landed softly on the ground in front of us.

"Michelle? Do I know a Michelle?"

Weston winced. "Sorry, bro."

"Did I step in something? There's so many of you, and you have detailed layers of secrets, that sometimes I step in it." Cale shook his head. "Sorry."

"No, it's fine. Michelle was my ex. We dated in high school, and then when I decided not to go to college right away and joined the army, I ended up deployed more often than not. It didn't work out between me and Michelle."

"I'm sorry about that. Truly. And thank you for your service," Cale tacked on, looking awkward.

I felt just as awkward. I didn't know what I was supposed to say when people mentioned that. It wasn't as if I felt like I had done anything. I was trying to do things now though, and I guess that's what mattered.

And I didn't add that I wasn't with Michelle because she had cheated.

And then she was dead. I couldn't just say those words.

It was Weston's turn to climb, and then my own, and by the end of the day, I had a few cuts and bruises, but I felt lighter than I had in weeks.

It was good to get out into the mountain air, to just

breathe for the first time. Spring would hit hard soon, and then summer, and I'd be working as usual.

I had a few projects in town that I needed to do, since Ms. Patty had roped me into more than one mural. And I would get it done. I would do anything for Ms. Patty.

She'd been the one to give me my first cup of coffee when I had moved to town, still in a sling, and glared at anybody who tried to talk to me. She'd ignored my barking, handed me coffee, patted my good shoulder, and told me I could come down from the mountains when I was ready.

I'd loved that woman, and all her gossip. Because while I had ignored my brothers, and pushed them away if they tried to feed me or give me anything, Ms. Patty had forced herself onto my land, driving her own four-wheel drive truck, in order to give me frozen meals and home baked food.

Then others had joined in, and my siblings and even my mother had done their best.

But it had been Ms. Patty who had been a force of nature. And she still was.

We made our way back down the trail, our guys' afternoon surprisingly peaceful. It wasn't that I disliked people in general, it was that I liked being alone. I wasn't lonely, I was happy and content in solitude.

Flynn and Weston were up front, talking about Weston's upcoming expansion, and I ended up in the back with Cale. Cale wasn't an outdoorsman by any stretch of the word, but he was trying, and he seemed like he was enjoying himself.

"You doing okay?" I asked, knowing that if I accidentally broke something on Sophia's husband, I would hear about it forever.

"I'm doing fine. I've only tripped twice today." He tripped again, and I reached out and caught him. "Sorry about that." He ripped his arm from my hand, and I knew he had to be embarrassed. Hell, I tripped all the time, but me saying that would just embarrass him further.

"I know you said that you and Sophia wouldn't be coming up to Cage Lake often, but we can still figure out a house for you to stay at that's yours. My dad was an asshole, we all know it. You guys deserve a place."

Cale gave me a look I couldn't quite read, and he shook his head. "Sophia spends most of her time with the girls or at the dance studio. And I'm traveling often. While having a place to relax would be nice, I don't think she would want a handout."

I frowned, knowing that I was probably walking on murky ground here. But it wasn't my decision. And maybe the group chat had more to say. Not that I was going to have any part of it.

I just nodded, and we made our way down the path to our respective cars.

Cale would be heading to Sophia and spending one

more night here. Flynn was going home to Denver, and Weston was going back to his place. He and Isabella would be traveling with the others and soon Cage Lake would be a few less Cages. Harper and Dorian were already in Denver, working on one of his clubs, and now that I thought about it, I might be the only Cage left for a little while.

I didn't know why that bummed me out. It never used to.

I made it home and figured I would go back to the studio and work, or maybe text Scarlett just to see how she was doing.

That was odd of me, but then again, I could still taste her on my lips. She had been working nonstop since our bike ride, and though we had texted and talked a few times on the phone, we hadn't spent much time together. Maybe that needed to change.

Of course I needed to figure out what the hell I wanted first. That would probably be a good thing.

My phone buzzed, and part of me hoped it was Scarlett, but when I saw my agent's name on the read-out, I groaned.

"Yes?"

"It's about time you answered. Now I've given you enough space, but you have to be at the show next weekend. It's in your contract, and I really don't want to have to play mean agent, but I need you to pretend that you can be sociable even if it's just for thirty minutes."

I had been avoiding this show and what it meant for months now. A high-end art dealer had found one of my pieces, and now I was starting to get a little more recognition. I hadn't been lying when I said I didn't need money. I got top dollar for my pieces, and if the rest of the town knew what I was making for the pieces that I sold through my agent, they would probably think twice about asking me to make so many murals. I paused in that thinking. No, Ms. Patty would probably ask me to make more. I snorted at that, and my agent finally snapped.

"This isn't funny, Hudson. I know you hate doing these, but I need you for just this once. Please. I don't ask you for much."

That was true. My agent was actually pretty accommodating. And I knew my success was helping him. Maybe Scarlett was right and I needed to stop acting like an asshole all the time. And that made me think. The whole weekend? Maybe getting out of Cage Lake would be good, and not just for me.

"I'll be there."

"Did I hear that right? No, don't answer that. I'm just going to go with a yes, and then I'm going to dance when we're off the phone."

My lips twitched. "Okay then. Just email me all the details?"

"Done. Thank you. You're not going to regret this. Well, you might later, but I don't care."

That made me laugh. "I get to bring someone, right?" I blurted.

My agent was silent enough for long enough that I was afraid the call had ended. "Yes. Your family?"

"No, I don't really know if I want to deal with all of my family at this. Then it will be a thing in the news."

I knew that my agent liked press, but the Cage family press when it came to my dad's death and the will and everything that came with it wasn't exactly the press we needed. Plus I liked making things work on my own, rather than on my name.

"That makes sense. Though your family is pretty great."

"They're okay," I said with a laugh.

"Did you just laugh? And you're asking if you can bring someone that's not a family member? Hudson Cage, are you seeing someone?"

I cursed under my breath and wondered why I had even said a damn thing. "Don't make it a big deal. We're not really seeing each other. I just want to take someone that's not Cage-like. And you're the one who wants me to do this show. Don't make it weird."

"I promise I'll be on my best behavior. Maybe. But don't worry you can bring the whole family if you want, you don't have a set number of tickets. But the show's sold out otherwise, and I'm excited for you." He paused, and I felt like squirming. "I'm happy for you. As long as this doesn't affect your art in a bad way."

That made me burst out laughing, exactly what my agent wanted me to do, since he wasn't one of those critiquing types who wanted me to be the starving or broken artist in order to produce things.

Instead he usually just let me be.

"Send me the details. I'll see you next week."

"Yes. And your date."

I hung up without saying anything and had to wonder if I was just setting this up for failure. I hadn't even asked her yet.

Phone still in hand, I texted her, hitting my large fingers on the tiny little buttons.

Me: I have a damn art show that I have to go to in Denver next week.

Me: I know it's the days you have off.

Me: Come with me.

Not exactly romantic, but I wasn't into romance. And I wasn't sure Scarlett was either.

And I hadn't truly asked her, more like ordered. Then again, maybe she liked that.

She didn't answer right away, and I figured she was either working, or ignoring me. Maybe I would just go down to her house later and annoy her in person.

My phone buzzed again, and I looked down at the readout, wondering if it was one of the one hundred family group chats.

It was. There were four new texts from them, and also one text that I was actually going to read.

Scarlett: Well. That's out of the blue. But okay. Is it overnight?

It didn't need to be, we could drive up late at night, but I had a feeling that's not what either of us wanted.

Me: I'll get us a nice hotel. Sorry, but there's only going to be one bed.

There, putting my intentions out there. Like an idiot.

Scarlett: I guess I'll have to figure out what to pack. If anything.

And with that, my cock pressed against my pants, and I groaned.

She-devil of a woman.

That was probably why I liked her so much.

I slid my phone in my pocket and whistled under my breath as I made my way to my studio.

Maybe I was making a mistake, but at least I would have fun along the way.

Chapter Eleven
Scarlett

"Is there a reason that you didn't want any of your family here?" I asked, my palms sweating.

Hudson raised a brow before lifting his chin at one of his paintings. "Because they've seen most of this. I don't need them to be here to bow at my feet or some shit. Or to pretend that they need to. That isn't what we do. I'd rather do shit for them than have them see this."

Another person came up to him, what felt like the one hundredth person at that point, and he grunted in thanks as his agent carried most of the conversation. I stood back in my red dress, wondering what the hell I was doing here.

Hudson's words were exactly who he was. He didn't like being the center of attention and would rather do things for others in his family than be forced to show that he was a talented man. Because goddess, his work was breathtaking.

I had always known that Hudson Cage could paint. I'd secretly wanted one of his smaller paintings that I could afford for my own house. I'd seen his murals around town, as well as some of the pieces he had done for his family and friends.

For a man who never spoke unless forced to sometimes, he communicated in his art.

I felt like I could walk through some of the paintings and stand in our forest. Many times it was landscapes, or pieces of life that others wouldn't be able to tell were from Cage Lake but spoke of home and family.

Other times his work would be slightly abstract, and perhaps you wouldn't realize exactly where it came from, until you focused and realized the painting spoke to you in a way you didn't understand.

I had never known an artist firsthand. I never realized that we could be friends like this.

When Hudson had invited me to his art show, part of me had wanted to ignore the text. Set my phone down and go about my day off like I normally would. With my mother, my sister, or alone. Because I would be better off that way. I had no idea what would happen next when it came to Hudson, but I had lied to myself in saying that I was fine. That I knew what I was doing.

Because here I was, saying yes to Hudson, and now I was in Denver with him.

And we would be staying overnight at the hotel we had barely seen after we had checked in. And it wasn't as if it was some dingy little hotel on the outskirts of town. No, it was the five star hotel near the gallery, and we had dropped off our bags before finding our way back here.

I'd only had a few moments to get ready, as traffic had been bad and yet, the look on Hudson's face when I walked out of the bathroom in my red dress, the one that fit my curves and made my breasts look amazing if I did say so myself, was worth the stress and the agony of the drive.

He had taken one look at me, growled, and then dragged me out of that hotel suite.

Because there was only one bed in that hotel suite.

And I knew as soon as we were finished with this art show, we would be using that bed.

We had danced around each other long enough, and I was tired of pretending that I didn't want Hudson.

This would break me in more ways than one when it ended. And it would end. I did not make good decisions when it came to men, and I was just like my mother after all. I didn't think Hudson would ever hurt me in that way, but he could break me in countless other ways.

He would break my heart without even trying, because we hadn't made each other promises. We hadn't truly spoken about what would happen.

Yet it would.

When his hand touched the small of my back, I pulled myself out of my worries and turned to his agent.

His agent was nothing like I had expected. Though I wasn't sure what I had expected.

Ellis had to be 6'5 at least, broad shoulders, and could fill out a suit perfectly. He'd also come with his husband and his wife, the three of them looking like damn models. In fact, all three of them had modeled for other artists in the past, and I knew their story had to be interesting as hell.

One of Hudson's brothers was in a poly relationship, so it didn't surprise me at all that Hudson's inner circle was welcoming. The other generations of Cages may have been bigoted assholes, but this generation? They were open, honest, and surprising.

It wasn't any wonder I was falling for him.

No, I wasn't. I could not fall for Hudson Cage. If I did so, I would make such a mistake that there would be no healing from it. I couldn't hide from Hudson as it was. Running away from him after finally giving into what I'd tried to hide would shatter everything that I had tried to build since Ronin and my father.

So no, I wouldn't fall for him.

But as I met his gaze and licked my lips, noticing the way his eyes went to the action, I *would* be going to bed with Hudson Cage tonight.

"Scarlett, I'm so glad that you could make it," Ellis said as he held out his hand. "This one has been quite secretive when it comes to you."

I rolled my eyes. "There are no secrets needed. I'm the one that he annoys when he comes to the resort I manage."

"I don't annoy you. You annoy me," Hudson grumbled.

Ellis looked over at his husband, who in turn, leaned down and kissed their wife on the cheek. "I annoy both of them on a daily basis," Ellis put in. "But that's how our relationship started."

I opened my mouth to tell him that Hudson and I weren't exactly in a relationship, that I didn't know what we were, but then again, here I was, at his art show when his family hadn't even been invited. I wasn't even sure they were aware it was happening. Not telling Isabella or Harper had been painful, but what was I supposed to tell them? That I was leaving town with Hudson, and I had no idea what I was doing? That would've been my truth at least. But Hudson was clear that he doesn't want to bother his family, and I didn't think overstepping the first time I left town with him on a trip like this would be appropriate.

Or maybe I was just terrified as to what the others would say. I didn't want to have them worry about me or Hudson.

"I can't believe you're trying to keep the family a secret," a slightly familiar voice said from behind us, and I turned as Hudson cursed under his breath.

Theo Cage stode toward us, wearing a suit without a tie. He winked at me before glaring at his brother. "You don't call, you don't write, you don't look at the group chat."

Hudson laughed, his whole face brightening. How the hell had that made him even more handsome?

I took a deep gulp of my champagne, and Ellis gave me a knowing look that I ignored pointedly.

"How did you know I was here?" Hudson asked before giving me a look.

I held up my free hand. "I didn't tell anyone. You asked me not to. I think that was a mistake, because now I feel weird for keeping secrets, but it wasn't me.

"She didn't tell me a thing, but I'm taking notes now," Theo said as he hugged his brother, and the two did that backslapping thing that I never understood, before Theo took my hand in his own and kissed my knuckles.

"Oh, Scarlett. It's lovely to see you."

I rolled my eyes because I knew he was just trying to get a rise out of Hudson, who in turn glared at his brother and put his arm proprietarily around my waist. I didn't dislike it. Yet it was just one more complication.

"How did you find out?" Hudson asked once again.

"I saw it on the flyers that went out. You do realize that I'm in the high-end restaurant scene, and sometimes we work with the gallery. I've catered here before." Theo gestured as he looked around the place. "You're stuck with me as the resident Cage." Then he pointed towards the man I hadn't noticed behind him, who also wore a suit without a tie. "Scarlett, I don't think you've met my business partner, Luke. Luke, Scarlett. And you know the asshole over here, Hudson. This is his work. Apparently, he's some brilliant artist."

He rolled his eyes as he said it, but I heard the pride in his tone. You couldn't help it. All of the Cages were proud of Hudson, even though they did their best not to show it. After all, Hudson would just get growly, and while I didn't mind some of the growls, I knew sometimes it was a little too much.

Of course, when had I learned to love those growls?

"Scarlett, it's lovely to see you." Luke took my hand just as Theo did, and this time Hudson grabbed my elbow, pulling me back.

"Hands off, Luke."

The hoop in Luke's nose glinted under the light as he laughed. "Well, well, well."

Theo winked, the tiny stud in his nose also shining underneath the strategic lighting of the gallery.

"It's good to meet both of you. And I do believe somebody else just arrived that's going to take focus away from both of you. Sorry." I winked as I said it, and the other two men turned.

Hudson closed his eyes and groaned. "Was there a bulletin in the group chat that I missed?"

I laughed, leaning into his side as Kyler Cage Dixon made his way into the gallery. Though he didn't have any of his team with him and was dressed in a suit with an open collar, where the tattoos on his chest and neck were easily visible, he didn't look quite like the rock star he usually did. Yet, there was no mistaking exactly who he was.

"Your group chats seem wild. But from what I heard, you don't pay attention to them. So maybe there was an alert in one, and you just missed it."

"Oh, I like her," Theo said with a laugh. "She has you there, bro."

"Don't bro me," Hudson snarled before turning to the resident rock star of the family.

"I didn't know you were in town," Hudson said as he lifted his chin towards Kyler. Kyler in turn lifted his chin back, and the two continued their male greeting. They might as well show their plumed feathers, and shake on it.

I held back a grin, my lips twitching. There was no need to tell them that they all resembled those birds from the Amazon with the black and blue feathers that would do the little dance to attract women.

"I know the manager," Kyler said in answer, and I laughed along with the others as Hudson sighed.

"If any other Cages walk through that door, we'll fill the whole place."

"I wouldn't mind that," Ellis said as he came to my other side. "And if those Cages like to buy things, the more, the better. We do have a couple other artists here that aren't Hudson, that are new to the area. We'd like to use Hudson's reach in order to help other artists."

I smiled at Hudson, who closed his eyes and pinched the bridge of his nose.

I moved my arm so I could squeeze his hand, and when he tangled his fingers in mine, I realized he was nervous.

The grumpy artist who likes to live in his cabin and not talk to anybody was nervous about this show.

Maybe I had made a mistake in not telling his entire family to arrive. But Theo and Kyler were here, so perhaps that would be enough.

I strategically took out my phone and snapped a few photos where Ellis said I could. I had my own group chat with some of the Cage women, so I would let them know what they were missing. And apologize that I hadn't told them to begin with.

"You should take a photo of the three of them," Luke whispered, and I turned to see Theo's business partner standing close to me.

"Oh?" I asked and swallowed hard.

The man was dreamy, though he had nothing on Hudson. Not that I would tell anyone that.

"I'm pretty sure they don't have a photo of just the three of them. In fact, I don't even know if this particular group has been together without the other Cages around."

I thought about that and sadness slipped over me. The expression must have shone on my face, because Luke reached out and squeezed my shoulder.

"I've always hated Theo's dad, not that I would ever tell the man to his face. Oh wait, I did." He winked, and I smiled.

"Really? You told him that."

"Of course I did. He was an ass to my best friend. Though he was worse to the others. At least from what I saw. But come on, capture this moment for one of the group chats. Or at least for Hudson. I think sometimes the old man forgets that he does have family."

I swallowed hard and snapped a few photos as the three spoke, looking so alike it was startling. I knew Hudson had a twin, and I liked Flynn, but in that moment, all three looked like full brothers, who had different personalities and individualities of their own.

What would it be like to not have known of each

other's existence until recently? The idea that these three had never been alone without the other Cages or some form of combination, astonished me. But then again since Hudson and Theo didn't live in the same town, and Kyler was rarely in the state, it made sense.

When Hudson glared over at me, that's when I realized Luke's hand was still on my shoulder. He dropped it, and I raised a brow at the other man as he just smirked at me.

"Just testing the waters."

"You better not be testing them with me. I don't take kindly to being the center of whatever male testosterone dance you guys feel like having."

Luke threw his head back and laughed, and then Hudson was at my side, and I couldn't help but nearly swoon at the sight of him. There was seriously something wrong with me.

"He's pretty amazing, good on you," Luke said before he went over to where Theo and Kyler were speaking to one of the other artists.

I looked at Hudson, who shook his head. "Theo invited us to dinner at his restaurant after this, but I declined."

I frowned. "I've always wanted to go to The Teal Door. It's hard to get in there. I'm just glad that he has another version of it in Cage Lake, or I would never have his delicious food."

Hudson grunted. "The man can cook I'll give him that. But no, I have other plans for you."

I pressed my thighs together and swallowed hard. "Oh?"

"Unless Luke has your attention."

I narrowed my gaze at Hudson, wondering why men could get so thick in the head. "He was teasing you. And if you think I'm the type of woman who would just flitter away with another man when you brought me down to Denver? You don't know me at all."

"You're right. But I want to know you."

I wasn't sure what else there was to say to that.

We stayed for a few more minutes, saying our goodbyes to Ellis and his spouses, as well as the Cages and Luke. I couldn't help but notice the multiple sold stickers on every piece of art around the gallery. Including the other artists who were here for their first show.

I had seen some of the costs of those paintings, and they had made me nearly drop my drink.

The Cages had money, that was for sure, but Hudson was turning out to be in a league of his own when it came to his career.

And I couldn't be prouder of him.

And more nervous for exactly what would be happening tonight.

One Quick Obsession

By the time we got back to the hotel, I could barely think. My thoughts went in a million different directions, scattered as if light through a prism. Or did a prism make light go into a rainbow? Why could I not remember basic science or the English language when I stood next to Hudson Cage?

Now we were walking into the hotel suite, as Hudson undid his tie, and I set my purse on the small table near the door.

"Do you want me to order room service?" he asked.

I turned to look at him, confused as to what he wanted or what I was doing in the first place.

"You did really good tonight, by the way."

He tilted his head as he looked at me, then toed off his shoes.

"I hate those things."

"Because you have to be the center of attention. But you're brilliant, Hudson. And I'm not saying that because I had two glasses of champagne. We know champagne doesn't do anything to me."

"I do know that. And I'm not brilliant. I can just use a paintbrush every once in a while."

"It's more than that. And if you want to play the humble artist, I'm fine with that. But you are a fantastic artist. And I've always been a little jealous because I can barely paint a rainbow when I have a color sheet."

"A color sheet?" he asked, sliding off his suit jacket.

I found myself undoing my bracelet and sliding out of my heels. We were both getting ready for the evening, finally stripping in front of each other. And yet we weren't saying a word about anything important. Why could Hudson do this to me? And why did I continually want him to?

"You know, with a coloring book? Where they draw the rainbow for you and you just have to fill in ROYGBIV."

His lips twitched as he moved forward and gently slid his finger along my jaw. I shivered and tilted my head back. When his fingers slid through the back of my hair, his thumb gliding over my jawline, I swallowed hard.

"Did you know they rarely teach ROYGBIV like that in some schools?"

I blinked, confused. "Seriously?"

"Seriously. Just like they don't teach Pluto in the solar system anymore. The earth is going to hell in a handbasket, and the main things we learned as children just don't make sense anymore. Even my times tables are now all messed up."

I grinned at that. "You don't have to memorize the numbers anymore. Not really. Now you can get there along a path that makes sense no matter what number's there."

"You said a bunch of words, and they don't make sense to me. But I was never good with numbers."

"Lucky for the resort, I am."

I licked my lips unconsciously, and then Hudson's mouth was on mine, and I moaned.

"Tell me you don't want this," he whispered against my mouth. "Tell me you want me to stop and I will. But if you kiss me back right now, I'm not stopping until I'm deep inside you, and you're riding my cock. You get that, Scarlett? I don't want to hurt you, so you need to let me know what you want."

I shivered, and then slid my hands up his chest, and dug my nails into his flesh through his white button-up shirt.

"I don't want to think of the consequences. I just want you."

"Good answer." And then he tugged on my hair, and I was lost.

He moved his free hand down my side, cupping my breast. When his thumb went over my nipple piercing through my bra and dress, I groaned.

"Damn it, I nearly forgot about these."

"Liar."

Then both hands were on my hips and then underneath my dress. When he palmed my ass, he froze. "You're not wearing any underwear."

"It was confining."

He let his head fall back as he groaned, rocking his erection against my belly.

Before I could say anything, he lifted me up with such ease that I gasped. I wrapped my legs around him, and he carried us to the bed.

"I need to taste you."

I nodded, unable to speak.

I was on the bed, dress at my waist, and I could barely think.

He knelt at the edge of the bed, my thighs pressed around his face, and then he was *moving*. He tongued my clit, taking his sweet time to explore my pussy as he ate me out to the point that my eyes nearly rolled to the back of my head. I slid my hand through his hair, forcing him closer to my cunt. His beard tickled my inner thighs, but it didn't matter. All I wanted was to come on his face, and then to touch him. I just wanted him.

He continued to explore me, until I could barely breathe, and when I finally came, I whispered his name, and he groaned against my flesh. He pulled back, and I blinked up at him lazily, my breasts heavy, my body flushed. He undid his shirt quickly, showing me those rock hard abs, his chest that I wanted to bite. I noticed the puckered scars there, the ones that I knew had come from bullet wounds when he had been overseas. But I didn't ask him. This wasn't the time. I didn't know if there would ever be a time.

I reached up and glided my hands over the hoops in his nipples, and he smiled.

"Like that?"

I nodded and reached back to unzip my dress.

"I need to get out of this."

"Then let's work on that."

He undid my dress, and I wiggled out of it, both of us tossing it to the side. Then he was undoing his pants, shoving them to the floor, and we were all over each other, our hands roaming, our mouths unable to stop moving.

I reached between us, gripping his cock, and realized that my thumb and forefinger didn't meet.

I groaned, sliding myself along him, leaving my wetness along his length.

"How long have you had your barbell there?" I asked, gently playing with the jewelry at the tip of his dick.

"A while now," he said softly, looking at where we met. He had one hand on my side, drawing circles with his finger, the other gently fingering me.

I rocked into him, needing a moment to catch my breath.

"Will I hurt you?"

He shook his head. "I can get myself off going pretty hard, Scarlett. You're not going to hurt me with those dainty hands of yours."

I rolled my eyes. "I don't want to hurt you, Hudson."

And there it was, the truth on multiple levels, but we did what we did best and didn't talk about it.

Instead he slid his fingers out of me and tapped them against my mouth.

"Open."

I did so and tasted myself on him. I nearly came right then, wondering what exactly this man did to me.

Instead he leaned back, and I straddled him.

"Farther up," he ordered, and I frowned, slowly rocking myself along his cock.

"Excuse me?"

"Sit on my face, Scar. I don't want to have to tell you again."

Eyes wide, I crawled up his body, pausing as he lapped at my nipples, tugging at the piercings.

He spanked me, and I laughed before moving forward to the edge of the bed.

"Hold on to the headboard if you have to but sit on my face."

I looked my legs, at that bearded face of his, and pressed my lips together.

"You're not going to suffocate me, Scarlett. And even if you do, it's not a bad way to go."

Laughing, I gripped the headboard, and did exactly what he asked, and sat on his face.

He held onto my thighs as I rocked myself over his

face, knowing that I was going to come again, and probably fall into a puddle.

I couldn't breathe, couldn't think, instead, I just rocked my hips, letting his tongue spear me, and before I could think, I was coming again, this time falling back.

Somehow Hudson caught me, keeping me in his arms. I had never come on a man's face like that, hadn't known it was even possible, truly, but Hudson was something else. And then I was on my stomach, thighs pressed together, and he was sliding deep inside me.

We both froze, and I realized what we had forgotten.

"Fuck," he growled. "Let me get a condom."

I reached around, unable to speak for a moment, as I caught his wrist.

I was so full, nearly stretched to the limit at this angle. He had filled me with one thrust, and it felt like I could burst. "You don't have to. I'm on birth control. I'm clean. I promise."

Hudson let out a curse through gritted teeth as he dug his palms into my lower back and ass.

"I had a vasectomy a few years ago. It's reversible, but I'm clean and I'm not going to get you pregnant. Not now."

I didn't know what the phrase "not now" did to me in that moment, but in the end, I lifted my hips slightly, drawing him deeper.

His piercing hit me and I nearly came again.

In his answer to my movement, he slid out of me, and before I could whimper at the loss, he thrust hard.

I gripped the duvet, hands shaking, as he slowly worked in and out of me, gently at first, before moving harder, faster. He pressed back to me, tangling one hand with my own, as he rocked his hips, both of us meeting each other thrust for thrust.

"You're so fucking tight at this angle, Scarlett."

"I can't, I can't," I whispered.

He pulled out of me then, pushing me onto my back and sliding into me before I could even think.

"I've never fucked anyone bare before. You're so fucking tight, so wet. I don't think I could ever go back to normal."

I looked up at him then, tears filling my eyes even though I hated myself for it. "I don't think there is normal."

He didn't pause as he continued to thrust, but as he slid one of my legs up so my ankle was at his shoulder, he moved forward and took my lips.

"Never normal. Just us."

And then he moved.

When I came again, clamping around his cock, he sped up, the bed rocking, and both of us clutching for each other.

He finally came, groaning into my neck, his breath warm, his body heavy along mine.

And I let myself come down from my orgasm, holding him as tightly as I could.

I hadn't asked for Hudson Cage, and as he kissed me softly and wiped my tears away, I knew he hadn't asked for me.

But in that moment, he was my obsession.

And walking away would break us both.

Chapter Twelve
Hudson

"It'd be better just to gut everything and start over." I ran my hand through my hair and looked over at my contractor, Frank. The man had been in the business for longer than I had been an adult and knew what he was doing.

He was also the father of one of the men I had fought beside. He'd lost his son the same day I took two bullets to my side and shoulder. I'd only spoken to the man a few times since, because what else were you supposed to say when you weren't quick enough to save your friend?

But Frank wanted to be part of this project, not for me, but for his son.

It would've been good for everybody, if his son would've been able to stay here.

Instead, his ashes lay on his mother's mantle, and

she dusted and polished the wood every day, and told her son exactly what had happened the day before, as if he could hear her.

She spoke to his ashes more than she had ever been able to speak to her son, and that was why his father did this. Because Frank and his wife deserved to stay here as well. Or maybe to just be able to fucking breathe after finally learning what grief was.

"The outbuildings and a few parts of the foundation are still good. The mudslide didn't take those away.

"You're right. And breaking into the side of the mountain like that to build something sturdy isn't going to be good for the land itself. So let's see what we can do. How many cabins are we thinking of?"

I took his tablet and tapped a few buttons on the screen. "I'm not the builder, you are. I can slap a couple coats of paint on after."

Frank gave me a look over that large mustache of his. "From what I know, you can do more than just slap on a couple coats of paint. I want to thank you again for letting me have that painting though. You should have let me pay."

I shrugged as I handed over the tablet, then put my hands into my pockets.

"Josh's sister was having a baby. And she'd always wanted something other than a print in her house." I remember Josh mentioned something like that.

"Katie loves it. And I got to be the best damn father out there for getting it for her. In reality, I lucked out."

"It was just a couple of weeks of work, so I don't mind."

"You need to start valuing yourself more than that." He let out a breath. "You seeing anyone yet?"

I frowned and turned to the older man. "What?"

"You settling down? I hear things about your family. Hard not to when they're always in the news." He raised a brow, but I didn't say anything. "I see some of your siblings are out there getting married. Having babies. Protecting the Cage legacy."

I snorted. "Some legacy."

"You're making your own. They hardly talk about your dad anymore. Now it's about the new set of Cages."

"My siblings are procreating enough for the rest of us. Don't you worry."

"So you're still single." I opened my mouth to say something, and a small smile spread over Frank's face. "Damn. What's her name?"

I shook my head. "It's...it's new. And it's not what you think."

"It never is until it slaps you in the face. But good for you. You deserve happiness, you know."

"I was happy before."

It was Frank's turn to snort. "We both know that you weren't. So you don't have to lie. You out here doing this thing for us? For your people? That is what will bring happiness to others. So maybe do it for yourself. With whoever this woman is. She has you confused and stuttering over your words. I like her."

"You don't even know her." I paused. "But I like her too. It's probably why it won't last."

"Because you like her?"

"Because she's fucking amazing. And it's early yet. I'm not good at keeping women. You know that."

Frank knew the story but not many others did. I had told Josh about Michelle and Jefferson, and the accident that had happened afterwards. Of course, Josh had only known part of it when he'd been alive. I had to tell his tombstone the rest. But in a moment of weakness, and far too much whiskey, I had told Frank.

And he hadn't judged me for it. If anything, he had been disappointed I'd not been able to finish everything with my own hands.

Maybe that's why I talked to Frank more than I talked to my brothers about certain things. And I talked to him a hell of a lot more than I ever talked to my father. Frank wasn't a father figure, but he'd lost his son, and I'd lost my best friend.

We both stared off into the distance, and I had to wonder if Josh was on his mind, or the future that we were trying to make.

"When do you think you can be out here again?" I asked, clearing my throat.

"Give me a couple of weeks to finish our current project, and then we'll be out here in force. We will take down whatever needs to be pulled away and start with zoning. You got all the permits that you need?"

I nodded. "I do. Thank you. Isabella helped there."

"Your sister-in-law is good at the whole spreadsheet thing. I liked the email she sent."

"Of course. She was good at it." I paused "I might ask Scarlett to help with a few things. She's a resort manager."

"Scarlett is it? Fascinating."

"Frank," I warned, and the other man just laughed.

"Come on, let's do one more round, and you can head out. I promised Mary that I would have lunch with her down at the diner. She's shopping now with a woman named Ms. Patty."

I couldn't help but laugh. "Your wife's been adopted by the town's Mrs. Mayor."

"Her last name is Mayor?" he asked, confused.

"No. Let me tell you a story about the small town of Cage Lake."

Frank just shook his head, and I laughed for the first time in a long while in this man's presence.

I mourned my friends, I mourned Michelle. But I didn't wallow in it. At least I didn't think so. Yet when it came to figuring out what would come next, sometimes I couldn't help but be stuck in the past. That was why we were making this retreat. Or whatever the hell we were going to call it.

Taking something broken, used beyond measure, and trying make it for good.

By the time Frank and I finished, it was noon, and I was hungry. I put together a quick sandwich, and planned on heading back to the studio, figuring I'd get a few hours of work in. The art show had done tremendously well, surprising me. My agent hadn't been surprised at all, and so I had more work to do. But I didn't have a direction. I could go anywhere I wanted with it, and I couldn't get Scarlett's face out of my mind.

I wasn't into portraits, but maybe it was time to start.

Before I could go out the back door, my front door opened.

"You should lock your door, twin."

I rolled my eyes and got out all of my sandwich fixings again to make Flynn one of his own. Even though he might've already eaten for all I knew, he'd want a sandwich if he saw one in my hand.

Flynn grinned and handed me a bottle of Coke.

"I got the fancy bottles too, with real sugar. How did you know I wanted a sandwich?"

I rolled my eyes. "I didn't, but I was having one, so I knew you would whine until you got one."

"You say the sweetest things. Thanks."

I bit into my sandwich and took a sip of the crisp, real sugar Coke.

"Damn that's good. My teeth are going to rot, but worth it."

"It's like candy." Flynn grinned.

I rolled my eyes. "You are the vice president of a billion-dollar corporation, and you're over here with a deli sandwich and a Coke like a kid."

"Hey, this is way better than Wonder Bread and off-brand Coke."

"True. This shit is fancy."

"Damn straight."

"Not that I don't love having you here, but why the hell are you here?" I asked, confused. It was the middle of the work week, and it wasn't like Flynn to show up like this. Oh, he showed up unannounced all the fucking time, but he usually didn't take off work.

"I was going through my mail and realized that I had something for you."

I frowned, confused. "What? People get us confused in person, but not when it comes to mail."

"I have a feeling our lawyer did it on purpose. Probably on Dad's request just to fuck with us some more."

I stiffened when I realized what Flynn held in his hand.

Our father had mixed us up constantly. It wasn't like with Sophia when she was exhausted and had to blink a couple of times to get the girls situated. And even then, now that the girls were getting older, and their faces were changing ever so slightly, even though they were identical, Sophia didn't make that mistake anymore.

But our father had purposely not cared enough to figure out who was who.

Though of course he'd make sure that the letter that I wanted nothing to do with would go to Flynn first. Fucking with us had been his favorite pastime in life, why not in death?

"I was wondering when that was going to show up," I said in lieu of anything else.

When our father had died, not only had we realized we had another set of siblings, but there had been countless addendums to the will.

The main one being that we had to have dinner once in a month as a group as we had been doing for the past few years. If anything, we'd made it our own, and I'd even participated enough that I'd learned to like them.

There were other parts of the will that some of my siblings had to deal with personally, ones that I knew they were keeping close to the vest or not wanting to speak of at all. I didn't blame them, not when my father could be so manipulative.

Another major component were these letters.

Each of our siblings had received letters from our father. Some more than one.

Our father could barely stand talking to me when he'd been alive, why would he bother when he was dead? Other than to find some way to hurt us, which was something he was so good at.

"Did you read it?" I asked, not bothering to reach for the letter.

"No. I thought about it. Not because I was curious and wanted to have a one-up on you."

"You're not like that, Flynn. You may joke, but you're not cruel. You're not him."

"You have no idea what it feels like to hear that. The only reason I wanted to read it was to make sure that he didn't fuck with you. But then I realized if I read it ahead of time, it'd feel like a betrayal."

"You could have read it, Flynn. You're allowed everything that I have. We shared a womb for God's sake."

Flynn grinned, though it didn't reach his eyes. "Womb to tomb."

"Damn straight."

"Will you take the fucking thing now? We can burn it together, but I thought you should get the choice. The will doesn't specify that you have to open it. Just that it has to get to you. But of course they went about it in a long fucking way because they're dumbasses that like to break us. Or at least pretend they're trying."

I snagged the letter from his hand and stared down at the handwritten addressee.

"At least he didn't call me dumbass on this," I said, trying to be funny and yet falling flat.

"Let's just burn it. I don't even know why I brought it here."

"You could have burned it on your own. But then you would've felt guilt. Because you have integrity. Unlike our father."

"With our parents, it's really shocking that we turned out in any form of normal."

"I love that you think I'm normal."

Flynn didn't rise to the bait, and I wasn't surprised. Neither one of us knew what we were truly doing.

"Are you going to open it?"

I nodded but didn't move to open the damn letter.

"He typed the others. Did he handwrite their names too?"

"I know Aston's was. I'm not quite sure about the others. I don't even know what most of them say. Probably not the best thing."

"All he does is berate us. Find a way to cut us from the beyond. He wasn't a good man, Flynn. Why should we care what he says?"

"I don't." Flynn paused. "I do. Talk about needing therapy."

"Do you go?" I asked, honestly curious.

Flynn shrugged. "Sometimes. You?"

"Not anymore. It got to be repetitive."

Flynn just gave me a look and I didn't bother answering. We all had our own reasons.

With a sigh, I tore open the envelope and pulled out the single sheet of paper.

"Looks like he spent a lot of time on this," I said, looking at the small paragraph.

"It could be worse, could be the receipts of your wrongdoing."

"No, Father just decided to do that himself with his own guilt and wrongdoing."

Flynn shook his head, and I cleared my throat and began to read aloud.

Hudson –

You failed me. You always did. But you proved yourself in the end.

You fought for our country, and that was something to be proud of. At least they say I should be proud of you as your father.

The one thing I'm truly proud of is that you were never caught.

In order to survive as a man in this world, you have to get your hands bloody. And you did so.

And they never found you.

That is what fills me with pride over your other siblings.

Maybe you're more like me than you ever knew.

- Loren Cage

I looked down at the note and burst out laughing.

"Well. He told me that he was proud of me. It's practically a declaration of love."

Flynn took the letter from my hand and shook his head. "So was he proud of you for being in the military or not? I have so many questions on his stance on the military and appointments."

"I have zero questions for that man. I have my own issues when it comes to that, and he never entered the arena of people that I cared about or their opinions when it came to military service. I can be as conflicted as I fucking want to be about what happened over there, and he has nothing to do with it. But the fact that he's proud of me because he thinks I killed a man? What the fuck?"

"So he never knew the truth?" Flynn asked, and I ran my hand over my chest.

"What truth is there? Michelle and Jefferson are dead. I might not have pulled the trigger, but he sure as fuck thought I did. Turns out I just need a hint of a felony and breaking one of the commandments for him to love me. Who knew?"

"I should have been taking notes this whole time?" Flynn said, laughter in his voice though it didn't quite reach his eyes.

We were both failing and trying to make this lighthearted, but hell. Our father had been insane. There was no other word for it.

Without another thought, I did what I had

planned on doing when I saw that letter and tore it into pieces before tossing in the trash. "Fuck him. Seriously. I got over Dad being a dick to me long ago. I have my own issues outside of him. Thank you very much."

"I have a feeling you probably shouldn't have tested the gods when you said that," Flynn muttered.

I frowned, then turned as footsteps echoed in my living room.

The day was a day of family reunions, because it looked as if hell had frozen over, and Melanie Cage had decided to walk on Cage Lake grounds after swearing to never come back to this hellhole—her words—again.

"I'm so glad I caught you." Her gaze went to Flynn. "You too."

"What are you doing here, Mother?" I ask, confused.

Flynn took a step to me, and in that moment, we were doing our twin thing again, two against one. And honestly, with this woman, I needed the support. *We* needed the support.

"I'm here because I'm asking for help."

If she would've said she'd murdered a man, I'd have believed before her asking for help.

"Why on earth would I help you?" I asked.

"What do you think we could do for you?" Flynn added right after.

"I've made mistakes, and I don't know how to fix

them. Everybody has cut me off, and I need to fix this. We cannot be a proper family if I don't fix this."

"How do you think I could help? It's not like you and I have ever gotten along," I said dryly.

"Hudson. That's not the case. And Flynn, I'm your mother. I love you both. All of you."

"You know, I've really had too much family for the day. Dad has already fucked up our family enough and you've made mistakes. You have been cruel to people in our family."

"I might have misstepped, but there has to be a way for me to atone," my mother added, and I shook my head.

"I'm not the one you need to apologize to. You decided that you didn't care about me long ago."

"That's not true, Hudson. I might not have understood why you joined the military. Or why you came back to Cage Lake. Or why you decided to be your own land baron out here by owning this property and the properties around you. But it made sense. You're a Cage. I might not understand everything, but I've never not loved you."

My mother kept speaking, but Flynn had stiffened beside me, and I realized that today was a day I really should have fucking locked my door.

Scarlett stood behind my mother in the open doorway, linen grocery bag in hand and a frown on her face.

I wanted to pinch my nose and groan. Because

Scarlett didn't know I owned the land. But as the wheels turned in that brain of hers, she knew now.

Secrets were never good, I knew that. They always broke those around them, but for once, why couldn't the world just let me breathe for a minute so I could handle things?

"Mom, Mom! *Mom!*" I repeated as my mother ignored me. "I'm not the one you need to deal with. That's on the others that you hurt. I don't know why you're here, but this isn't the time."

My mother frowned at me before she turned back to look at Scarlett. "Oh, Scarlett Blair. Is there something that you need with the resort? I didn't know you were making house calls with my son."

Scarlett's face drained of color before she narrowed her gaze and opened her mouth to say something.

I knew that whatever she did, it would just egg my mother on. Because no matter how much my mom wanted to apologize right now, she couldn't help but cut people down. She had married my father for a reason.

But Scarlett already had to deal with enough people in her life. Scarlett already had to deal with enough people in her life who tried to break her. I wasn't going to let my mother be one of them.

"Mom. Get out. You said your peace, but it has nothing to do with me. And as you can see, I have plans for the evening that don't include you."

"Hudson!" she gasped, trying to come closer.

Then Flynn was there taking her by her elbow. "Come on, Mom. Let me walk you out."

Flynn raised a brow as he stared at me, and I gave him a chin nod. We would talk about everything, but first, I needed to fucking fix what my mother had decided to shatter. She might not have realized what she was doing, but she would have enjoyed the consequences nonetheless.

As Flynn practically dragged my mother out, Scarlett stood to the side, studying me.

"Hudson?" she asked, and I rub my fingers over my temples.

"This has been the longest day, and I have no idea why everybody decided to do this at once."

"You own the land underneath my home."

With a sigh, even though it wasn't yet dinner time, I reached to my cabinet and pulled out two glasses and a bottle of decent bourbon.

"I'm going to need a drink if I'm going to continue this day. You?"

"I guess so. And then you can tell me what the hell was just going on. What was your mother doing here?"

I poured two fingers of bourbon in each, before taking the glasses and walking over her. I handed her one, took the tote from her hand, and set it on the counter. Flynn had thankfully shut the door behind him, leaving the two of us alone.

"You knew the Cages owned the land. It's what we do."

She looked down at her bourbon and then up at me. "I didn't know you did."

"Because I didn't want you to hate me more than you already did." And with that, I tossed the bourbon back, even though it was more of a sipping kind. It didn't burn, but I already regretted the action. I set the glass on the counter. Scarlett stared at the amber liquid, before doing the same thing I had. When she didn't flinch, I was afraid I had fallen just that more much in love with her.

Scarlett Blair was some kind of woman, and she scared me.

There, that was as honest as I was going to be in that moment.

"It's been a really fucking weird day, Scarlett."

"Tell me about it. There's a power issue at the resort, and we finally got it fixed. I had to come home and change. I thought I would bring my groceries for later, and here I am drinking in the middle of a workday."

With a sigh. I put my hands on her hips and drew her near.

"I own the land. I'm sorry for not telling you. There're a lot of things that I own in this town because it was going to go to waste if I didn't. Or a developer was going to come in and hurt this town. But things just added up. I didn't want you to hate me before, and then I didn't want you to feel like you owed me. So I didn't tell you. Even though I was trying to think about when I would. I'm sorry."

Scarlett set down her glass and cupped my cheeks. "Okay. Okay."

I raised my brows. "That's it?"

"Between the look on your face, and the fact that your mother was here even though I know she's estranged from the family, I have a feeling that you had a longer day than I have."

"Maybe. Probably. Do you need help with the resort?" I asked, knowing that if she'd had to change, she'd had a hell of a day.

"No, we have it figured out. But of course you would offer."

I leaned down and brushed my lips against hers. "It's been a hell of a day."

"Why don't you tell me about it?"

"You don't want to hear it, Scarlett."

"I really do. So please, tell me. And then I'll totally forgive you for not telling me about the property."

I raised a single brow. "A bribe?"

"Damn straight."

I leaned down, lips twitching, and took her mouth with my own.

"Should I start with the letter, the ghost, or my mother?"

"That sounds like the start of a really bad joke. I'm in."

And with that, I pulled her into me and did something that I never did with anyone other than Flynn, I told her about my day.

And afterwards, she did the same for me, and neither one of us tried to fix the other.

And I had no idea what that meant.

Chapter Thirteen
Hudson

If you asked any of my exes, they would tell you that I wasn't good at dating. And it wouldn't be a complete lie. I wasn't good at dating. I had no idea what the hell I was doing most times. But I tried. Tried to the point that I probably failed more often than not.

But here I was, at Scarlett's front door, package in hand, hoping to hell I didn't fuck this up.

I took a deep breath and frowned at the slight breeze in the air. It was chillier than usual, and I didn't like that. It was still early enough in the year that there could be a blizzard at any moment, but the weather app hadn't sensed one, and the radar looked clear. So today's hike should be fine, but then again, snow could show up without warning. That was what happened when you lived in the mountains.

The sun shone brightly, not a cloud in the sky, and it was warm enough that it canceled out the breeze, and honestly, we'd end up with a sweat after our date. But I was still going to check the weather one more time before we headed out.

I knocked on the door, waiting for her to answer.

I hadn't expected to be in a relationship, or whatever the hell we were to each other. We had been very careful not to put labels on this thing, other than the fact that we were only with each other at this moment. We weren't going to be sleeping with anyone else, or fighting with anyone else like we did. That was maybe the fun part. Or I was losing my damn mind.

I didn't want to be in a relationship. I wasn't good at them. But I had never expected Scarlett Blair. And perhaps that was the problem. There was nothing usual or expected about her. I didn't want her to become an obsession, but she was quickly becoming one. And that was the problem. I didn't know where we stood, or if there should be a change at all. But I couldn't fix that right now. I just had to focus and not fuck this up.

And I had a feeling I would be the one who fucked things up before she did. She always had a plan. A list. A goal.

I was trying not to drown.

We weren't equals, and I knew she was better than me. But that was just fine. I liked the fact that she was better than me. Except she probably needed to learn the truth before long. About who I was. And that was going to be a problem.

Scarlett opened the door, a small smile on her face. "You're here."

I frowned. "Of course I'm here. I said I would be."

She rolled her eyes, leaned forward, and put her hand on my chest. When her lips brushed mine, I sighed.

"Okay, grumpy."

"I'm not grumpy," I lied.

"Of course you're grumpy, that's what I like about you."

"Sure. We can go with that."

She just smiled, before looking down at what I held in my hand.

"What's this?"

I shrugged. "Something I thought you might like. You can hate it. It's fine."

The problem was, I didn't want her to hate it. I wanted her to love it. And want more of it.

This was a problem. After all, Scarlett was so much better than me. I knew that, the town knew, and my family would know if they actually paid attention.

Yet yelling at them about wasn't going to help anyone.

She needed to know the truth about me. About everything had happened. She might not believe she did at this point, but I knew it. Pretending the worst hadn't happened wouldn't help anyone. It would just make it harder for me to leave when the time came, so I needed to tell her the truth. And maybe today would be the day. Or maybe I'd be just as much of a coward as always.

I finally blinked out of my own thoughts and looked up at Scarlett who frowned at me.

"What's wrong, Hudson?"

"Nothing." I cleared my throat. "Do you mind if I set this inside before we go out?"

"Of course not. What is it?"

"It's nothing much," I said with a shrug, as I moved passed her into her home. It smelled of coffee, fresh flowers, and that scent that was all Scarlett.

When she finally left me after she realized the type of man I was, it would take forever for me to get that scent out of my brain.

"Can I open it?" she asked, her hands outstretched.

I nodded, suddenly self-conscious that she'd hate it, and wondered what the hell I was doing, before she finally took it from my hands.

She gently set the large rectangular package on the kitchen island and began to slowly undo the brown paper wrapping it.

"You don't have to be too careful with the paper. It's not fancy or anything."

"I just don't want to damage what's beneath it."

There was an odd note underneath her tone, and I realized her hands shook.

"Scarlett?"

"No. I'm fine. Totally fine." As she began to blink quickly, I realized she now stared at the front of the painting.

"Hudson." Her voice cracked, and I cursed under my breath.

"You don't have to like it. Or even take it. You just mentioned that you wanted a painting, and I like to paint. It's sort of what I do. So, here you go. It's yours if you want it."

She just stood there, holding the painting without a word, as tears began to trickle down her face.

I cursed again and reached for the painting. She clutched it to her chest and shook her head.

"Don't take it. I love it. Mine. It's all mine."

"What?" I asked on a whisper. "If you hate it, you don't have to tell me. Hell, you can tell me if you want to. I just thought you'd like one."

"You are such a generous, amazing man, and I hate you for that."

I blinked, confused as always when it came to Scarlett.

"What did I do?"

"You painted me our afternoon."

She turned the painting so I could see it even though I knew exactly what was on it as I'd been the one to create it. The mountains, the path next to the creek, the picnic bench where we had eaten, and I had taken her mouth with such an abandoned ease, that I'd nearly taken her body right there.

"I thought you'd like it, but you don't have to keep it. I promise."

"You are not taking this away from me," she said, shaking her head. "This is mine. Now I have an original Hudson Cage. And nobody will know the true meaning behind it other than us. They can ask about the color of blues and what exactly that tree means, but they'll never know. Because this is just ours, and I'm going to start crying again, so you're going to have to deal with it."

With a sigh, I gently tugged the painting away from her, set it on the table, and then pulled her into my arms.

"You're a menace."

"And I love it so much. So if I cry a little bit, just let it happen."

"Like I can stop you from doing anything. We both know that's a lost cause."

She snorted against my chest and wrapped her arms around my waist. I rubbed my chin on top of her head and breathed in that scent of hers that I couldn't get enough of.

"You're ridiculous you know," I said after a moment.

"You are. But that's fine, I'll let you call me that, because I love it so much."

"You love that we're ridiculous together?" I asked, trying to lighten the mood since I had no idea what the hell was going on.

"I love that you thought of me. That you painted that on a whim, just because I've said I wanted to buy one when I had enough money."

"You never have to buy anything from me, Scarlett."

"Then you say things like that, as if I'm not supposed to fall at your feet in tears."

"You know I hate tears. Don't cry."

"I promise never to use them as a weapon, but I am going to cry."

I lifted her chin with my finger and took her mouth with my own.

She moaned into me, as my tongue slid against hers, and the tension eased out of her shoulders. My cock stiffened, but I ignored him. He'd have to wait until later.

"Well then," she whispered against my mouth.

"I know we have a plan for the day, but if you'd like to show me exactly how thankful you are..." I trailed off.

She pulled back, laughing, and shoved playfully at my shoulder. "Menace," she said again, before kissing my jaw. "Let's go for our hike, and then when we come back, I can show you exactly how thankful I am."

My cock paid attention once again.

"Okay then. Sounds like a plan."

She reached between us, rubbed her hand along my shaft. I closed my eyes and groaned.

"That's just mean."

"I really am mean. I hope you can hike with a hard-on."

In answer, I reached between us and rubbed the seam of her jeans over her clit.

She let out a shocked gasp, and I grinned, loving the way her eyes dilated.

"Payback's a bitch. And that clit of yours is going to be rubbed every time you take a step. Poor baby."

"I should hate you right now, but I can't really catch my breath."

"And now we're even." I smacked a kiss on her lips and took her hand. "Let's start our hike. I'm going to drive to the edge of the trail, that way we don't waste most of our hiking time getting through the property."

"You're the one who knows what he's doing. I'll just follow along."

"I like the sound of that."

She shoved at me again, before she picked up her backpack. "I went through the checklist that you gave me, as well as one that I found online. I should have everything for an afternoon hike."

I frowned and lifted the bag. "It's a little heavy. You going to be okay with that?"

"Of course. I even practiced on my small treadmill to see if I could handle it."

My lips twitched. "Of course you did. I know you do a few hikes with the resort, but we're going to be on the trail that heads off to the off-gridders."

Her eyes widened. "We're not actually going to go to the off-grid camp, are we?"

I shook my head. "No. These guys aren't the dangerous ones. They are off-grid when it comes to most things, but they're not the scary guys that believe they're forming their own independent country within the United States. Or any other shit like that."

"Oh good. They just don't like being on the electrical grid or something?"

"Pretty much. They own the land that they're on, so there's nothing much that others can do about it."

"You know, when they told me that you were a growly mountain man, I assumed you were with the off-gridders."

I shrugged as we got into the truck and made our way to the trail.

"I thought about it to be honest."

Her eyes widened, and I gripped the steering wheel a little bit harder.

"Some of them have the right idea. Getting away

from people and just figuring out what the hell you want with your life."

"So why didn't you?"

I met her gaze, before turning back to the road. We parked in a small spot that wasn't really a parking lot at the edge of the trail.

"As much as I like to be alone, and to hide, well, maybe not hide, but to get away, my family would never let that happen. Even before my dad died, my brothers and I were all decently close. When my youngest brother Ford went through all that hell, well, somebody had to be there for him. Even if he tried not to let us. And then it was one thing after another, and here I am, doing family dinners."

"I'm glad that your family was there for you. Because you're always there for them even if you don't think you are."

I let out a breath and didn't say a word as we got out of the truck and began on the small trail that would lead us in a circle after a couple of miles. The wind started to pick up, and I frowned, checking the clouds.

"What's wrong?" she asked as she tightened the straps on her backpack.

"Just making sure that we're okay on the weather. We should be."

"That doesn't sound ominous at all," she said dryly.

She slid her fingers through mine, and I didn't let

go, instead I rubbed my thumb along the space between her thumb and forefinger, and frowned.

"You see a good person when you look at me. Even when we yell at each other, I don't think you see the person I used to be. The person I try not to be." I hadn't meant to say the words in quite such a transparent way, but they were out, and there was no going back.

She paused, frowning at me as we stood at the edge of a clearing.

"What on earth are you talking about?"

"I haven't always made the best choices. There's a reason that I came back to Cage Lake and didn't go to Denver near the family."

"Will you tell me about those choices?" she asked.

I opened my mouth to say something, yet my throat tightened, and I couldn't say a damn word.

She studied my face, and I was afraid I'd see disappointment in hers, instead she pushed back my hair and smiled softly though it didn't reach her eyes.

"I know all about making poor choices. I thought Ronin loved me. I thought I'd finally found someone that was perfect for me. And then he hit me that first time. And I didn't walk away."

"Scarlett. You don't have to talk about him if you don't want to." And frankly if I kept hearing about him, I was going to find him and murder him. Which wasn't the best thing in the world.

"I sometimes need to talk about him. Because I didn't walk away. I'd always internally blamed my mother for not doing that. But then I realized that she had tried. She had tried so hard, and my dad had pulled her back in. She hadn't even realized she'd been closed in until it was too late. And I had found myself down that same path. I talk to my therapist all the time about this, how I'd somehow become a statistic, and yet every statistic has a story. There's a depth and a breadth to those points in a spreadsheet. We aren't just numbers, we aren't just tragedies. We're human beings who make mistakes and yet realize that those mistakes were also made upon us. I found myself in the same strange life that my mother had been in, and I found a way out. Yes, he's still around and I want to scream every time I see him or my father—"

"You haven't seen him recently, have you?" I asked as I gripped her shoulders.

"No. I haven't. I promise. I'd have told you. Even though I like to deal with things on my own, you're growlier than me."

"Damn straight," I growled, adding emphasis to the words, which made her smile. Exactly what we had both needed at that moment.

"The fact I'm even here with you right now freaks me the fuck out."

I froze. "Why?"

Though I was just as freaked out.

"Because I'm afraid I'm making those same mistakes. Not that I believe you'd ever do that. But finding trust in a way that I could believe in myself again isn't something I thought I'd allow myself to do. He irrevocably changed me, and yet I have to find myself forcing a new change. Altering who I am so he isn't the last mark upon my soul."

I leaned forward and did the one thing I could do in that moment, I brushed my lips along hers.

"I hate the word strong. Because they always put it on somebody who's trying to dig their way out from hell, as if strength is the only thing that matters. But you are strong. And you're erasing those marks from your soul, from everything he touched. You do know that, right?"

"There will always be scars left behind."

"As someone covered in scars, maybe that's okay."

"I like when you speak with wisdom. It's kind of hot since you're such a brute."

I rolled my eyes and took her hand, continuing the trail.

"Will you tell me about what you meant before?" she asked after a moment, and I let out a breath, letting the sounds of nature do what they were meant to do. "I'm not a murderer, but sometimes I feel like I am."

She nearly tripped over her feet, then turned to me. "Because of the deployments?" she asked, her words so careful.

"Not exactly." I ran my free hand over my face, and finally at least tried my best at speaking the words that refused to come. "I did what I had to do over there. What I was ordered to. And there will always be horror in my heart and soul over what I did for somebody else's actions. But that's not what I'm talking about." She didn't say anything, giving me a moment to breathe. "I've had one serious girlfriend in my life. And her name was Michelle."

Scarlett's eyes widened, and I had a feeling she hadn't known what direction this conversation was taking.

"Okay."

"We met in high school, we were sweethearts, voted most likely to get married and be boring in our school yearbook. All of the little things like that." Her lips twitched, but she didn't laugh, and neither did I. "I didn't know what I wanted to do when I graduated high school. Everyone had assumed I would go to college, continue the Cage legacy, but I was so mad at my father for so many things, and I didn't want to go into business, I wanted to paint. I wanted that artistic lifestyle that had nothing to do with being a starving artist. And that's not something my dad could understand. So I didn't go to college right away. I joined the military, and I left. I left Michelle behind, with a promise that I would be back to her. And she kissed me, said she loved me, and that she would wait. We did video calls, wrote letters, emails, did all the things you do on deployment."

"Hudson—"

I shook my head. "I came back, and I found out she was with somebody else. While she was with me, well, albeit while I was overseas, she was with Jefferson. A man I thought was my friend."

"That's terrible. I'm sorry. No wonder you don't want to date anyone else."

"If that was merely what had happened, maybe I'd find a way through it. Without being the asshole that I've become. But no, it turns out that it was worse."

"You don't have to continue if you don't want to."

I wasn't going to tell her everything. I couldn't. Not when I could barely even speak the words.

"I came back again and met up with her. She had bruises on her body." Just like Scarlett had when I had seen her in the mirror. When I'd walked into her office, and our worlds had shifted.

"Oh, that poor woman."

"I beat the shit out of Jefferson, I had so much anger, and nowhere to put it. Josh, one of my friends who I'd been deployed with, pulled me back, was the only reason that Jefferson didn't die." That day. "And so when I got deployed again, I thought she was safe. But she wasn't."

Tears filled her eyes, and I wiped away the single

tear. "He killed her. He killed her and he got away with it."

Thunder thrashed above us, and I cursed. "We should head back." The storm I had a feeling was coming in had finally made it.

"Hudson. I don't have any words."

"I don't either. I don't really know what to say. Other than she died and I wasn't there. So that's why I am who I am. Why I'm that asshole."

"It's not the same you know. With Ronin? It's not the same, Hudson. That much I can promise you."

"I can handle that promise." I leaned down and took her lips as snow began to fall. Because of course it would be thunder snow in the mountains in spring in Colorado.

"And let's get back before we both freeze to death?"

"And I think I promised you a little reward for that painting, didn't I?" she asked, and I knew she was trying to lighten the mood.

So I grinned like she wanted me to, and we ran down the trail as snow fell, and the tension in my shoulders began to ease. Not forever, I knew that would never happen.

But it was something.

After all these years, it was something.

Chapter Fourteen
Scarlett

Water slipped down my back as I slid my finger over Hudson's jaw. He looked down at me, the steam rising between us, and grinned.

It was so weird to see a smile or any form of emotion other than a snarl on his face. There had been so many months where looking at him would anger me, and not because he had truly done anything cruel. No, that was not Hudson Cage. Instead his presence had just annoyed me. Or perhaps annoyed me because of how he could affect me. There was probably something wrong with me when it came to that, but there was no turning back now.

Not when his hand moved between us, cupping my pussy.

"You were already wet before we got in the shower, and now look at you. Soaked." He speared me with two fingers before I could even say a word, and my mouth parted.

"That's it. Look how you take my fingers." I looked between us, and watched his fingers disappear deep inside me. I clenched my inner muscles, and he smirked.

"Good girl."

"Giving me praise? I didn't realize that was our kink."

"We can make it our kink." He licked my lips, before parting them, and I moaned into his mouth, unable to focus on anything but him.

I shivered in his hold even as the water began to heat, but I didn't need anything else but his touch in this moment.

When he continued to circle his fingers, pressing that small bundle of nerves, my toes curled, and I rocked myself on his hand.

He moved his mouth down, over my jaw, nibbling gently, before taking one nipple into his mouth and sucking. He twisted his lips in a way I hadn't even thought possible, and then I was coming, riding his hand as he continued to fuck me with his fingers.

"I love watching you come. Your eyes get all hazy, and your mouth parts."

"I would be embarrassed, but I just had an orgasm and can't really think about much else."

"That's my girl."

I held back a sigh at that, unsure what to say. Because him calling me his? That did something to me that worried me.

Because I was falling in love with Hudson Cage, and it had nothing to do with how he worked my body. But dear God, this man could work my body.

In answer, I went to my tiptoes, letting his fingers slide out of my cunt, before moving so I could go to my knees.

"I don't want you to hurt yourself in here," he warned as he took my hair in his fist, guiding me to his rock-hard cock.

"You say that as if you're not eager for my mouth on your dick." I cupped him then, letting his balls sit comfortably in the palm of my hand as the water began to get into my eyes. Without another word, he shifted slightly, blocking the stream of water so I could see, and my heart did that pitter-pat thing again. Of course he would notice, and of course he would fix it.

Because that was Hudson. Always trying to fix things even when it wasn't his fault.

It was no wonder that I was falling in love with this man.

He leaned down and played with the piercing on

my nipples, and I remembered the last time he had done that with his tongue, making me come from that alone. I had never come from breast play before, but here I was, continuingly to do so. This man was my menace. My drug.

And I wanted more.

Only I was afraid of what would happen if I asked for it.

With a grin on my face, I licked at the ring at the tip of his dick, and he moaned. His fist tightened around my hair, and I continued my exploration.

I loved going down on Hudson. Yes, his cock was slightly too big for my mouth, and my jaw always ached afterwards, but then he'd take care of me, and I wouldn't care about the inconvenience. But whenever I was on my knees in front of him, he let me pretend I was in control for those few moments. And as someone who constantly needed to be in control of her own life, at work, in reality, and everything connected, it was nice to give in. Because I was the one leading his orgasm, but he was the one guiding my head. As if he were reading my thoughts, he tilted my head slightly, and I opened my mouth, letting him guide himself in. I flattened my tongue as the tip of his cock and the ring hit the back of my throat.

"I'll have to take that out if we ever want to go harder," he teased.

I nodded, even as my mouth widened around the length of him, and continued to bob my head. When he angled my head once more, keeping me steady, I looked up at him, mouth wide, as he fucked my mouth, slowly, and then a little harder. The piercing didn't hurt when it was angled. It didn't catch on anything. If anything, I loved the fact that I could slightly feel it as I swirled around his dick. And when I contracted those muscles, he moaned, as if nearly on the edge. Kneeling at his feet, I spread my legs and then slid my free hand down to cup my breast, tugging on my nipple rings.

He grinned at me, moving quicker, as he ran his fingers along my jaw, then my neck, as if gently preparing me for his onslaught.

When I knew he was nearly there, I sucked harder, hollowing my throat, but then he moved back, not letting himself finish.

I wanted to pout, but I couldn't think, instead I was on my feet again, breasts pressed hard against the glass of the shower, and before I could say anything, I was on my tiptoes, and he was spreading me. He slammed into me from behind, one stroke that nearly sent me over the edge, and I placed my palms on the glass, trying to keep steady.

"I want to come inside you. While I love coming down that pretty throat of yours, I want you to feel my come in that sweet cunt, knowing I'm the one that filled you up. Do you want that? Do you want my cum dripping down your thighs?"

"Just get on with it," I bit out, teasing.

He leaned forward, gently grazing his teeth along my shoulder, before he pulled back out and slammed into me again.

I gasped, trying to find purchase on the wet wall, but then he was there, keeping me steady. I knew Hudson would never let me fall. And when he pounded into me from behind, I arched my back, needing him to go even deeper. He licked up my spine, and I shivered, needing more.

"I'll keep you steady, use one hand to play with your clit. I want to see your ass move as I fuck you."

My pussy clenched as my breath quickened. "The way that you talk makes me want to come right here and now."

"I'm not stopping you, Scar."

I closed my eyes, loving the way that he filled me, stretching me with his cock, and then I couldn't think. I slid my middle finger over my clit, and before I could even say his name, I was coming, my pussy clenching around his cock as I tried to catch my breath. Hudson moaned before pulling back and sliding out of me.

"You didn't come," I whispered, my knees shaking.

"I needed something first," he whispered. Then he speared me with two fingers, catching me off guard. He fucked me hard with those wide fingers of his, but before I could question what he was doing, he slid them out of me and then slammed his cock home. I gasped, trying to catch my breath. Then he used his newly lubed fingers to play with my ass.

I froze, my pussy tightening.

"Hudson?"

"I'm going to fuck your ass one day. We both know it. But first, let's get you ready."

My eyes rolled as he slowly worked his way in and out of me, just to the knuckle with his index finger, and I swallowed hard at the sensation. It burned slightly, and yet it was a good ache. I could not even fathom what it would feel like with his dick though. He was far too large for that, and I thought we had both known that. But I couldn't help but wiggle back.

That rough chuckle made my toes curl, and then he moved his finger away, gripped my hips, and continued to shift.

Our breaths came in pants as he worked me, and before I could reach for him, or ache for him further than I ever thought possible, he was leaning forward, face buried in my neck as he came. He cupped one breast in his hand as he wrapped his arm around me, his hips tilting up as he filled me with his cum, both of us shaking in the now cooling water.

I stood there, trying to catch my breath, as I leaned back against him.

"Good morning," I teased.

He kissed my neck, my jaw, and I closed my eyes, hoping he couldn't see my reflection in the mirror, grateful that there was still a little bit of steam left.

I couldn't let him know. Couldn't let him see that I loved him.

"Good morning," he whispered, and when he kissed me, tilting my head back so he could reach, I closed my eyes once more and promised myself I wouldn't get hurt.

Only I had a feeling I had just lied to myself once again.

SORE THROUGHOUT THE DAY, WORK DRAGGED ON. I had countless things to do, but that was what I liked. Working through problems and making sure the resort had everything they needed for the upcoming seasonal change meant that I didn't have too much time to worry about my feelings for Hudson.

Of course, as soon as I tried not to think about Hudson Cage or any of the Cages, Isabella and Sophia walked in, smiles on their faces.

Feeling slightly haggard because I had just ran around with one of my assistant managers, trying to help a family deal with lost luggage and a screaming toddler, I tried to clean up my hair, and smiled at the two women who had quickly become good friends.

"Hey there. I didn't know you guys would be here."

"I promise we're not catching up on you," Isabella teased as she hugged me tightly, before moving out of the way so Sophia could do the same.

They were both so beautiful, though they looked different. Isabella with all curves and shorter hair, while Sophia had that long willowy look of a former ballerina. Considering she had been a principal dancer for the Denver Ballet, I was always in awe of her grace. She still had that same aura, even after birthing twins, but I knew she ran herself ragged with the kids, her husband, and the studio.

I barely slept these days, and I had no idea where she found the time to do so.

"It's so good to see you. Sorry for dropping in on you like this. But the nanny kicked me out of Isabella's house, so she could watch the babies, and I could have a girls' day. Although getting Isabella to not work on her actual day off was like pulling teeth. But we're on our way to your spa to get our nails done."

"The Cage family Resort Spa is quite wonderful. And both girls on staff today are our two best. Not that we would ever hire anyone not the best." I winked at Isabella, who just laughed.

"I've been here before, and you know I love it. It's still so weird that I'm part of the family that owns this, but I'm figuring it out."

"Don't remind me, I'm still not used to it either," Sophia put in. "And I don't even live in town."

"It is still so good to see you both."

"And I know we're taking up all of your time. And you have to be busy, I know you have a full house," Sophia added.

"And we're just here to hug you because we love you, and don't want to get in your way. Although we will want details about you dating our brother soon, but I'm not going to mention that out in public. Oops, already did."

I froze, blinking quickly. "Oh. Right. That."

"We've given you plenty of time as just the two of you, without encroaching, but you do realize you have to come to the next Cage family dinner," Sophia put in solemnly.

"What? Oh. But he didn't invite me."

"Of course Hudson won't invite you," Isabella said with a roll of her eyes.

It felt as if someone had kicked me in the chest, and I tried to keep my smile on my face. "Oh. I mean I'm not surprised. We're just not there yet."

The blood drained from Isabella's face, and she held up both hands. "I meant, he would just assume you're going. Because that's the Hudson that we've gotten to know over the past few years. I honestly think he's a little surprised that we've given him this much space.

But this is the final Cage dinner, and the entire family's going to be there. And you're coming too. Sorry."

My mind whirled, trying to catch up. "Final? You guys aren't having dinner together again?"

"She means this is the final one proposed by the will. At least for this segment. For all we know there's a whole other segment coming because that's the type of games Dad liked to play. However, this is the final one of the three-year mark. I still can't believe Dad's been gone for three years."

Isabella reached out and squeezed Sophia's hand, and I swallowed hard, trying to catch my breath, and wondered why they thought Hudson would want me there.

"You're coming. And this way you can get all of the 'what's it like dating our recluse brother' questions out of the way."

"I don't know if we're dating or not. We're just," I blew out a breath and pinched the bridge of my nose, "I have no idea what we are because we purposely don't talk about things like that. But we're doing fine. I don't really want to, you know, hurt things."

"You won't. I promise." Sophia smiled brightly. "We want to hear all about it. You look so happy, if not stressed out that we're here, but that's neither here nor there."

I just let out a laugh and stared at the two women

who had become so close to me, and yet I felt like a chasm separated us in this moment.

It had nothing to do with them though, and all to do with the fact that I was falling in love with their brother and couldn't tell anyone. Because everybody that I would tell was somehow connected to him. I could talk to Ivy and Luna. Yes, I would go to that group chat.

But how was I supposed to put that into a group chat? In a text. No. It had to be in person. But neither one of them were here. What the hell was I doing?

"And you're spiraling." Isabella nodded while Sophia didn't let go of my other hand. "We love you. You're coming to dinner because you're our friend. We love you. You're doing an amazing job with the resort. So stop stressing."

"I thought you said you were my friend."

Both women gave me an odd look.

"Stress is how I breathe. I don't know how to do anything other than that."

Sophia just smiled as Isabella rolled her eyes.

"We love you. Seriously. You're doing amazing. This place has never run as efficiently as it has since you've become manager. And I'm a forensic accountant. I should know. Now, we get to do the personal things. And you can't get out of it."

Before I could say anything, the girls' phones buzzed, and they were called off to go get their manicures. I tried to look as if I wasn't having a panic attack, as I waved them off and told myself that I could do this.

Everything was just fun.

My phone buzzed then and I looked down at it as I walked to my office, knowing I had to get a few things done before I came back out.

Hudson: I have family dinner tomorrow. Want to come?

I froze where I stood right by my desk and swallowed hard.

Tears pricked my eyes, and I licked my lips. He'd asked.

He'd asked.

I let out a shaky breath, ready to reply.

Someone tugged my ponytail, and my phone dropped to the floor, as a scream was nearly ripped from my mouth.

But then a large hand covered my mouth, and I kicked out.

"Shut up. Just shut up."

I froze, knowing that voice.

The same voice that had echoed throughout my nightmares since I had been a little girl. The same voice that had broken my mother.

"That's a good girl," he whispered.

The fact that it was the same words that Hudson had used made me want to throw up.

"Now. You're going to be the girl that I raised, and do as I say."

I had dropped my phone, and with the door closed behind him, nobody would truly be able to hear me if I screamed. That's when I realized something sharp pressed against my lower back, and tears threatened.

He was going to kill me. I didn't know what he wanted, but he had something sharp against my back, and this man was going to kill me.

"Now, I know you have a safe in here, or a way to get cash. You're going to get me that. And then I'll leave. I'll leave your mom and your sister and everyone else alone. But you're here with these little Cages now. You've got access to money. I want my due. I'm the one that raised you and now you owe me."

Bile rose up my throat as his words played in my head. He hadn't raised me. He'd done nothing but beat my mother and threaten Luna and me my entire life. His demented worldview made him think that he was owed just for us surviving childhood.

And I hated him.

"Now I'm going to lower my hand, and you're not going to scream. You can feel this knife, can't you? You've always been my smart girl. Just remember that. I'll do what I have to. Don't make me angry."

He was a narcissistic selfish asshole, and I wasn't going to let him break me. And yet everything hurt. My heart, my head.

Every ounce of the soul and strength that remained within me.

"We don't have cash here. That's not how the resort works."

"Don't fucking lie to me. I know you're fucking that Cage, who has money from being a bitchy artist or something. Pansy."

"I don't have his money here either." He pulled on my hair, and I held back a scream as the knife dug in slightly. A sharp sensation slammed into me, and warmth spread on my side.

"Fuck. You're fine. I only broke the skin. You're fine."

My lips trembled. He was really going to kill me. He didn't care about me at all and was truly going to kill me if I didn't do what he wanted.

"Now, tell me where the money is."

"It's not in here but I can get it."

"Don't lie to me."

I risked everything and began to turn. His hand let go of my hair, and I let out a breath, grateful that he let me face him.

His eyes were bloodshot, and he looked a decade older than he was. While my mom had aged thanks to the terror that he had put her through, drugs and alcohol had taken everything else from my father. And yet he had looked so charismatic even weeks before. He had fallen into something hard since, and I wanted to feel bad about it. But all I wanted him to do was to vanish from my life.

"Okay. It's in the room next door, where our financial officer is."

All lies, and I had to hope my father couldn't see through them.

He narrowed his gaze, and terror slid through my veins.

"I'll be right behind you."

I nodded, wondering what the hell I was going to do now. I took a step past him, aware that the knife was close, and hoping to hell that the cut on my side wasn't too deep. Then he was behind me, the knife right against where he'd already cut me, and I moved a little quicker, trying to get away.

I went to open the door, and he tugged on my ponytail.

"Don't fucking lie to me."

Without thinking, I slammed my head back into his face, the crunch of bone satisfying if not terrifying. The knife slid through my side deeper this time, and I called out, a scream ripping from my throat.

"You bitch!"

I whirled, punching out like Hudson had taught me, slamming my fist into his jaw. He staggered back, swiping out with the knife. I moved out of the way, barely avoiding being grazed by the blade, as I turned again and reached for the door. He pulled at my ponytail, blood spraying from his hand as he whirled it in the air, and I threw open the door, hitting him in the face again.

My office was situated at the end of the hallway, and unless someone was in their office, they weren't going to be able to hear me. So I screamed and ran smack into a wall of muscle. Shaking, scared that my father was behind me and was going to hurt this person too, I looked up to see Hudson.

He gave me one look, lifted me by my elbows, and set me to the side, before stomping towards my father.

My dad let out one high-pitched scream, before he thudded to the ground, and Hudson hit him once, twice, and kicked him in the side for good measure.

Before I could say anything, Sophia and Isabella were there, Isabella on the phone, while Sophia pressed her palm to my side.

I tried to figure out what the hell had just happened, but then I realized I was having a panic attack, my breath coming in so quickly I couldn't catch up.

"Scarlett," a deep voice said from beside me, I turned to see Hudson, the glare on his face frightening, and yet I knew it had nothing to do with me.

"Breathe."

I opened my mouth to do so, and then black spots settled in front of my eyes, and before I could say anything, Hudson cursed and caught me as I fell.

"She's fine. She's going to be just fine," Isabella said for the fifth time. I finally opened my eyes and realized I was now in the hospital.

"What happened?" I asked, as I reached out, and noticed I had an IV in my arm. I could barely feel any pain but something felt off.

"You're awake. I'm going to go get the nurse," Sophia said as she left the small room, and I frowned at my best friend.

"What happened?"

"You fainted. I think from adrenaline. Not from blood loss thankfully. You didn't even need stitches on your side. And we're going to add so much fucking security to the resort it's going to be insane. People are going to complain about the amount of security and I won't care." And then Isabella burst into tears, before reaching forward and cupping my face.

"Never do that again."

"I promise I won't. I can't believe I passed out."

"I can't believe I didn't," Isabella said right back. "The rest of the family will be here soon. As will your sister. So don't worry. They should let you out of here soon actually. They said you had just passed out, and you would be fine, and you came to a couple of times, but I've been worried. You know me. I always worry."

I frowned again and stared at Isabella. "Where did

Hudson go?" I asked, trying to figure out everything that had just happened.

Isabella froze, and worry covered me.

"He left, didn't he?"

He had left. I had been too much for him, and he had left. I didn't blame him for that. How could I? But some part of me had broken.

Hudson had left.

"He isn't here right now. But I'm sure he'll be right back."

"What happened, Isabella?" Even I could hear the lack of emotion in my voice.

Isabella didn't comment on it, instead she just squeezed my hand. "You had your phone open to your text with Hudson and it called him instead of texting back somehow. I do that sometimes with Weston when I press the wrong button. And so when he answered he heard your dad's voice and his threats. He had already been on the way to the resort to grab you for dinner tonight or something. I'm not sure, I kind of missed that part of the conversation. But he heard what happened, called the police, called us, and then he was there. You had apparently already saved yourself because I love you and you're amazing. So he knocked your father out, made sure he was tied up thanks to Weston and some of the staff, and then helped you into the ambulance."

My mind whirled, and yet, Hudson had come. He had tried to save me.

"And then he left."

Isabella winced. "For a good reason."

I wasn't even sure she believed that.

Before I could say anything, the nurses and doctors were there, telling me that I was just fine, and I could go home. I listened to them and they explained things, and then I spoke with the sheriff, and knew I would have to talk with him again.

And it felt like I spoke to countless people, except for the one person I wanted to speak to.

Nearly ready to be checked out, nausea whirled, and I realized that I was going to have to go home.

Alone.

Because it wasn't as if Hudson would be there for me.

Before I could say anything, there was a knock at the door, and it felt like the floor had fallen out from beneath my feet.

Hudson stood there, a scowl on his face, a storm in his eyes, but he wasn't who had surprised me.

My mother walked towards me, her face deadly pale, eyes wide, but then her arms were around me, and I was holding her, and I broke into tears.

"I'm so sorry. I'm so sorry. But I'm here now. I'm out of the house and I'm here now. You are safe. And I love you so much."

"Mom." That was the only word I could say, my voice cracking.

And as we held each other, I looked up and met Hudson's eyes and realized why he had left.

He had brought my mom to me.

The one person in the world who would understand.

And I knew right then and there I loved Hudson Cage with all of my heart.

And I would never get over him.

CHAPTER FIFTEEN
HUDSON

"We shouldn't have come. We should have just stayed at the house, so you could have your feet up, and you didn't have to deal with the stress. My family is more than enough for anyone, and after everything you just went through, you seriously don't need this right now."

Scarlett merely turned to me while we sat in the cab of my truck, idling in front of Aston's lake house, and blinked slowly. "I'm fine. If I have to sit down and keep my feet up, I will be bored out of my mind and will wallow in everything that just happened. I would rather move on. Can we please just move on?"

"You can't even turn to me fully without wincing, Scarlett."

She set her hand on her side over where I knew her

bandage lay and shook her head. "Yes, that's true. But I didn't get stitches, and I'm perfectly fine."

"Don't lie to me." I gripped the steering wheel tighter, the whites of my knuckles showing. "You were hurt. And if I hadn't been there in time, you could have been hurt even more."

"Everything worked out, and I'm already stressed out your entire family knows the fact that my father is a terrible person. So I would rather put this past us and not think about it. Okay?"

"Considering we're going to a family dinner that's going to continue to go over all the bullshit that my jerk and adulterer of a father has put us through, you don't need to be worried about standing out with father issues."

Scarlett's lips twitched, even as her eyes softened. "That's true. We can do shots later about who has the worst daddy issues, and I honestly don't know who would win right now."

I leaned forward and brushed her hair back from her face.

"Let's just go inside, to this huge dinner with people that I should know all of their names and I haven't figured them out, and then go home."

"Okay. Let's do that. Mostly because I know I will never be able to convince you otherwise."

"You're learning so much. I'm so proud of you." She fluttered her elashes, and then let out a scream as I flinched when Flynn rapped on the window with his knuckles.

"Is there a reason that you're in here and not in the house? I assumed you were making out, but no. So confusing."

I flipped off my twin, before reaching down to undo Scarlett's seatbelt. "Let's go inside before I have to murder him."

"Do you mean let's go inside so you don't murder him?"

"I said what I said."

She grinned then, some of the tension on her face finally easing.

I got out of the truck and stomped my way around the front of it, pushing past Flynn so I could help Scarlett down.

The fact she had waited for me instead of jumping down as usual, told me she was in far more pain than she'd let on. I gently sat her feet on the ground and then took her hand.

Flynn looked down at the gesture and smiled. "You guys are so precious. I love it."

"Flynn," I warned.

"What? I'm just stating the obvious. Precious."

This time Scarlett moved forward, slapped him on the shoulder gently, then hooked her arm with his. "Okay, boys, lead me inside. I'm having an out-of-body experience right now."

"What?" I asked, confused as Flynn threw his head back and laughed.

"The twin thing?"

"Exactly. Two strong men leading me into the house. I mean, what more does a girl want?"

"I have so many questions."

"If you ask any of them, I will break you," I warned my twin.

Flynn merely winked before leading us into the house.

Aston's lake house was the largest of the Cage family homes. It made sense since he was the eldest, and when we had built it, it was because we knew whenever we visited, we would most likely do our dinners at his place. We hadn't taken into account the extra set of siblings and all of their spouses, but we were learning.

It was odd that my parents didn't have a home here. Yes, Dad had owned the Ackerson place, but it hadn't been for Mom. Mom did not have a place here, and frankly, she was never going to. At least not until she wised up and learned how to be a human being.

She hadn't our entire lives, and I had a feeling the only maternal figure we would have in our lives was the other Cage mother who was currently playing with Sophia's twins.

Constance Cage had known about the secret family, and had willingly gone along with it because she had loved my father for some reason. I wasn't sure if every one of her children had forgiven her, but she was here now, and the one grandmother for everybody. Hell, she even had Ford's son Micah with her. They had no blood relation, but she was a grandmother to him.

And I knew she would be for each of the kids that came along in our generation. If I even decided to have kids.

I nearly choked on air at that moment, wondering where the hell that thought had come from. No, thank you. I wasn't trying to think about that. There was no way I would be having kids. Right? No. Never.

Yet as Scarlett leaned into me, I realized that saying never had gotten me to this point.

"You're here." Isabella moved forward and stole Scarlett from me, and suddenly I found myself with a beer in hand, and James and Flynn on either side of me.

"You ready for this?" James asked as he studied the rest of the family.

"You continually force me to come to family dinners, so no. I'm never ready for this."

"But you brought a woman," Flynn added.

I raised a brow. "And?"

"You've never brought a woman before. Ever. To any family function. Let alone the final Cage forced dinner."

"It's a step." James nodded tightly. "A big step."

"You guys have been working together for so long that you're starting to sound like twins who finish each other's sentences. It's a little weird." I shook my head. "And everybody here knows Scarlett. Of course I was going to bring her. I don't want her to be alone."

Worry washed over James's face as Flynn let out a deep breath.

"He's behind bars?" Flynn asked softly.

"Yes. And will be for a long while. I think this was the final straw in terms of the legal shit." I gritted my teeth. "At least it better be."

"I'm surprised you didn't rough him up a bit," Flynn said after a moment.

My hand squeezed on my beer bottle, and I forced myself to relax. "I did. A little. But Scarlett needed me more."

Flynn whistled through his teeth. "Noted."

"No. Nothing to noted. We're just… I don't know. I have no idea what the fuck I'm doing, okay?"

"Do you love her?" James asked, and I cursed under my breath, looking around in case anybody had heard.

"We're not… I don't know. That seems like a big…" I wave my hands around. "*thing*. Let's just have this dinner, read the ridiculous next step of the will, and go home."

"Whatever you say," Flynn drawled out, and I shoved at his shoulder, before stomping towards Aston.

"Can we get this part done?" I asked, interrupting Aston and Kyler's conversation.

The fact that Kyler had even been able to take time off his tour to be here, spoke volumes. We all wanted this will to be done. Having our father hovering over us for any period of time was our own circle of hell.

"Sure. We can make that happen."

Aston cleared his throat, and just like that, the noise in the room lowered.

All twelve siblings, the spouses, and even the kids quieted to a murmur.

Constance held Ford's son in her arms, while the twins played at her feet, and yet, everybody's attention was still on Aston.

"I have the final paperwork here," Aston said after a moment, staring down at the envelope in front of him. Blakely moved to him, her hand on the round of her stomach as she came to lean against her husband.

"The lawyer didn't need to be here?" Theo asked from his seat on one of the couches next to Emily and Phoebe. Phoebe's husband stood behind her, his hands on her shoulders.

Dorian and Harper sat on the love seat next to them as others began to mill about. Cale came forward and stood next to his wife, an odd expression on his face I couldn't read.

This whole thing was a farce, and a weird fucking

way to begin a dinner, but that was our father, making everything far more complicated than it needed to be.

I looked around the room once more and took a few steps to the right to be near Scarlett. She slid her hand into mine, and I didn't miss the fact that others had seen. I squeezed her hand and waited for Aston to continue.

"No lawyer. This is just us. He knows we're all here. We'll do the photo just to annoy the fuck out of him like always." His lips twitched as everybody gave an awkward laugh. "I know the kids are in here, so I'll try to keep my language a little tamer." Aston winced. "Our father was not a good man. We all know that. He made his decisions, ones that we didn't have a say in."

I risked a glance over at Constance as she swayed with Wyatt in her arms, but her face was blank.

Maybe she didn't have the same say in her circumstances as our mother had. I didn't know her, but I had a feeling with the gravity of my father's presence, and the way my mother could manipulate, perhaps Constance hadn't had a choice in the way that we had all thought.

Though I didn't know why that idea had just come to me in that moment.

She met my gaze, gave me a sad smile, and then slowly began to take the kids out of the room.

Aston's shoulders relaxed at that moment, and once again I was grateful for a woman that I didn't know.

"In front of me is the next step of the will. Because there's always hoops to go through when it comes to Loren Cage."

"Do you want me to read them?" James asked, his voice low. "Or we can just burn everything."

"And break the company? No. Never." Although there was an odd humor in Aston's voice as he said it. "This man was a liar. A manipulator. But we're here. Together. Maybe it's what he wanted, or maybe he never thought we could, but we found a way to make this work. We are a family. All one hundred and ten of us."

I smiled as others laughed, Scarlett squeezing my hand.

"So let's read the next phase."

He opened the envelope as Blakely wrapped her arm around his waist.

Aston cleared his throat and began, the legal jargon going over my head in some cases, but some things made sense.

Loren Cage was truly a maniacal asshole.

"So, the dinners are done," Aston said after a moment. "We have a few charity and committee options that we need to perform in order to keep the town and company intact, but we no longer need monthly dinners where a ratio is important." Aston met each one of our gazes in turn, and I cleared my throat before raising my beer in a toast.

"To figuring out a dinner plan on our own. Because I have a feeling you guys are never going to let me leave the group chat. Or these family dinners."

And with that, the tension that had risen broke ever so slightly, and people laughed, standing up to hug, and continued the conversation.

Because there was no way we'd be ending these family dinners.

Maybe we wouldn't have to focus on how many of each family line was there, but we weren't cutting ties anytime soon.

Hell, my brothers were right. I had brought Scarlett to this, and that meant things were changing.

Only I wasn't sure exactly what would happen next.

By the time we had dinner and made plans for the next family dinner that would be in Denver, I was exhausted, and I knew Scarlett was beyond tired. She might not have needed stitches, but she was still in pain.

We made our way back to my house, driving up the winding road past her smaller place.

"So are you going to be on a charity committee?" Scarlett asked, her voice fatigued but still teasing.

"If they know what's good for the family, they won't. Isabella and Blakely will probably have fun organizing it. They like their spreadsheets."

"Spreadsheets save lives. I'll help them too if you

want." She paused. "If that's not stepping on toes. I mean, I'm not family. And well, you and I are... You know what, I'm too tired for this conversation."

I reached out and gripped her hand, squeezing. "I'm sure they'd love the help. And you're right, we're both a little too tired for this conversation."

"I suppose we should have it at some point."

I let out a breath. "Yes. Just not after a Cage family dinner with one hundred and ten people invited."

"That is true."

As I took the turn to pull into my house, I frowned, realizing there was an SUV already there.

"What the hell?"

"Who's here? All of your family was at Aston's."

"Stay in the car," I ordered, knowing exactly who it was.

I frowned, trying to figure out why the hell they would be here, and then the date clicked.

Shit. Grief slammed into me like a two-ton semi, as I slid out of the truck and ignored Scarlett's questions.

Michelle's mother got out of the SUV, her face ragged, her eyes red. Then Michelle's brother got out of the driver's side.

"How could you forget? How could you do this to her?"

In two quick steps, Michelle's mother was there, her palm swiping across my face as she slapped out.

I didn't move, and I let her have that one hit. After all, I deserved it.

"Shirley. Robert."

"You should have saved her. You knew what was happening to her and you did nothing. How could you?"

Then she began to scream, and I could barely understand the words. Scarlett got out of the truck, and I nearly closed my eyes in resignation. She hadn't known the whole story, had only known parts of it, but not all of it.

And now she would finally realize what kind of monster I was and walk away. Maybe that was for the best.

"You forgot her birthday," Robert snapped as he moved forward and took his mother into his arms. "How could you?"

"I'd say I'm sorry, but you've never believed me when I said it before." The lack of emotion in my voice echoed throughout the area, but I ignored it. Scarlett stood behind me, and as Shirley locked eyes on her, her gaze narrowed.

"You've moved on? Just like that. With her?"

I took a step to the right to somewhat block Scarlett. "You both need to go. I'm sorry that it's Michelle's birthday. I'm sorry about everything. But it was a long time ago, and there's nothing we can do now. You coming here in the pain that you are is not going to help you grieve."

"What do you know about grief? You let our baby die."

"You knew what he was doing to her, and you left her there," Robert added.

Each word was like a blow to the chest, but when Scarlett put her hand on the small of my back, bile rose in my throat. I didn't deserve her trust. Her comfort.

"I thought she was safe," I said after a moment, not knowing what else there was.

"She wasn't. And you let her die." And with that, Robert forced his mother back into the SUV, as he spun out of the parking area.

I stood there, not realizing my hands were shaking until Scarlett wrapped her arms around me.

And that was why I had never deserved Michelle. Or Scarlett. Or a future.

I had been too late before. Hadn't seen the signs.

And the woman that I had once loved was dead, and her family would never heal.

I'd almost lost Scarlett, just like I had lost Michelle.

I'd nearly been too late.

And I knew there was nothing left, as I wasn't the man Scarlett needed.

Just like I wasn't the man I had needed to be for Michelle.

Chapter Sixteen
Scarlett

There is a moment in every person's life where a transition meant the end, the beginning, or an absence of both.

I hadn't said a word when that mother and her son had been there. There hadn't been anything for me to say. Hudson had stood up for himself in a way, and yet hated himself in every other way. I had wanted to do something, to help, but what was there for me to do? The day was Michelle's birthday, the woman that he had lost. He had lost her long before she had died, but some part of him still reached for her. Still grieved for her. And I didn't blame him for that grief. How could I? I grieved the person I had been before Ronin, the person I had been before I had realized life wasn't fair.

But it wasn't the same.

And as Hudson refused to look back, to turn

towards me, I realized that this could be the end. All of this could be the end.

So he would walk away now, because he didn't think he was good enough.

It was funny, because I had been the one to think that for so long. That I wasn't good enough. That I made terrible choices.

I had fallen in love with him and there was no going back.

But if he didn't turn around, I knew he would walk away.

So I reached out and pressed my palm to his back. His shoulders stiffened, flinching, and I nearly pulled away.

"Hudson."

"I forgot it was her birthday today. It's been how many years? And I forgot. I didn't even think about her today."

He turned then, and the ravaged anguish on his face nearly undid me.

"I'm so sorry. I have no idea what to say other than I'm sorry."

"I didn't even realize they knew where I lived. Silly, because it's not like I hide it. I hide from the world, but not from everyone. It's pretty easy to find me."

"Do you want to go inside? Let me make you some coffee."

"I don't need coffee, Scarlett," he snapped. My

hand dropped and he cursed under his breath before reaching for it.

"I'm sorry. I'm not angry with you, I'm not anything. I just can't think right now."

"Then let's talk it out." Please, anything. *Just talk to me, Hudson.* Though I didn't say those words out loud.

"What has talking ever done?"

"Maybe it's doing something. I don't know. But you've told me so much, and yet there has to be something I'm missing. About why they're here to begin with. It wasn't your fault. You didn't hurt her."

"But I wasn't there. I didn't kill him when I had a chance."

My hand went to my mouth and I shook my head.

"You wouldn't have killed him." Though I wasn't quite sure if that was the case. Because if somebody had hurt someone that I loved, I wasn't sure what I would do. If my father came after my mother again, I was afraid I would be the one to end him. What did that make me? Maybe the person that I needed to be, but then again, this wasn't about me. Not right now.

"I'm sorry. I'm so sorry."

"I didn't tell you everything. About Michelle."

Chills slid up my spine and I nodded. "Okay. You can tell me now. You can tell me anything." *I love you.*

But it wasn't the right time to say that. And I was worried that there would never be a time.

"When I found out that Jefferson killed her, and got off on a technicality, I was livid. I was still in a damn sling from being shot, and Flynn couldn't even hold me back. So I found him, and I beat him. I tried to kill him, and in the end, I couldn't do it. I couldn't kill him. I wanted to. I held his life in my hands, threatening to choke him until he quit breathing, just like he had done to Michelle, but it wasn't enough. I couldn't do that."

"Because you're not a murderer, Hudson. You're not the darkness that you think you are."

"I could have though. One quick movement and he would've been dead. But I let him go."

"Hudson."

"Then he came at me with a knife, and I ducked. Instinctively, even in pain because I wasn't taking my meds after being shot, I ducked. And Jefferson fell right off the side of the cliff. Slipped with a single scream that I can still hear in my dreams. A scream that ended abruptly when he hit the jagged rocks below. He's dead. Michelle's dead. Her parents and brother will never forgive me for it. And it's been years. Years of this. Years of dreaming of everything that had happened. So yes, that's my penance. That's why I've been hiding."

Tears began to slide down my cheeks, but then he moved forward and wiped them from my face.

"Don't cry, Scar. I don't want any more tears."

"Then you're going to get them."

"I don't know what I'm supposed to do."

"I don't know either. I've never... I've never felt like this before. And I don't know what I'm doing. Because I thought I trusted someone before, and I was wrong."

He staggered back as if I'd hit him, and I reached forward, gripping his hand.

"I know you aren't going to hurt me. I'm not comparing you two. I'm just talking about my feelings, like you're talking about yours, and I'm all twisted inside, but I don't want you to blame yourself, Hudson. You didn't do anything wrong. You have to believe that."

"I want to. It's so weird. Because after so many years of you and me fighting, I never thought you'd be the one that I would need to tell me that you trust me. That you believe."

"I find it ironic as well, because I usually like yelling at you more. But Hudson, you didn't do anything wrong."

"Part of me knows that, and then things like this happen."

I move forward and reached up to cup his face. I winced though, forgetting I had the cut on my side, and his eyes went stormy.

"Let me get you to bed. You need to rest."

"As long as we're okay. Because you told me something that I know you've been hiding. That I know has to hurt. And I'm so grateful that you trust me."

"I trust you with everything, Scarlett."

My throat tightened. And I knew I needed to tell him I loved him. Soon. Not now. Not when everything was so raw, so shattered.

"I just want you to be okay."

"That's what I was thinking about you."

"Then we'll figure it out. I'm sorry. I'm sorry about Michelle, about Jefferson. About your dad. About my dad. I feel like we need time away from here. Just to breathe. It's been ridiculous."

"Tell me about it. I never expected you, Scarlett Blair."

His hands were on my face again, and I leaned into his touch.

"You are more than unexpected, Cage."

He smiled, then, and brushed his lips against mine. I moaned into him, needing him. Trusting him with everything.

It was odd that I could trust him and yet sometimes couldn't trust myself. But maybe that's what love was.

"I'm going to tuck you in, okay? You need rest."

"Are you going to rest with me?" I asked, a frown on my face.

"I will. I just, I need to paint." He took a step back, running his hands through his hair. "I know that's stupid, but whenever things are like this, I just need to paint. I hate being the whole temperamental artist thing, but sometimes it's just there. You know what I mean? I'll talk to you. I swear I will once I figure shit out."

I didn't take a step back. I didn't even feel a blow. Because he was telling me his truth. Something I was afraid that he had never told anyone else. Because he trusted me. So I cupped his face and took his lips with mine.

"Okay. But can I sleep in my own bed? After everything that's happened, I just want my own bed."

He opened his mouth to say something, and I kissed him again. "And then you can meet me there later."

He smiled, his shoulders finally relaxing.

"Okay. Let me tuck you in and maybe give you an orgasm. Just saying."

I threw my head back and laughed, leaning into him. And so we walked hand in hand down to my home, and I let him tuck me in, gently kissing me until I felt safe, at home.

And when he walked away, I knew it wasn't forever.

Because he allowed me to see part of himself he didn't show others.

The world was dark, and sometimes felt like an unending twisted pain, but I wasn't alone.

And I was finally starting to think he understood he wasn't either.

I nuzzled into my pillow, knowing he would be back soon, and smiled.

When the hand slid over my mouth, I opened my eyes and tried to scream. And then another hand went around my throat, squeezing, and I kicked, shoving, but I couldn't see his face.

I only heard that deep laugh, and I knew who it was. When he dragged me out of my room, and I tried to scream, tried to reach for the edge of the door so he wouldn't take me away, I only hoped that Hudson would hear.

"Don't you dare, you bitch," Ronin whispered into my ear as he pressed the gun to my side, and I quieted, wondering if Hudson would know I was gone. But I had to believe. I had to trust.

But I was so afraid that Hudson would be the one hurt in the end.

And so I let Ronin drag me away, even as my heart leapt in my throat and tears slid down my cheeks.

And Hudson's name was the last thing I thought of before Ronin knocked me out, and there was nothing.

Chapter Seventeen
Hudson

The pounding on the door echoed throughout my house, and growling, I stomped my way towards the front. When I swung open my front door, Flynn pushed his way inside.

"Well hello to you. I didn't realize you were in town this late. What the fuck's going on?" Alarm shot through me, and I pulled at his arm. "Are you okay? Is something wrong? Is it Blakely and the baby?"

I was already emotionally drained from my day, and hell, all I wanted to do was lay near Scarlett and get through the rest of the day, telling myself everything was okay, I had to remember... I couldn't help but think of the fact that my family was growing leaps and bounds day by day. How the hell was I supposed to even function when there were so many around me that cared. They wanted me in their lives, and worried about me just as I worried about them. For somebody who had done their best to be a hermit and not be on the minds of everybody around them, I certainly failed at actually succeeding in that.

"What? No. She's fine. I'm here because I'm pissed off about something, but it has nothing to do with Blakely." He glared at me. "Should I be worried about Blakely and the baby? Let's call Aston now. Because what the fuck?"

"No, no." I ran my hands over my face, trying to catch my breath and frankly, trying to just catch the fuck up.

"I don't know why the hell you're here, storming in like that. I thought something was wrong with somebody. And since Blakely's pregnant, she's the first person that came to mind."

"I think she's fine. I haven't heard otherwise. But now I'm worried, so let's call."

I held up my hand and tried to focus.

"No, we're good. You're good. I'm just losing my fucking mind. Why are you here?"

"I was at the restaurant, dropping off a few things for Theo because apparently I'm now an errand boy for the family."

"Only now?" I teased, trying to feel lighter than I did. My heart ached, and I knew I just needed to get over to Scarlett's. Letting her go to sleep alone was a damn mistake. So what if I needed to focus and maybe just paint? I could do that near her. I didn't have to leave her alone when we were both emotionally bruised from our talk. But I could still see Michelle's brother's face as he laid into me, screaming at me.

It didn't matter that I hadn't been the one to kill her, I hadn't been the one to save her.

And yet I hadn't been able to lean on Scarlett the way that she'd needed me to.

"Anyway, Luna was there, and she got a weird call from Scarlett, saying that she needed to talk to her tomorrow, for sister time or some shit, so Luna got worried, yelled at me, so now I'm here to yell at you."

I blinked. "Scarlett called Luna? Fuck."

"Damn straight. What did you do? I thought things were going great between the two of you. Are you fucking kidding me right now?"

"It's not that. We're fine. I think. Hell."

"Talk to me. Are you guys okay or not? Because when Scarlett goes to talk with Luna tomorrow, what the hell's she going to say?"

"Nothing. We're fine. We're fucking fine. I think."

"Then what? What the hell is going on?"

"Fine. When we got back from dinner, fuck."

"Talk to me."

"Michelle's brother and mom were at the house. Here. Because it's her birthday and I had forgotten that today Michelle would've turned a year older, but she didn't. Because I wasn't there."

"Don't, don't put that on your fucking shoulders. You didn't kill her. Jefferson did."

"I know that. I know he beat her. She cheated on me, left me for him, and I would've found a way to be fine. If that's who they needed to be together, then fine. But he was a worthless piece of shit and didn't deserve her. And he killed her. He killed her and I wasn't there to save her. By the time I got back, there was nothing I could do."

"It wasn't your fault. You were overseas."

"And she was alone. Alone and screaming and in pain, and I wasn't there. And when I got home, I couldn't even go to the funeral. Couldn't go to her grave without her mother and brother shouting at me."

"So they thought it was okay to come here on her birthday and take it out on you? They're in pain, God knows they have a right to be, but they don't get to blame you for it."

"Maybe I should take some of the blame."

"Is that what you told Scarlett? Because she was here, right? For all of it? Did you push her away because you're afraid she's going to get hurt? Because that's the stupidest fucking thing I've ever heard."

I staggered back at the venom in Flynn's tone. "No. I don't know. She's sleeping next door. But we're fine. I promise. We kissed and said we were going to see each other in the morning. I just need to fucking paint or breathe or do something."

"Then why is Scarlett trying to talk with Luna?"

"Because it was a lot to deal with? I don't know. We're not over." Panic settled in my chest. "We better not be fucking over."

"So you're going to fight for her?"

"Damn straight. I didn't fight for Michelle because I thought that's what she wanted. And she's dead. I might not have been the one to kill her, but I didn't see Jefferson for who he was."

"No one did. I was here, remember? Left behind. I was friends with her too. We're twins, Hudson. Everything we had together we did together. I didn't see the man for who he was, and he killed her. But Jefferson's dead too. You didn't kill that man."

"I wish I would have."

I said it out loud again, knowing it was the truth. I wish I could have had Jefferson's blood on my hands, rather than Michelle's or Josh's or anyone else I had lost along the way.

"I wish I would've killed him too. I might not have loved Michelle the way you did, but she was yours therefore she was mine too. The twin thing."

"Scarlett's not yours," I tried to tease, and Flynn just smiled softly.

"In case you ever can't step up to the plate I will do my manly twin duty."

"I should punch you, but I'm exhausted."

"I can see why. Family drama in all ends. But us

Cages are going to be okay. And you and Scarlett better be okay. You should go to her tonight, make sure she's not alone."

I pinched the bridge of my nose and nodded. "You're right. Fuck."

"Good. Now you can tell Scarlett to tell Luna to stop yelling at me."

"I have nothing to do with it. It's their twin thing."

"I guess," Flynn said dryly. "Come on, let me go walk you to Scarlett's place because I parked down the street."

I frowned. "Why?"

"With the storm last night, some of the rain washed out part of the edge of the street. I'm surprised you didn't see it on your way here."

"It wasn't like that before. What do you mean part of the street?"

"There's a bunch of branches, and a downed tree." Flynn paused and tilted his head. "That's weird, right?"

The hair on the back of my neck stood on end, and I nodded. "Let's go down to Scarlett together. You can show me the street on the way there."

"Let's do that."

Alarmed, I grabbed my keys and phone and headed down the path to Scarlett's house. Hopefully she'd see me on the security soon and come out to us. But when she didn't, I kept frowning.

Then my legs nearly went out from under me as ice

slid up my spine, a steely resolve taking over as I tried not to panic. Only clear thinking would get us out of this even as I knew there would be no clarity in this moment. "Call the cops."

"What?"

"The door is open, Flynn. And that window is broken. Fuck."

"Do you think it's her dad? Or hell, Michelle's brother?"

Bile coated my tongue as Flynn pulled out his phone. I immediately went down the deck stairs and tried to see if there were any tracks.

"It's got to be Ronin. He's the only one left. I knew he was being too fucking quiet."

"Hudson."

The ice in my twin's tone nearly broke me, and I finally followed his gaze to the smoke slithering through the tops of the trees.

"Fuck. That's the Ackerson place."

"I'm already on the phone with the cops. Then I'll call Sheriff Macon. Fuck."

"I'm going."

"I'm right behind you. Can't be a coincidence."

I shook my head, even though he couldn't see me, as we ran through the trees, and I had to pray that I wasn't too late.

It wasn't that far down the path. Branches slammed into us, little twigs slicing into our skin, but we kept moving, and I was damn glad that I had worn my boots. Flynn wore nicer shoes than me, since we had been at dinner, but he didn't slow down, and I would forever be grateful for that.

As we broke through the side of the property, I cursed under my breath. The entire original structure, at least what was left of it, was on fire.

"Holy fuck. If we don't take care of this, it's going to take a shit ton of forest too," Flynn whispered, and I pulled out my phone. "I need to tell the authorities that they're going to need to send everybody."

A scream echoed through the clearing, and ice froze my blood.

Scarlett. That was Scarlett.

And then I was moving, phone in hand, as I ran towards the burning building.

Flynn was right on my tail, but before I could do anything, a body shot out of the side of the building and slammed into me.

Ronin's fist connected with my jaw, and I twisted, kicking at the man.

"She's mine. You asshole. Don't you see? You Cages think you know everything, but now you're not going to get anything. You have nothing."

Scarlett screamed again, and fear etched its way onto my soul as I elbowed Ronin in the gut and continued to try to get through him. Flynn was there, pulling Ronin off me, but then my twin froze, hands raised.

"You don't need to do that, Ronin."

That's when Ronin staggered forward, gun in hand.

"But I really do. She ruined everything. She got me fired. My family hates me. Nobody will have me. So now nobody gets to have her."

I stood up, as Ronin swayed, gun in hand, but I knew if I wasn't quick enough, we were going to be too late to save Scarlett. And I'd be damned if I lost someone else.

Out of the corner of my eye, I saw Flynn move. I wanted to tell him to stop where he was, that I could handle this, but Ronin lifted his gun towards me and fired.

Everything moved so quickly, but as the body slammed into me once again, and I rammed into the ground, Flynn let out a shout.

Scrambling, I stood up and slammed my fist into Ronin's jaw.

The other man staggered back and fell, the gun dangerously swaying from his hands. I took the gun, tossed it away, and continued to ram my fist into Ronin's face.

When Ronin finally stopped moving, though his chest rose and fell, telling me he was at least alive, I forced myself to stand up and look towards my brother, hoping to hell I hadn't just lost the other half of me.

Flynn lay on the ground, clutching his leg. "I'm fine. I swear." He gasped, his face deathly pale.

I reached out, knowing Flynn needed me, as Scarlett's scream echoed through the air once again, and I turned towards the burning building. As Flynn gave me a nod, I pushed my way through the door, into the smoke, knowing I would be too late. For us both.

Chapter Eighteen
Scarlett

The rope dug into my wrists, as smoke began to fill the side of the house. Ronin had dragged me to the old Ackerman place, and I still couldn't catch up. My thoughts kept blending, and I knew the blood seeping down my face meant whatever cut he'd added there when he'd hit me, hadn't stopped bleeding. I didn't think I had a concussion, but for all I knew, it was worse than I allowed myself to believe.

The place Hudson had bought was still somewhat erect. Though half of it had been destroyed in the mudslide, the other half had been torn apart while they had done their best to save as much of the materials as possible. Ronin had found the dirtiest place of it all and tied my arms around one of the metal poles that were keeping the roof up. At least that's what I thought the point of those were. Honestly I couldn't quite figure it out, and as smoke continued to fill the room, everything hurt, and I knew I needed to get out of here soon. If not, I was going to die of smoke inhalation long before the flames hit.

Coughing once again, I tugged on the rope, using whatever strength I had to pull and try to make a way out of here.

Nobody knew I was here. Nobody knew that I was going to die in a place filled with memories that everybody kept burying. And they should. Hudson was going to make this place full of life and love and happiness, now I was going to die within its walls.

And he would blame himself for not being there. Because after everything that had happened, we had needed a moment to breathe, because we trusted and loved each other enough for that. And I was going to die here, weak and unable to protect myself, because I couldn't figure out how to get out of the tightening rope.

I tugged on the binds again, trying to get myself loose. No one was going to save me. I needed to do it myself.

"Come on. You can do this. Why can't I be like one of those people in an action movie that always has a knife or a shard of glass on them, even in their pajamas?" I coughed again, the room beginning to heat up. Sweat and blood leaked down my temples as I continued to work on the ropes, rubbing them at the corner edge of the hole. It wasn't going to be enough. There were no jagged parts of the metal for the rope to snag on, and I couldn't break my wrist or dislocate my thumb or do anything that an action star would be able to figure out.

I was going to die. Ronin was going to have the last word after all, and I was going to die here.

I would never forgive myself for what this was going to do to Hudson. Because I knew that he would never let himself feel again.

Damn Ronin. Damn this house, and damn everything.

The sound of a gunshot echoed through the room, and the forest, and I froze, smoke seeping through the walls.

I coughed again, my nose itching, eyes burning. "Hudson!" I screamed.

Because it had to be him out there. I just knew it. Who else would Ronin be shooting at in this moment? Maybe I was delusional, maybe it was the smoke, but Hudson had to be out there. We had saved each other before, maybe we could figure out how to do it again. I tugged harder, twisting my arms to try to create friction. A few strands began to unravel, and tears streamed down my face as I continued to pull, kicking at the bottom of the pole to try to get it loose. The flames were getting higher, and the roar of them echoed through my brain.

I wasn't going to die here. I couldn't die here. I wouldn't let Ronin have the satisfaction. I shoved again, pushing and shouting.

There was a scramble of feet, a shout, and more screaming.

"I'm in here! Help!"

Coughing, I shoved and kicked, crying as the rope refused to budge.

Damn Ronin. Damn everything.

"Scarlet!"

I froze in that instance, my throat tight. That wasn't Hudson's voice.

It was Luna's.

Another gunshot, or perhaps it was a tree snapping, I couldn't tell. Dizziness began to set in, the smoke too thick.

It couldn't be Luna. Ronin was not allowed to touch my sister. I planted one foot on the pole, gripped the rope, and screamed as I pulled, using all of my strength. Another part of the rope snapped, but not all of it.

"No. I refuse. No, no, no, no, no."

"Scarlett!"

Another shout, this one deeper.

I turned, coughing as my shoulders shook, and then Hudson was there.

"Get out of here!" I called out. "The flames are too high."

"Not without you." Hudson pulled a knife out of his pocket, and I let out a watery laugh that held no humor.

"Of course he would have a knife. Why couldn't I just sleep with a fucking knife?"

"We'll make sure you have weapons on you at all times."

"I know you're placating me, but we're going to have to do this. Okay?"

"Keep your head down, the smoke's getting thick. I've got this."

And then the ropes were loose, but instead of sighing in relief, I pushed Hudson down and threw my body on top of him.

"What—" he began as part of the roof caved in, landing where Hudson had just been kneeling.

Then he rolled us over, covering me as well, as we both tried to stagger to our feet.

"We have to get out of here," he called out over the flames, coughing.

He shoved off his flannel and covered my head with it. "Keep low."

"What about you?" I asked, my throat so raw that dizziness started to seep in.

"I've got you, Scarlett. I've got you."

My knees buckled, as the smoke was nearly too

much, and then Hudson had me in his arms, as he ran through the back door that laid nearly on its side.

"Scarlett!"

Hudson set me down on the ground, moved the flannel off my head, and I blinked at Luna's voice before turning back to the old Ackerson place.

The roof continued to cave in, as the walls licked with fire, the sounds of glass and stone being charred or breaking filled the small open space.

I coughed, my whole body racking as Hudson ran his hands over my body, checking for wounds.

"Where are you hurt?"

"Head. Lungs," I rasped between coughs.

"I got you."

He kept saying those words, and I wanted to say them back. But I couldn't think. Instead I just sat there, body shaking, lungs threatening to burst, as Hudson put pressure on the wound on my head, and the sounds of sirens filled the air.

I finally turned to see Luna on the ground, holding Flynn as blood seeped from a wound on his leg.

I had no idea what had just happened, or where Ronin was, but we were out of the fire, at least for now.

As the authorities worked on the now unsalvageable home, Sheriff Macon came forward, a frown on his face.

"Get in the ambulance," he snapped at Flynn, who waved him off.

"Scarlett first. I just have a slight flesh wound."

"You were shot in the leg, dumbass," Luna snarled. "And there are two ambulances now. Get in the damn thing."

"You do like me," Flynn said with a grin, though I knew he had to be in pain.

"I'd like you much more if you stayed alive. So please? Listen to the paramedics."

"It's okay, I'll just knock him out. We went to school together, I'm allowed to do that," one of the male paramedics said with a wink, and Flynn narrowed his gaze.

"Jack?" he asked as he leaned against the back of the stretcher.

"Oh good. You remember me. You always did like to one-up me in school when it came to grades. So I decided to move to your town and annoy the fuck out of you."

"I believe that's true, he also married Rumor, who's a townie," Luna explained, and I realized they were talking about things that didn't truly matter in this moment to distract Flynn as they carted him towards the ambulance.

Sheriff Macon stood between the two stretchers, hands on his hips.

"Scarlett, they're taking you to the hospital in the next town over, same with Flynn. If we have to take you down to Denver to see specialists, they will."

"Damn straight we will," Hudson growled.

I reached out and gripped his hand, as I wasn't allowed to speak. They put oxygen over my mouth, and since it was the only thing keeping me awake at this moment, I wasn't going to move the mask.

"We'll talk about everything soon," Sheriff Macon ordered. "But Ronin's not going to be a problem." He said the words with such finality, I realized that while Ronin might not be dead, he wasn't going to step foot in Cage Lake again anytime soon. If ever.

My father and Ronin weren't our problems anymore. Though I knew my mother was probably worried out of her mind, she would meet us anywhere that we needed now. Because she loved us more than our father scared her. Or maybe it was just the idea that our brains could finally let us breathe after years of trying to suffocate us.

I watched as Flynn was put in the ambulance, and Luna stepped in with him.

I frowned, and Hudson shook his head. "The family's on their way, but I said I would ride with you. Luna will ride with Flynn. She offered to flip a coin to see who would ride with you, but I love you, so I win."

My eyes widened as they stuffed me into the back of the ambulance. Sheriff Macon spoke with some of his deputies, and I finally lowered the mask.

"You love me?"

He scowled, even as the paramedic helped put the mask back on my face.

"Of course I love you. You saved my life in there too you know."

I pulled the mask back and waved off the paramedic. "I love you too. But I thought we would say this in a way more romantic way."

"I don't know, stayed with each other through a fire and a kidnapping sounds pretty romantic," the paramedic said, and I narrowed my gaze at her.

The other woman just winked. "If you keep the oxygen mask on, I promise I'll stop with the commentary." And then she was sliding an IV into my arm, and Hudson rubbed the back of his knuckles on my cheek.

"You scared the hell out of me. But I love you, Scarlett Blair. And from now on, you don't sleep outside my bed. Those are the rules. Because I swear to God, I'm never going to let anyone hurt you again."

I scowled at him, before slowly lowering the mask despite the paramedic's glare.

"Fine. We can sleep in our bed together from now on. But I love you too. Jerk. You don't need to growl at me all the time."

"I think I do. Mask on."

I rolled my eyes and did as I was told, as my entire body hurt.

Ronin had almost killed the both of us. Had almost killed Flynn and maybe Luna from what I could see. I wasn't sure how the timeline had played out, but I did know that the people I cared about most in the world had nearly died because of a man's anger and addictiveness.

But as Hudson held me close, and we made our way to the hospital, I leaned into him, knowing that I wasn't ever going to let him go.

I had made many mistakes in my life, and Hudson Cage wasn't one of them.

And now, once we were cleaned up, stitched up, and healed, we had the rest of our lives to figure out what was next.

And I for one had a feeling nothing was going to be normal about this anytime soon, or ever.

And I didn't truly mind. Not with Hudson Cage holding me, and both of us knowing that we could save each other. Even if I knew he would do his best to make sure nothing like this happened again. Hudson was mine. And I was finally able to give in.

I let him hold me, and knew it was only the beginning.

Chapter Nineteen
Hudson

Sometime later

I gripped Scarlett's hips, squeezing tightly as I thrust, sweat slicking down my back.
"That's it. Take me. Take all of me."
"Hudson."
"You're almost there. Almost there." I leaned forward and slid my fingers over her clit as she let out a moan, grinding herself into me.
Lips twitching, I leaned back and smacked her on the ass.
"Needy, aren't you?"
"I swear to God if you don't let me come soon, Hudson Cage, I'm going to scream."
"We both know you're going to scream anyway.

And I let you come right before I started fucking you. I thought we were doing okay."

"You're ridiculous."

"That is true."

I pulled back, before slamming hard into her again, and we both let out a groan. And then we were moving, and there were no more thoughts.

I'd never been the person to laugh or even think about laughing during sex like this. That wasn't really what I had thought we needed.

It wasn't what I thought I deserved. Happiness? Hell no. A connection with someone where it felt like we could take on anyone? Never.

Scarlett moved back, both of us kneeling as she pressed her back to my front, and I slid one hand down, flicking my middle finger over her clit, the other holding her close as I cupped her breast.

"Come. You earned it."

"So greedy," she teased right back, and then she was coming, her beautiful cunt clamping around my cock as I slid in and out of her, both of us shaking from the exertion. But I wasn't done with her yet. I slid out of her, and then moved her to her side. With wide eyes, she reached for me, and I lifted one leg and slid deep into her.

"That's it. So fucking tight."

"I'm going to have to do more Pilates and yoga I

think," she teased, but then she was moaning, her eyes rolling in the back of her head as I slid in and out of her, this position deeper than usual.

We rolled into each other, and I found myself on top of her, cradled between her thighs as I moved slowly, taking her lips with mine as we continued to move.

And when she finally came again, tears sliding down her cheeks, I slammed home one more time and filled her. We laid there, my hips slowly working in and out of her as I continued to fill her with my cum, and I took her lips.

"You're sleeping on the wet spot," she teased.

Smile deepening, I kissed her hard on the lips, and then rolled us so we were at the side of the bed, still joined.

"We don't have time to sleep. We have a full day, and then the dreaded family dinner."

"Oh yes. The family dinner."

Nestled in my arms, neither one of us really wanted to get up, but then our alarms went off, and I groaned.

"Yay for to-do lists. But you get to wash the sheets."

I reached around and smacked her ass, loving the way that her inner muscles clenched around my still semi-hard cock.

"You can spank me all you want, but you're still doing the sheets."

With a grin, I slid out of her, and then moved her so she lay over my lap.

"If you say so."

"Hudson Cage. Now I have your cum running down my inner thigh, and you better not spank me. Ouch!" she screeched as I smacked her hard on the ass, once, twice, and then she moaned.

"Oh, look at that, so pink and ready for me." I speared her with two fingers, and she wiggled on my lap.

"Are you kidding me right now?" she asked, panting. "The alarms are going off, and you don't really think that you're going to—"

She moaned again, as I slid my thumb over her clit and continued to fuck her with my fingers. And when she came again, squeezing me tight, I pulled out of her, smacked her on the ass just once more for good measure, and pulled her into my lap as she sat there, shaking.

"If I fall asleep because I did not get any last night, I will blame you."

"You say the sweetest things. Of course they're going to blame me. They know that I keep you up all night with my cock."

"I mentioned something along those lines to Ivy once, and your brother overheard, but you really need to stop repeating that around."

"What do you mean? That my cock is so amazing that you just can't sleep at night?"

"Hudson Cage."

"I love it when you get all grumpy with me." I smacked a kiss on her lips and stood up, carrying her to the bathroom so we could get ready for the day.

I turned on the shower and let her begin her process that took far longer than mine, before going back, shutting off the alarms, and stripping the bed.

Like I would let her do laundry while she was walking bow-legged like that.

I tossed everything into the washer, began a cycle, and then headed to the shower. She was finishing up, when I walked right in and took her mouth.

"Good morning."

"You and your cock better stay five feet away from me right now. I cannot be late for my half day at work."

"I can't believe you're taking part of a vacation day."

She shrugged, a small smile on her face. "I promised Luna and Mom that we would go shopping together. And if Mom's going to leave the house, I'm going to be there."

I kissed her softly and nodded, no words needed.

Her mother wasn't healed or a hundred percent the way she used to be. She never would be. None of us would. We each had scars of our own, the ones on my shoulder always going to be ridged, the scar on Scarlett's hairline forever hidden by her bangs, but still there if you looked hard enough.

But Mrs. Blair left the house more often than she ever had, all because she loved her girls and was trying.

That was a damn strong woman, and I liked her a lot. The Cages may overwhelm her, but they overwhelmed me, so it wasn't like I could say much about it. However, she was great and did her best to try to be in her daughter's life.

And for that, I'd love her to the end of my days.

In the months since the fire, things had moved quickly in some areas but slowly in others.

Scarlett had moved in with me, because there was no way I would let her out of my sight. She rented out her home to people with long-term rentals, because the town wouldn't allow short-term rentals. And I knew she was thinking about selling the place, though since I owned the land itself, it would make sense just to keep it as another place for the Cages. Not that I had been the one to think that. No that had been Flynn, and his ever-present wanting to make sure the Cages owned everything and increased their connections. He was like our dad that way, but in the best ways possible and not the ways that made you want to tear your hair out.

After the authorities were finished with the Ackerson property, my friends had come in with their bulldozers, and the contractors had leveled everything that needed to be. And although part of me had wanted to sell the damn place and never allow any part of that memory back, it had been Dorian of all people—the one with the most connections to the place—that had convinced me to continue on with my plan.

A few of the cabins were already set up and ready to go, and a few others would be starting soon. There would be a main building, one for larger families, and that was taking a little longer, but it'd only been a few months.

Some of the people that I had served with who had made it home were already requesting time to stay, and I knew that seeing them wasn't going to be easy, but introducing Scarlett to them? That would make the awkwardness worth it.

Michelle's family hadn't been back, and I didn't think they would. And if they did, I would deal with it. I couldn't blame myself for the rest of my days, I knew that. I would always hold some of that blame. Of that guilt. There was no getting around that. But the fact that I could even speak the words, and talk it out with Scarlett, meant that maybe I was figuring shit out.

Scarlett seemed to be changing everything. Not only was the resort adding more events that were gaining recognition among certain circles, but she was now working on a charity aspect of the resorts, and Isabella and James had jumped right into it.

I loved that woman, and one day she would be my

wife, if she let me that was, but she was already part of my family.

I ran my hand over my heart as I stood in my studio, knowing I had work to do, and wondered how the hell I'd gotten here.

I had hidden in Cage Lake for a reason. And those reasons would always be there. But now I wasn't hiding. I was here because I wanted to be. Because I loved a woman who loved Cage Lake, and maybe being a Cage of the infamous Cages wasn't all that bad.

My phone buzzed and I ignored the text from my agent, wondering when we would talk about the next showing in a month, but I would get back to him soon.

See, that was growth.

My phone buzzed again, and this time while I wanted to ignore it, I knew I couldn't.

The infamous group chat, one of the thousands, lit up my phone, and I sighed.

Flynn: 6:00 PM at Aston's?

Aston: Yes. You're welcome to be there early, you know the code in case we're not there yet.

Isabella: We've already opened it up for you guys though, just to make sure that it was ready to go.

Sophia: I have the list. We're good here.

James: All of us will be there. And we're bringing food, though I know that Aston already has food there. Right?

Dorian: Harper and I are bringing the food that

needed to be cooked ahead of time. Don't worry. We have a plan.

Ford: Should I be afraid of the plan? And I'm sorry that the family can't be there, but with the sniffles going around, we didn't want to travel with the whole crew.

Isabella: Poor baby. I'm glad that you'll be there though.

Phoebe: And you're hitching a ride with us so we'll talk about that in the other group chat.

Theo: That makes me sad that I'm not part of the group chat.

Kyler: You do realize that my body has no idea what time it is and I was currently sleeping. How many texts do you guys do a day?

Emily: Way more than you would ever know. But don't worry, I'm forcing you to come with me, so you can't escape a family event.

Flynn: And look at that, Kyler's joined the group chat along with Emily. We have now reached everyone.

Aston: Except the person that has lived in Cage Lake the longest.

Me: I'm looking at the group chat now. Stop freaking out. I'll see you tonight. Don't know why we need to have an entire conversation before we'll all be together for the first time in months. Just saying.

Flynn: It's a miracle!

James: He's alive!

Kyler: Oh good. They can make fun of you now.

Emily: Don't worry, I will always make fun of you.

Isabella: I'm going to text Scarlett with more of a list, okay?

Me: Okay. Not quite sure why you needed to tell me you're going to text her.

Dorian: It's a girl thing.

The group chat continued to explode, so I muted it like the good brother that I was.

While we didn't have to have these family dinners anymore, it was nice to at least continue part of them. I didn't know why the entire group was going to be there tonight, but I honestly didn't mind.

That really was growth.

Though as soon as they annoyed me, I would probably get grumpy and leave. That would mean I would leave Scarlett behind however, so maybe I'd be forced to stay. Well then.

I shook my head and got back to work.

By the time my alarm went off that told me I needed to get ready for dinner, I felt good about the painting in front of me, and had even texted my agent back.

With a sigh, I walked back to the house, showered, and smiled as Scarlett walked into the house.

"Oh good. You're ready to go. And I see Ranger has been keeping you company."

I looked down at the nearly one-year-old stray cat

we had found in the woods a couple of weeks ago, and shrugged.

"He's okay."

Ranger looked up at me and meowed. He then shook slightly, lifted his leg, and began a stretch that I wasn't even sure Scarlett could do.

"You love that cat. You know it."

"I think he needs a friend," I said with a shrug. "I mean, he stays in the house all day, and we won't let him go outside because there are predators out there, and he doesn't really like the studio because I have to carry him over there. Maybe I can build something so he can just have a little cat walkway the whole time."

Scarlett put her hands over her mouth, eyes wide.

"What?"

"You're going to build a cat walkway just for the baby?" she asked as she lifted Ranger into her arms.

The orange tabby purred and rubbed his head under her chin, and I narrowed my gaze at the cat.

He didn't let me pet him like that.

"What? I don't want him to be alone. That's why I wasn't going to get a pet in the first place."

"The cat distribution system made sure we got this one. But you're right. He does need a friend. Would you like that, Ranger? Another cat? Or maybe a dog?"

"No, another cat. And a boy cat. This way they can be friends, and you don't have to deal with dominance things that you do when a female cat enters the house.

And we don't know if he's going to get along with dogs, and I don't want to have that be an issue right away."

Scarlett just blinked at me.

"What now?" I asked.

"You've done research on this. You know things. I'm just so confused."

"What? Ranger's a family member now. A Cage."

"A Blair Cage," she corrected.

"Whatever. I'm just not going to screw up this cat's life. Right, Ranger?"

Ranger yawned, showing me his teeth.

"Okay, we'll find him a brother. A little Cage brother. Who knew?"

"Okay, enough with that," I said with a laugh, before I kissed Sophia hard on the mouth, rubbed Ranger's chin, and went to get ready for the day.

After leaving Ranger with his dinner, water, and a new toy, we headed to Aston's lake house.

There were far too many cars parked around the area, and I knew Aston was already thinking about a way to make this work for the long term, but I would leave it up to him. I didn't have the space for that many Cages, so I didn't have to worry about it. At least that's what I told myself.

As soon as we walked inside, everybody said their hellos, and Scarlett was immediately enveloped into the family.

I leaned down, lifted Hazel onto my hip, and grinned.

"Hello there, Hazel."

She smiled and rubbed my beard with her tiny little hand. "Hi, Uncle Hudson."

When Violet pulled at my jeans, I leaned down and lifted her onto my other hip before making my way into the living room.

I ignored Blakely taking a photo of me holding the girls, but only because she had to be hormonal considering she was ready to pop any day now.

"Where's your mama?" I asked, searching for Sophia.

As if I'd conjured her, Sophia came around the corner and grinned. "Hello there. I see you've attacked your uncle."

The girls hugged me tightly, babbling about something, and I just shook my head.

"They let me pick them up, unlike Ranger."

"That cat will let you pick him up one day," she teased as she brushed Violet's hair from her face.

"Maybe. We'll see. Where's Cale?" I asked, searching for my brother-in-law.

"Oh, work trip." She said it with a shrug, and I frowned, but forced myself to blank my face since the girls were in my arms.

When Hazel was plucked from my arms and tossed around the room in her Uncle Kyler's embrace, I didn't scowl. He didn't get to see the girls as often as I did. And considering I didn't live nearby, that was saying something.

Everybody milled about, looking happy, as if we had done this countless times before. Maybe we had, just not in this sense.

I knew this wasn't what my father had envisioned when he had forced this upon us. He had expected us to fail. There was no doubt about that, but he had been wrong.

I set Violet down, and she ran over to Theo, who picked her up and continued his conversation with Emily.

There was a bountiful amount of food and drinks around the house, and the volume increased with each laugh and joke.

As Scarlett wrapped her arm around my waist, continuing her conversation with Phoebe, I took a sip of the beer offered by Flynn.

I hadn't expected this type of family, this type of future, had never thought I deserved it.

And now I was never going to let go. Scarlett and I had fought for each other, and come out scarred, and yet whole at the same time.

She was my everything, and my family was just the same.

We had community projects to attend to, and countless other small things that were required of a

Cage, but I was no longer running from it. I would do what I had to in order to keep my family safe, and to keep us together. And as I placed an absent kiss on the top of Scarlett's head, and she smiled up at me before continuing her conversation, I knew I would fight to hell and back to keep Scarlett in my life.

She had been my obsession, my desire, and my enemy.

And now she was just mine.

Forever.

Chapter Twenty
Sophia

Leg extended, I leaned into the stretch, my joints aching for more than one reason today. But the world didn't need to know why. I let out a breath and sank deeper into the stretch, before moving out of the angle and deepening my breath so I could continue my movement.

It had been a long day of classes, the twins needing a thousand things, and just exhaustion in the head. School had just finished, and that meant that everybody's priorities were shifting. Oh, many students would come back for their favorite classes, and continue on during the summer, but others wouldn't return until the fall semester.

Some of my middle schoolers would begin the path toward advanced classes, and even private tutoring.

While I was no longer a principal ballet dancer for the Denver Ballet, I still danced to my heart's content as much as possible.

So I didn't have as much time as I once had.

But that made sense. I was a mom of two, owned my own business, and was doing my best to make my marriage work.

I rubbed my temples, telling myself that it was working.

Yes I made a few mistakes here and there, but those couldn't be helped. I wasn't the sweet, affable Sophia that Cale had married so few years ago. I was no longer dancing full time, or in the same shape I had once been. I had let myself go when the babies had come, and was working on strengthening everything that I could. It's what Cale needed from me. He worked long hours and went on countless business trips to provide for our family.

When we had gotten together, I'd had a decent savings from my time dancing, but it wasn't until my father's will had been read that I'd been able to be financially solvent enough to find balance in everything that we'd wanted.

But that was okay. We were learning this new life of ours.

I did a few of the moves, letting the music sing its way through my bones. I loved dancing. Ever since I had been a little girl, I had tried to stand on my toes, plié, and jeté. I wanted to be the graceful dancer in a skirt and tutu, gliding and flying over the dance floor as if I could walk on air.

I had been blessed in my career and had gone out on top. I still danced with a local troupe, one filled with retired dancers who no longer wanted to dance professionally but still had the bug.

I couldn't join often these days, not with the twins at home, and a husband who needed to be looked after, but I did my best. Besides my family, dance was the one thing that could truly be mine.

I smiled at myself, letting one final move take me, before bending down for my towel to dry off the sweat.

I needed to shower, get presentable, and then head home so I could feed the girls, and get ready for dinner. Cale had been out of town for the past week. He'd had a tough trip, with his bags being lost on the way there, and having to change hotel rooms halfway through, so I knew he would be excited to get home and see me and the twins.

My lips curved into a smile as I thought about our babies.

I never thought I would be a mom. It wasn't that it had been a definite no, it was that my priorities had shifted. I had only worked towards being a dancer. My sister Isabella, as well as my mother, had done everything they could to ensure that I had the childhood I needed in order to find balance. I had been competitive and determined. Much like my brother Kyler, we had gone into the arts and never turned back. Kyler was still out on a world tour, and had just won yet another Grammy, because of course he did. I couldn't wait until my little brother came back to visit, but until then, I would be the artist at home. Even if I didn't do it professionally anymore.

Violet and Hazel, however, had changed my life. They were my babies, my darlings, and were somehow, over two years old. They were little people now, rather than infants, who were developing their tiny personalities. And they were changing day by day.

I knew Cale missed spending as much time with them as he wanted to. He was always on the road, doing what he could for his companies, and that meant he missed out on a few firsts.

I rubbed my shoulder, an odd pain that I pushed back. But he would see other firsts, and as soon as we finished with the next step of my father's will, Cale said he would pause and take more time to be with the family. After all, we would have more money now, thanks to my philanderer of a father.

I pressed my lips together, doing my best not to think about that. I had loved my father as a little girl. He had doted on me and called me his little princess.

And then he had ignored me so he could focus on his business, and his other family.

I hadn't neglected naming him in my thoughts when I had imagined who had helped me push myself to where I was today. My father's ambitions might not mirror my own, but he had similar determination. And that had been pretty much the only similar things about us.

But he was dead, his secrets long buried, and now thanks to my brothers and sisters who actually knew what they were doing when it came to business, Cale and I would be far more comfortable in our financial standings, and we would be able to breathe more.

Cale wouldn't have to work as hard, and I would be able to spend more time at home with the girls, just like he wanted me to.

I rolled my shoulders back and headed to the small shower area that I'd had added to the office space above my dance studio.

I did not like traveling covered in sweat, and Cale hated when I came home looking like I had drenched myself in a pool. So it was best all around if I did my hair and makeup and got ready for the evening while still at the office. I checked my watch and winced. I had danced on my own a little bit too long, and the sixteen-year-old girl I was privately tutoring had been on such a roll, that we had gone over time. Her parents had been thrilled, but now I was a little behind.

I showered as quickly as I could, and thanked the Lord that Kyler had gotten me this fancy blow-dryer for Christmas. My thick hair could sometimes take nearly an hour to dry, even with the best blow dryers out there, but I was grateful that now it wouldn't take as long.

Minutes later, I was as ready as I was going to be, but I still put my hair back in a low ponytail.

I dabbed some concealer over the bruise on my jaw and ignored the ache there.

I had hit my face on the floor when I had fallen, but it was a hazard of the job.

I met my gaze once more, the shadows there no longer surprising me. No, I was fine. Everything was fine.

I grabbed my things and headed out to my car after locking up. If I hurried, I would make it home to relieve the nanny before Cale got there. Neither one of us liked having a nanny, even part-time, but the girls were too big for me to wear them both while at the dance studio. And it wasn't like Cale could bring them into a business meeting. He was a very important person in his job.

A small part of me wondered exactly where those voices had come from. Or why I was even saying them. It didn't sound like me.

But I pushed those away because the more I dug into them, the harder it would be for everyone. If I just gave in a little bit, it would be easier. And soon we would both be home more, and it wouldn't be like this.

Everything was just fine and working how it should. My hands fisted on the steering wheel as I turned into my driveway and pulled into the garage.

Everything had to be fine.

I turned off the engine and grabbed my bag.

When I walked in, the sound of little girls screaming hit my ear, and I paused, realizing that Cale's luggage was in the front foyer, and I had failed to realize that the nanny's car hadn't been parked in front of the house.

It was late.

This wasn't going to be good.

No, it was going to be just fine. Cale would understand. He always did.

I set my bag down next to his and walked into the living room. Cale stood in the kitchen, facing the window, a glass of whiskey in his hands. Both Violet and Hazel were in their playtime pen, their heads thrown back as they screamed. Their little faces were red, their hands fisted at their sides, and I moved quickly towards them, heart thudding.

"What's wrong, little girls? Your daddy's home. You should be happy."

Hazel launched herself at me, and I caught her before reaching down and pulling Violet into my arms.

I kissed the tops of both of their heads and swayed back and forth.

"They're crying because their mother wasn't here like she promised."

I swallowed hard, rocking my baby girls as they quieted down.

"I must have lost track of time. But it's so good to see you home."

I turned, so focused on the babies I had missed him moving closer.

The blow caught me off guard, the back of his hand slamming into my cheek. I staggered back, one step, two, until I was falling. Horror rocked through me as I tried to maneuver so I would fall on my back, or even on my side, doing anything to protect my babies.

Hazel and Violet had both quieted down, but were now screaming in my ears, and yet everything moved so slow.

My butt hit the ground first, and the momentum pushed me back, the back of my head slamming into our hardwood floor.

Stars shot from beneath my eyelids, and I realized that blood coated my mouth. I had bitten my tongue, and tears stung my eyes.

I sat up quickly, ignoring the nausea, as I looked down at my baby girls.

"Are you okay?"

"Mommy tripped, girls."

Cale moved forward, as if to reach for them, and I turned, moving so they were both behind me.

"I've got it. Don't touch them," I snapped.

My voice chilled, and Cale just looked at me, tilting his head. One blond lock fell over his gaze, and he smirked at me.

"Excuse me?"

"Don't touch them. I didn't fall." Words tumbled out of my mouth, and I realized if I didn't say them, I wouldn't ever.

Who was this person? The one who had cowered, and would have most likely leaned into the idea that I had tripped.

But he had nearly hurt my babies. And I would never allow that to happen.

I ignored the thoughts that whispered to me that I had already done so by staying. By trying.

"Don't be so melodramatic."

The girls crawled behind me, and I stood up, still woozy.

"Don't touch me. Or my girls."

"*Our* girls. You forget that I'm the father, don't you? Or were you spreading your legs for someone else."

I blinked, wondering exactly how many drinks he'd had before this. And when exactly had I allowed his venom to pierce me.

"Get out. Just get out."

"Why? Why should I leave when it's my house? Oh

wait, it's not. Your family money helped us with the down payment, didn't it? I'm the useless one, who has to sleep with his wife in order to gain anything? Is that what your family thinks? Why they allow me to be in their presence? The beautiful and brilliant and billionaire Cages. They don't care who they step on to get where they are. You're nothing. You're the left behind Cage, that's getting the scraps. Why the fuck do you think I've stayed this long though? Because those scraps are worth far more than you. And they'll be mine soon. So don't find your damn spine now. You know you'll fall at my feet whenever you remember exactly what I can do to you, or exactly what I would do to take your kids. Because those girls are half mine. Remember?"

"Get out." I knew there was more I needed to say to stand up for myself. But it was all I could do to try to put any distance between him and the girls.

I had known that Cale was changing. That the shadows that had coated him had long since fallen away. My family hadn't found out, and I'd done my best not to let them see too closely, but I was failing.

I had failed my babies, failed my girls. And I wasn't going to let it happen again.

Hazel moved forward, past my legs, and towards him, and when Cale smirked, reaching for her, I pushed out, slamming my palms into his chest.

"Don't touch her."

"You think you can hurt me?" Cale snapped out, before he fisted his hand and punched me in the face.

I fell back, both girls screamed their little hearts out, and Cale hovered over me.

"You're going to clean up this mess, put the girls to bed, and make dinner. And then you're going to remember that you're my wife. The only Cage we need is the one that will help us sustain where we need to be in society. But you are *mine*. Remember that. You might not have taken my name because you wanted to show that you were a part of your precious fractured family. But I'm the one that let you do that. I own you. Just like I own these little girls. I'm tired of pretending to be the weak one in your family so they feel better about themselves. Remember exactly who I am."

I tried to crawl away, to cover both girls with my body, but Cale just sighed, grabbed my ankle, and pulled.

A scream ripped out of my throat as I scrambled to get away from him, but I had forgotten how strong Cale was.

"Are you really going to make me do this the hard way?" With a sigh, he leaned down and punched me again.

Darkness welled over me, and I tried to shift. Everything moved as if I was in a fog. I reached out, trying to grasp anything, but it was too late. Everything was just too late.

There were a few whispers, and the babies crying, but I couldn't do a damn thing.

"Come on, girls. You're coming with me."

I tried to scream, tried to wake up, but there was nothing.

Hot breath coated my face, and my eyes were forced open.

"You're spending too much time away. You don't remember your place. So I'm going to have to ensure you always remember."

My eyes widened, clarity sliding through me as I looked for my babies but couldn't find them.

And then Cale was in front of me again, the baseball bat that was always in the front closet in his hand.

I screamed, trying to scramble away, but I was too slow. The first break made my eyes roll to the back of my head as nausea swept over me.

And then he hit me a second time, and I knew I would never dance again.

Unconsciousness took me under once again, and all I could think about was my babies.

"Please don't take my babies."

"Sophia? Oh my God."

"What the fuck do you think you're doing?"

The first voice had been familiar, but I didn't know the second.

One of my eyes was swollen, but I still could crack open the other.

My brother. Flynn was here. Horror etched on his face as he touched my cheek, but I had to warn him.

"Cale," I rasped.

"It's okay. The cops are on their way."

"Babies. Girls." Why couldn't I talk? Why couldn't I say what I needed to?

"Carson took care of Flynn. And he's getting the girls. The girls are safe. You're going to be okay," Flynn whispered, though his voice cracked.

I didn't know who this Carson was, and I didn't trust him with my babies. I didn't trust anyone.

But then Flynn was holding me, and a man with dark hair moved forward, both of my girls in his arms.

And they weren't crying.

He had his hands underneath them and was whispering something about not looking.

And I was grateful.

My babies were safe.

But Cale would take them.

"Cale's not going to take them. He's tied up. And the cops are right here. Stay with me, Sophia. Stay with me."

I tried to fight. Tried to stay awake for Hazel and Violet.

And I met the gaze of that stranger, those green eyes piercing.

"Stay awake," the stranger ordered, and tears slid out of my single working eye.

"I'm going to go let the cops in. I'll be right back," Flynn said, and then he was moving, and nothing made sense.

I couldn't breathe, could barely think.

But my girls were safe, and not crying while they sat in a stranger's arms.

And I wasn't sure what else there was to say.

"I'M GOING TO KILL HIM," ASTON SNAPPED. "KILL him."

"Aston, be quiet."

"Funny you're saying that, Isabella, when you're the one that shouted earlier and nearly got us all kicked out," Aston growled.

They were speaking so quickly, and it was hard to catch up, but this wasn't the first time that I had been awake since coming to the hospital.

"I'm okay," I said after a moment, and everyone stopped speaking and shouting at each other to stare at me.

"Sophia," Isabella whispered, and I swallowed the lump in my throat.

"The girls?" I asked.

"Blakely has them."

"Okay. Okay." Tears threatened again.

"Cale's in custody. We'll make sure he stays there,"

Flynn warned, his gaze intense. Flynn was always the smiling brother, the laughing one. I'd never seen him so serious. But then again sometimes it felt like I was just getting to know my brothers.

And I didn't want them to know me like this.

"I'm sorry," I whispered.

"It's okay, don't be sorry. Everything's going to be okay." Isabella reached out as if to cup my cheek, and I flinched.

I wanted to crawl in a hole and die at the pitying look on her face. But I wouldn't. I had already failed Violet and Hazel before, and I wouldn't do it again.

Unconsciousness swept over me again. By the time I woke up again, there was only one man in the room, and for an instant I thought it was Cale. But I recognized those green eyes.

"Who are you?" I asked, my voice hoarse.

The stranger moved forward, grabbed the pitcher of water, and poured a glass. When he gestured for me to take it from his hands, I forced myself to sit up slightly, and nodded in thanks, ignoring the pain in my head.

"I heard you say you were sorry earlier. You don't get to say that again. You understand me?"

I frowned, ignoring the tug of the stitches on my forehead.

"I know you don't know me from Adam, and that's fine. But your family's going to be back in here hovering, because that's what they do. So you're going to let them because I have a feeling that's what you do. And maybe that's what you need. But don't apologize. I'm the one that needs to apologize."

"I don't even know you."

His lips quirked into a smile that didn't reach his eyes. "No, you wouldn't. That's fine."

"Then why are you apologizing?"

"Because I didn't kill the bastard when I had a chance. Get well, Sophia Cage. Those little girls are too cute for words. And they're going to need their mom."

And with that, he walked out, leaving me just as confused as ever.

But he was right.

My little girls did need their mom.

And that meant I needed to figure out exactly who Sophia Cage was. Broken, lost, and shattered as she was.

Next in the series: Sophia gets her HEA. And her peace in Pretend it's Forever

AND IF YOU'D LIKE TO READ A BONUS SCENE YOU CAN FIND IT HERE! I LOVE THIS SCENE SO MUCH!

If you'd like to read the next Generation with the Montgomery Ink Legacy Series:

Bittersweet Promises

In the mood to read another family saga? Meet the Cage Family in The Forever Rule!

In the mood for more small town romance? Check out the Ashford Creek series with LEGACY. Or as I like to call it "The Small Town of Single Dads".

A Note from Carrie Ann Ryan

Thank you so much for reading One Quick Obsession.

Hudson & Scarlett's romance flew off the pages for me. It was so odd, honestly. Because I'd thought Hudson would be the problem for me. No. Of course not. Instead it was Scarlett. Because she had to be the strong one, as many of us know.

I am so grateful for all of you and the fact that you've embraced the Cages as you have!

The next book is Sophia's book. I have known the path of her story since the start and I've been anticipating and dreading it ever since. I fully cannot wait for her to find her HEA in Pretend it's Forever. You won't be disappointed.

In case you'd like to read Phoebe's romance, you can read about her and Kane in His Second Chance!

And Ford finds his match with Greer and Noah in Best Friend Temptation!

The Cage Family
Book 1: The Forever Rule (Aston & Blakely)
Book 2: An Unexpected Everything (Isabella & Weston)
Book 3: If You Were Mine (Dorian & Harper)
Book 4: One Quick Obsession (Hudson & Scarlett)
Book 5: Pretend it's Forever (Sophia & Carson)
Book 6: Wish it Were You (Flynn & Luna)

If you want to make sure you know what's coming next from me, you can sign up for my newsletter at www.CarrieAnnRyan.com; follow me on twitter at @CarrieAnnRyan, or like my Facebook page. I also have a Facebook Fan Club where we have trivia, chats, and other goodies. You guys are the reason I get to do what I do and I thank you.

Make sure you're signed up for my MAILING LIST so you can know when the next releases are available as well as find giveaways and FREE READS.

Happy Reading!

From One Way Back to Me
Eli

When my morning begins with me standing ankle-deep in a basement full of water, I know I probably should have stayed in bed. Only, I was the boss, and I didn't get that choice.

"Hold on. I'm looking for it." East cursed underneath his breath as my younger brother bent down around the pipe, trying his best to turn off the valve. I sighed, waded through the muck in my work boots, and moved to help him. "I said I've got it," East snapped, but I ignored him.

I narrowed my eyes at the evil pipe. "It's old and rusted, and even though it passed an inspection over a year ago, we knew this was going to be a problem."

"And I'm the fucking handyman of this company. I've got this."

"And as a handyman, you need a hand."

"You're hilarious. Seriously. I don't know how I could ever manage without your wit and humor." The dryness in his tone made my lips twitch even as I did my best to ignore the smell of whatever water we stood in.

"Fuck you," I growled.

"No thanks. I'm a little too busy for that."

With a grunt, East shut off the water, and we both stood back, hands on our hips as we stared at the mess of this basement.

East let out a sigh. "I'm not going to have to turn the water off for the whole property, but I'm glad that we don't have tenants in this particular cabin."

I nodded tightly and held back a sigh. "This is probably why there aren't basements in Texas. Because everything seems to go wrong in these things."

"I'm pretty sure this is a storm shelter, or at least a tornado one. Not quite sure as it's one of the only basements in the area."

"It was probably the only one that they had the energy to make back in the day. Considering this whole place is built over clay and limestone."

East nodded, looked around. "I'll start the cleanup with this water, and we'll look to see what we can do with the pipes."

I pinched the bridge of my nose. "I don't want to have to replace the plumbing for this whole place."

"At least it's not the villa itself, or the farmhouse, or the winery. Just a single cabin."

I glared at my younger brother, then reached out and knocked on a wooden pillar. "Shut your mouth. Don't say things like that to me. We are just now getting our feet under us."

East shrugged. "It's the truth, though. However much you weigh it, it could have been worse."

I pinched the bridge of my nose. "Jesus Christ. You were in the military for how long? A Wilder your entire life, and you say things like that? When the hell did you lose that superstition bone?"

"About the time that my Humvee was blown up, and when Evan's was, Everett's too. Hell, about the time that you almost fell out of the sky in your plane. Or when Elliot was nearly shot to death trying to help one of his men. So, yes, I pretty much lost all superstition when trying to toe the line ended up in near death and maiming."

I met my brother's gaze, that familiar pang thinking about all that we had lost and almost lost over the past few years.

East muttered under his breath, shaking his head. "And I sound more and more like Evan these days rather than myself."

I squeezed his shoulder and let out a breath, thinking of our brother who grunted more than spoke these days. "It's okay. We've been through a lot. But we're here."

Somehow, we were here. I wasn't quite sure if we had made the right decision about two years ago when we had formed this plan, or rather *I* had formed this plan, but there was no going back. We were in it, and we were going to have to find a way to make it work, flooded former tornado shelters and all.

East sighed. "I'll work on this now. Then I'll head on over to the main house. I have a few things to work on there."

"You know, we can hire you help. I know we had all the contractors and everything to work with us for some of the rebuilds and rehabs, but we can hire someone else for you on a day-to-day basis."

My brother shook his head. "We may be able to afford it, but I'd rather save that for a rainy day. Because when it rains, it pours here, and flash flooding is a major threat in this part of Texas." He winked as he said it, mixing his metaphors, and I just shook my head.

"You just let me know if you need it."

"You're the CEO, brother of mine, not the CFO. That's Everett."

"True, but we did talk about it so we can work on it." I paused, thinking about what other expenses might show up. "And what do you need to do with the villa?"

The villa was the main house where most things happened on the property. It contained the lobby, library, and atrium. My apartment was also on the top floor, so I could be there for emergencies. Our innkeeper lived on the other side of the house, but I was in the main loft because this was my project, my baby.

My other brothers, all five of them, lived in cabins on the property. We lived together, worked together, ate together, and fought together. We were the Wilder brothers. It was what we did.

I had left to join the Air Force at seventeen, having graduated early, leaving behind my kid brothers and sister. After nearly twenty years of doing what we needed to in order to survive, we hadn't spent as much time with one another as I would have liked. We hadn't been stationed together, so we hadn't seen one another for longer than holidays or in passing.

But now we were together. At least most of us. So I was going to make this work, even if it killed me.

East finally answered my question. "I just have to fix a door that's a little too squeaky in one of the guestrooms. Not a big deal."

I raised a brow. "That's it?"

"It's one of the many things on my list. Thankfully, this place is big enough that I always have something to do. It's an unending list. And that the winery has its own team to work on all of that shit, because I'm not in the mood to learn to deal with any of the complicated machinery that comes with that world."

I snorted. "Honestly, same. I'm glad there are people that know what the fuck they're doing when it comes to wine making so that didn't have to be the two of us."

I left my brother to this job, knowing he liked time on his own, just like the rest of us did, and went to dry my boots. I was working by myself for most of the day, in interviews and other "boss business," as Elliot called it, so I had to focus and get clean.

I wasn't in the mood to deal with interviews, but it was part of my job. We had to fill positions that hadn't been working out over the past year, some more than others.

Wilder Retreat was a place that hadn't been even a spark in my mind my entire life. No, I had been too busy being a career military man—getting in my twenty, moving up the ranks, and ending up as a Lieutenant Colonel before I got out. I had been a commander of a squadron, and yet, it felt like I didn't know how to command where I was now.

When my sister Eliza had lost her husband when he was on deployment, it had been the last domino to fall in the Wilder brothers' military career. I had been ready to get out with twenty years in, knowing I needed a career outside of being a Lieutenant Colonel. I wasn't even forty yet, and the term retirement was a misnomer, but that's what happened when it came to my former job.

East had been getting out around that time for reasons of his own, and then Evan had been forced to. I rubbed my hand over my chest, that familiar pain, remembering the phone call from one of Evan's commanders when Evan had been hurt.

I thought I'd lost my baby brother then, and we nearly had. Everett had gotten hurt too, and Elijah and Elliot had needed out for their own reasons. Losing our baby sister's husband had just pushed us forward.

Finding out that Eliza's husband had been a cheating asshole had just cemented the fact that we needed to spend more time together as a family so we could be there for one another.

In retrospect, it would have been nice if Eliza would have been able to come down to Texas with us, to our suburb outside of San Antonio. Only, she had fallen in love again, with a man with a big family and a good heart up in Fort Collins, Colorado. She was still up there and traveled down enough that we actually got to get to know our sister again.

It was weird to think that, after so many years of always seeing each other in passing or through video calls, most of us were here, opening up a business. And all because I had been losing my mind.

Wilder Retreat and Winery was a villa and wedding venue outside of San Antonio. We were in hill country, at least what passed for hill country in South Texas, and the place had been owned by a former Air Force

General who had wanted to retire and sell the place, since his kid didn't want it.

It was a large spread that used to be a ranch back in the day, nearly one hundred acres that the original owners had taken from a working ranch, and instead of making it a dude ranch or something similar, like others did around here, they'd added a winery using local help. We were close enough to Fredericksburg that it made sense in terms of the soil and weather. They had been able to add on additions, so it wasn't just the winery. Someone could come for the day for a winery tour or even a retreat tour, but most people came for the weekend or for a whole week. There were cabins and a farmhouse where we held weddings, dances, or other events. We had some chickens and ducks that gave us eggs, and goats that seemed to have a mind of their own and provided milk for cheese. Then there was the main annex, which housed all the equipment for the retreat villa.

The winery had its own section of buildings, and it was far bigger than anything I would have ever thought that we could handle. But, between the six of us, we did.

And the only reason we could even afford it, because one didn't afford something like this on a military salary, even with a decent retirement plan, was because of our uncles.

Our uncles, Edward and Edmond Wilder, had

owned Wilder Wines down in Napa, California, for years. They had done well for themselves, and when we had been kids, we had gone out to visit. Evan had been the one that had clung to it and had been interested in wine making before he had changed his mind and gone into the military like the rest of us.

That was why Evan was in charge of the winery itself now. Because he knew what he was doing, even if he'd growled and said he didn't. Either way though, the place was huge, had multiple working parts at all times, and we had a staff that needed us. But when the uncles had died, they had left the money from the sale of the winery to us in equal parts. Eliza had taken hers to invest for her future children, and the rest of us had pooled our money together to buy this place and make it ours. A lot of the staff from the old owner had stayed, but some had left as well. Because they didn't want new owners who had no idea what they were doing, or they just retired. Either way, we were over a year in and doing okay.

Except for two positions that made me want to groan.

I had an interview with who would be our third wedding planner since we started this. The main component of the retreat was to have an actual wedding venue. To be able to host parties, and not just wine tours. Elliot was our major event planner that helped with our yearly and seasonal minute details, but he didn't want anything to do with the actual weddings. That was a whole other skill set, and so we wanted a wedding planner. We had gone through two wedding planners now, and we needed to hire a third. The first one had lied on her résumé, had given references that were her friends who had lied and had even created websites that were all fabrication, all so she could get into the business. Which, I understood, getting into the business is one thing. However, lying was another. Plus, we needed someone with actual experience because we didn't have any ourselves. We were going out on a limb here with this whole retreat business, and it was all because I had the harebrained idea of getting our family to work together, get along, and get to know one another. I wanted us to have a future, to be our own bosses.

And it was so far over my head that I knew that if I didn't get reliable help, we were going to fail.

Later, I had a meeting with that potential wedding planner. But first, I had to see what the fuck that smell was coming from the main kitchen in the villa.

The second wedding planner we hired was a guy with great and *true* references, one who was good at his job but hated everything to do with my brothers and me. He had hated the idea of the retreat and how rustic it was, even though we were in fucking South Texas. Yes, the buildings look slightly European because that was the theme that the original owners had gone for.

Still, the guy had hated us, hadn't listened to us, and had called us white trash before he had walked away, jumped into his convertible, and sped off down the road, leaving us without help. He had been rude to our guests, and now Elliot was the one having to plan weddings for the past three weeks. My brother was going to strangle me soon if we didn't hire someone. And this person was going to be our last hope. As soon as she showed up, that was.

I looked down on my watch and tried to plan the rest of my day. I had thirty minutes to figure out what the hell was going on in the kitchen, and then I had to go to the meeting.

I nodded at a few guests who were sipping wine and eating a cheese plate and then at our innkeeper, Naomi. Naomi's honey-brown hair was cut in an angled bob that lit her face, and she grinned at me.

"Hello there, Boss Man," she whispered. "You might need to go to the kitchen."

"Do I want to know?" I asked with a grumble.

"I'm not sure. But I am going to go check in our next guest, and then Elliott needs to meet with the Henderson couple."

"He'll be there." I didn't say that Elliot would rather chew off his own arm rather than deal with this, considering we had a family event coming in, one that Elliot was on target with planning. The wedding for next year was an important one, so we needed to work on it.

Naomi was a fantastic innkeeper, far more organized than any of us—and that was saying something since my brothers and I knew our way around schedules, to-do lists, and spreadsheets. Naomi was personable, smiled, and kept us on our toes.

Without her, I knew we wouldn't be able to do this. Hell, without Amos, our vineyard manager, I knew that Evan and Elijah wouldn't be able to handle the winery as they did. Naomi and Amos had come with the place when we had bought it, and I would be forever grateful that they had decided to stay on.

I gave Naomi another nod, then headed back to the kitchen and nearly walked right back out.

Tony stood there, a scowl on his face and his hands on his hips. "I don't understand what the fuck is wrong with this oven."

"What's going on?" I asked as Everett stood by Tony. Everett was my quiet brother with usually a small smile on his face, only right then it looked like he was ready to scream.

I didn't know why Everett was even there since he was part responsible for the financials side of the company and usually worked with Elliot these days. Maybe he had come to the kitchen after the smell of burning as I had after Naomi's prodding.

Tony threw his hands in the air. "What's going on?

This stove is a piece of shit. All of it is a piece of shit. I'm tired of this rustic place. I thought I would be coming to a Michelin star restaurant. To be my own chef. Instead, I have to make English breakfasts and pancakes with bananas. I might as well be at a bed and breakfast."

I pinched the bridge of my nose. "We're an inn, not a bed and breakfast."

"But I serve breakfast. That's all I do these days. That and cheese platters. Nobody comes for dinner. Nobody comes for lunch."

That was a lie. Tony worked for the winery and the retreat itself and served all the meals. But Tony wanted to go crazy with the menu, to try new and fantastical items that just weren't going to work here.

And I had a feeling I was going to throw up if I wasn't careful.

"I quit," Tony snapped, and I knew right then, it was done for. I was done.

"You can't quit," I growled while Everett held back a sigh.

"Yes, I can. I'm done. I'm done with you and this ranch. You're not cowboys. You're not even Texans. You're just people moving in on our territory." And with that, Tony stomped away, throwing his chef's apron on the ground.

I was thankful that the kitchen was on the other side of the library and front area, where most of the guests were if they weren't out on one of the tours of the area and city that Elliott had arranged for them. That was the whole point of this retreat. They could come visit, and could relax, or we could set them up on a tour of downtown San Antonio, or Canyon Lake, or any of the other places that were nearby.

And yet, Tony had just thrown a wrench into all of that. I didn't know what was worse, the smell of burning, Tony leaving, the water in the basement that wasn't truly a basement, or the fact that I was going to smell like charred food and wet jeans when I went to go meet this wedding planner.

"You're going to need to hire a new cook," Everett whispered.

I looked at my brother, at the man who did his best to make sure we didn't go bankrupt, and I wanted to just grumble. "I figured."

"I can help for now, but you know I'm only part-time. I can't stay away from my twins for too long," Sandy said as she came forward to take the pan off the stove. "I wish I could do full time, but this is all I can do for now."

Sandy had come back from maternity leave after we had already opened the retreat. She had been on with the former owners and was brilliant. But she had a right to be a mom and not want to work full time. I understood that, and I knew that Sandy didn't want to handle a whole kitchen by herself. She liked her position as a sous chef.

I was going to have to figure out what to do. Again.

"I'll get it done," I said while rubbing my temples.

"You know what we need to do," Everett whispered, and I shook my head.

"He'll kill us."

"Maybe, but it'll be worth it in the end. And speaking of, don't you have that interview soon? Or do you want me to take it?" His gaze tracked to my jeans.

I shook my head. "No, help Sandy."

Everett winced. "Just because I know how to slice an onion, it doesn't mean I'm good at cooking."

"I'm sorry, did you just say you could slice an onion? Get to it," Sandy put in with a smile, pointing at the sink. "Wash those hands."

"I cannot believe I just said that out loud. I just stepped right into it," Everett said with a sigh. "Go to the interview. You know what to ask."

"I do. And I hope we don't get screwed this time."

"You know, if we're lucky, we'll get someone as good as Roy's wedding planner, or at least that woman that we met. You know who she is." Everett grinned like a cat with the canary.

I narrowed my eyes. "Don't bring her up."

"Oh, I can't help it. A single dance, and you were drawn to her."

"What dance? You know what? No, I don't have

time. We have to work on lunch and dinner. Tell me while you work," Sandy added with a wink.

Everett leaned toward her as he washed his hands. "Well, you see, there was this dance, and he met the perfect woman, and then she got engaged."

Sandy's eyes widened. "Engaged? How did that happen? She was dating someone else?" she asked as she looked at me.

I pinched the bridge of my nose. "It was at Roy's place when we were looking at the venue to see if we wanted to buy the retreat here." I sighed, I knew if I just let it all out, she would move on from this conversation, and I would never have to deal with it again. "Somehow, I ended up at a wedding there, caught the garter. This woman caught the bouquet, and she happened to be the wedding planner. We danced, we laughed, and as she walked away, her boyfriend got down on one knee and proposed."

"No way!" She leaned forward with a fierce look on her face, her eyes bright. "What did she say?"

"I have no clue. I left." I ignored whatever feeling might want to show up at that thought. Everett gave me a glance, and I shook my head. "Enough of that. Yes, the wedding that she did was great, but I honestly have no idea who she is, and she has a job. She doesn't need to work here." And I didn't know what I would do if I saw her again or had to work with her. There had been such an intense connection that I knew it would be awkward as hell. But thankfully, she had her own business and wasn't going to come to the Wilder Retreat for a job.

I left Sandy and Everett on their own, knowing that they were capable, at least for now. And I knew who we would have to hire if she said yes, and if my other brother didn't kill me first.

I washed my hands in the sink on the way out, grateful that at least I looked somewhat decent, if not a little disheveled, and made my way out front, hoping that the wedding planner who came in through the doors would be the one that would stick. Because we needed some good luck. After the day we've had, we needed some good luck.

I turned the corner and nearly tripped over my feet.

Because, of course, fate was this way.

It was her.

Of all the wedding planners from all the wedding venues, it was her.

In the mood to read another family saga? Meet the Wilder Brothers in One Way Back to Me!

From Bittersweet Promises
Leif

"Not only did you convince me to somehow go on a blind date, it became a double date. How on earth did you work this magic on me, cousin?" I asked Lake as she leaned against the pillar just inside the restaurant.

Lake grinned at me, her dark hair pulled away from her face. She had on this swingy black dress and looked as if she were excited, anxious, nervous, and happy all at the same time. Considering she was bouncing on her toes when usually Lake was calm, cool, and collected, was saying something. "I asked, and you said yes. Because you love me."

"I might love you because we're family, but I still think we're making a mistake." I shook my head and pulled at my shirt sleeves. Lake had somehow convinced me to wear a button-up shirt tucked into gray pants, I even had on shiny shoes. I looked like a damn banker. But if that's what Lake wanted, that's what I would do.

Lake might technically be my cousin, even though we weren't blood-related, but we were more like brother and sister than any of my other cousins.

I had siblings, as did Lake, but with the generational gap, we were at least a decade older than all of our other cousins. That meant, despite the fact that we had lived over an hour apart for most of our lives, we'd grown up more like siblings.

I loved my three younger siblings and talked to them daily. Unlike some blended families, they *were* my brothers and sister and not like strangers or distant family members. I didn't feel a disconnect from the three of them, but Lake was still closer to me.

Probably because we were either heading into our thirties or already there, where most of our other cousins were either just now in their early twenties or still teenagers in high school. With how big we Montgomerys were as a family, it made sense that there would be such a widespread age group. That meant that Lake and I were best friends, cousins, practically siblings, and sometimes the banes of each other's existences.

We were also business owners and partners and saw each other too often these days. That was probably why she convinced me to go on a blind double date.

But she had been out with Zach before. I, however, had never met May. Lake had some connection with her that I wasn't sure about, and for some reason Lake's date had said yes to this double date.

And, in the complicated way of family, I had agreed to it. I must have been tired. Or perhaps I'd had too many beers. Because I didn't do blind dates, and recently, I didn't do dates at all.

Lake scanned her phone, then looked up at me, all innocence in her smart gaze. "You shouldn't have told me you wanted to settle down in your old age."

I narrowed my eyes. "I'm still in my early thirties, jerk. Stop calling me old."

"I shouldn't call you old since you're only a few years older than me." She fluttered her eyelashes and I flipped her off, ignoring the stare from the older woman next to me. Though I was a tattoo artist, I didn't have many visible tattoos. Most of mine were on my back and legs, hidden from the world unless I wanted to show them. I hadn't figured out what I wanted on my arms beyond a few small pieces on my wrists and upper shoulders. And since tattoos were permanent, I was taking my time. If a client needed to see my skin with ink to feel comfortable, I'd show them my back. My body was a canvas, so I did what I could to set people at ease.

But I still had the eyebrow piercing and had recently taken out my nose ring. I didn't look too scary for most people. But apparently, flipping off a woman, growling, and cursing a time or two in front of strangers probably made me appear too close to the dark side.

"Yes, I want to settle down, but this will be awkward, won't it? Where the two of us are strangers, and the two of you aren't?" I wanted a life, a future, and yeah, one day to settle down with someone. I just didn't know why I'd mentioned it to Lake in the first place.

"If it helps, May doesn't know Zach, either. So it's a group of strangers, except I know everybody." She clapped her hands together and did her version of an evil laugh, and I just shook my head.

"Considering what you do for a living and how you like to manipulate things in your way, this makes sense. Are you going to be adding a matchmaking company to your conglomerate?"

Lake just fluttered her eyelashes again and laughed. Lake owned a small tech company that made a shit ton of money over the past couple of years. And because she was brilliant at what she did, innovative, and liked pushing money towards women-owned businesses, she owned more than one company at this point and was an investor in mine. I wouldn't be surprised if she found a way to open up a women-owned matchmaking company right here in town.

"It might be fun. I can call it Montgomery Links."

Her eyes went wide. "Oh, my God. I have to write that down." She pulled out her phone, began to take notes, and I pinched the bridge of my nose.

"You know I trust you with my actual life, but I don't know if I trust you with my dating life."

Lake tossed her hair behind her shoulder as she continued to type. "Shut up. You love me. And once I finish setting you up, the rest of the family's next."

"Oh, really? You're going to get Daisy and Noah next?" I asked, speaking of two more of our cousins.

"Maybe. Of course, Sebastian's the only one of the younger group that seems to have a serious girlfriend."

I nodded, speaking of our other familial business partner. Sebastian was still a teenager, though in college. He had wanted to open up Montgomery Ink Legacy with me, the full title of our company. There was a legacy to it, and Sebastian had wanted in. So, though he didn't work there full-time, he was putting his future towards us. And in the ways of young love, he and his girlfriend had been together since middle school. The fact that my younger cousin was better at relationships than I was didn't make me feel great. But I was going to ignore that.

"You're not going to start up a matchmaking service, are you? Or maybe an app?"

"Dating apps are ridiculous these days, they practically want you to invest in coins to bid on dates, and that's not something I'm in the mood for. But maybe there's something I can try. I'll add it to my list."

Lake's list of inventions and tech was notorious, and knowing the brilliance of my cousin, she would one day rule the world and might eventually cross everything off that list.

"Oh, here's Zach." Lake's face brightened immediately, and she smiled up at a man with dark hair, piercing gray eyes, and an actual dimple on his cheek.

Tonight was not only about my blind date, but me getting the lay of the land when it came to Zach. I was the first step into meeting the family. Oh, if Zach passed my gauntlet, he would meet the rest of the Montgomerys, and we were mighty. All one hundred of us.

"Zach, you're here." Lake's voice went soft, and she went on her tiptoes even in her high heels as Zach pressed a soft kiss to her lips.

"Of course, I'm here. And you're early, as usual."

Lake blushed and ducked her head. "Well, you know me. I like to be early because being on time is late," she said at the same time I did, mumbling under my breath. It was a familiar refrain when it came to us.

"Zach, good to meet you," I said, holding out my hand.

The other man gripped it firmly and shook. "Nice to meet you too, Leif. I know you might be the one on a blind date soon, but I'm nervous."

I chuckled, shaking my head. "Yeah, I'm pretty nervous too. Though I'm grateful that Lake's trying to look out for me."

My cousin laughed softly. "You totally were not saying that a few minutes ago, but be suave and sophisticated now. Or just be yourself, May's on her way."

I met Zach's gaze and we both rolled our eyes. When I turned toward the door, I saw a woman of average height, with black straight hair, green eyes, and a sweet smile. I didn't know much about May, other than Lake knew her and liked her. If I was going to start dating again after taking time off to get the rest of my life together, I might as well start with someone that one of my best friends liked.

"May, I'm so glad that you're here," Lake said as she hugged the other woman tightly.

As Lake began to bounce on her heels, I realized that my cousin's cool, calm, and collected exterior was only for work. She was bouncing and happy when it came to her friends or when she was nervous. I knew that, of course, but I had forgotten how she had turned into the mogul that she was. It was good to see her relaxed and happy.

Now I just needed to figure out how to do that for myself.

May stood in front of me, and I felt like I was starting middle school all over again. A new school, a new life, and a past that didn't make much sense to anyone else.

I swallowed hard and nodded, not putting out my hand to shake, thinking that would be weird, but I also didn't want to hug her. I didn't even know this woman. Why was everything so awkward? Instead, I lifted my chin. "Hello, May. It's nice to meet you. Lake says only good things."

There, smooth. Not really. Zach began to move out of frame, with Lake at his side as the two went to speak to the hostess, leaving May and me alone.

This wasn't going to be awkward at all.

The woman just smiled at me, her eyes wide. "It's nice to meet you, too. And Lake does speak highly of you. Also, this is very awkward, so I'm so sorry if I say something stupid. I know that your cousin said that I should be set up with you which is great but I'm not great at blind dates and apparently this is a double date and now I'm going to stop talking." She said the words so quickly they all ran into one breath.

I shook my head and laughed. "We're on the same page there."

"Okay, good. It's nice to meet you, Leif Montgomery."

"And it's nice to meet you too, May."

We made our way to Lake and Zach, who had gotten our table, and we all sat down, talking about work and other things. May was in child life development, taught online classes, and was also a nanny.

"I'm actually about to start with a new family soon. I'm excited. I know that being a nanny isn't something that most people strive for, or at least that's what they tell you, but I love being able to work with children and be the person that is there when a single parent or even both parents are out in the workforce, trying to do everything."

I nodded, taking a sip of my beer. "I get you completely. With how my parents worked, I was lucky that they were able to get childcare within the buildings. Since they each owned their own businesses, they made it work. But my family worked long hours, and that's why I ended up being the babysitter a lot of the times when childcare wasn't an option." I cleared my throat. "I'm a lot older than a lot of my cousins," I added.

"Both of us are, but I'm glad that you only said yourself," Lake said, grinning. She leaned into Zach as she spoke, the four of us in a horseshoe-shaped booth. That gave May and me space since this was a first date and still awkward as hell, and so Lake and Zach could cuddle. Not that that was something I needed to be a part of.

"Oh, I'm glad that you didn't judge. The last few dates that I've been on they always gave me weird looks because I think they expected a nanny to be this old crone or someone that's looking for a different job." She shrugged and continued. "When I eventually get married and maybe even start a family, I want to continue my job. I like being there to help another family achieve their goals. And I can't believe I just said start a family on my first date. And that I mentioned that I've been on a few other dates." She let out a breath. "I'm notoriously bad at dating. Like, the worst. Just warning you."

I laughed, shaking my head. "I'm rusty at it, so don't worry." And even though I said that, I had a feeling that May felt no spark towards me, and I didn't feel anything towards her. She was nice and pleasant, and I could probably consider her a friend one day. But there wasn't any spark. May's eyes weren't dancing. She wasn't leaning forward, trying to touch my hand across the table. We were just sitting there casually, enjoying a really good steak, as Lake and Zach enjoyed their date.

By the end of dinner, I didn't want dessert, and neither did May, so we said goodbye to the other couple, who decided to stay. I walked May to her car, ignoring Lake's warning look, but I didn't know what exactly she was warning me about.

"Thanks for dinner," May said. "I could have paid. I know this is a blind date and all that, but you didn't have to pay."

I shook my head. "I paid for the four of us because I wanted to be nice. I'll make Lake pay next time."

May beamed. "Yes, I like that. You guys are a good family."

"Anyway," I said, clearing my throat as I stuck my hands in my pockets. "I guess I'll see you around."

May just looked at me, threw her head back, and laughed. "You're right. You are rusty at this."

"Sorry." Heat flushed my skin, and I resisted the urge to tug on my eyebrow ring.

"It's okay. No spark. I'm used to it. I don't spark well."

"May, I'm sorry." I cringed. "It's not you."

"Oh, God, please don't say that. 'It's not you. It's me. You're working on yourself. You're just so busy with work.' I've heard it all."

"Seriously?" I asked. May was hot. Nice, but there just wasn't a spark.

She shrugged. "It's okay. I'll probably see you around sometime because I am friends with Lake. However, I am perfectly fine having this be our one and only. You'll find your person. It's okay that it's not me." And with that, she got in the car and left, leaving me standing there.

Well then. Tonight wasn't horrible, but it wasn't great. I got in my car, and instead of heading home where I'd be alone, watching something on some streaming service while I drank a beer and pretended that I knew what I was doing with my life, I headed into Montgomery Ink Legacy.

We were the third branch of the company and the first owned by our generation. Montgomery Ink was the tattoo shop in downtown Denver. While there were open spots for some walk-ins and special circumstances, my father, aunt, and their team had years' worth of waiting lists. They worked their asses off and made sure to get in everybody that they could, but people wanted Austin Montgomery's art. Same with my aunt, Maya.

There was another tattoo shop down in Colorado Springs, owned by my parents' cousins, who I just called aunt and uncle because we were close enough that using real titles for everybody got confusing. Montgomery Ink Too was thriving down there, and they had waiting lists as well. My family could have opened more shops and gone nationwide, even global if they wanted to, but they liked keeping it how it was, in the family and those connected.

We were a branch, but our own in the making. I had gone into business with Lake, of course, and Sebastian, when he was ready, as well as Nick. Nick was my best friend. I had known him for ages, and he had wanted to be part of something as well. He might not be a Montgomery by name, but he had eaten over at my family's house enough times throughout the years that he was practically a Montgomery. And he had invested in the company as well, and so now we were nearly a year into owning the shop and trying not to fail.

I pulled into the parking lot, grateful it was still open since we didn't close until nine most nights, and greeted Nick, who was still working.

Sebastian was in the back, going over sketches with a client, and I nodded at him. He might be eighteen, but he was still in training, an apprentice, and was working his ass off to learn.

"Date sucked then?" Sebastian asked, and Nick just rolled his eyes and went back to work on a client's wrist.

"I don't want to talk about it," I groaned.

The rest of the staff was off since Nick would close up on his own. Sebastian was just there since he didn't have homework or a date with Marley.

"Was she hot at least?" Sebastian asked, and the client, a woman in her sixties, bopped him on the head with her bag gently.

"Sebastian Montgomery. Be nice."

Sebastian blushed. "Sorry, Mrs. Anderson."

I looked over at the woman and grinned. "Hi, Mrs. Anderson. It's nice to see you out of the classroom."

She narrowed her eyes at me, even though they filled with laughter. "I needed my next Jane Austen tattoo, thank you very much," the older woman said as she went back to working with Sebastian. She had been my and then Sebastian's English teacher. The fact that she was on her fifth tattoo with some literary quote told me that I had been damn lucky in most of my teachers growing up.

She was kick-ass, and I had a feeling that she would let Sebastian do the tattoo for her rather than just have him work on the design with me as we did for most of the people who came in. He had learned under my father and was working under me now. It was strange to think that he wasn't a little kid anymore. But he was in a long-term relationship, kicking ass in college, and knew what he wanted to do with his life.

I might know what I want to do with my work life, but everything else seemed a little off.

"So it didn't work out?" Nick asked as he walked up to the front desk with the clients after going over aftercare.

"Not really," I said, looking down at my phone.

The client, a woman in her mid-twenties with bright pink hair, a lip ring, and kind eyes, leaned over the desk to look at me.

"You'll find someone, Leif. Don't worry."

I looked at our regular and shook my head. "Thanks, Kim. Too bad that you don't swing this way."

I winked as I said it, a familiar refrain from both of us.

Kim was married to a woman named Sonya, and

the two of them were happy and working on in vitro with donated sperm for their first kid.

"Hey, I'm sorry too that I'm a lesbian. I'll never know what it means to have Leif Montgomery. Or any Montgomery, since I found my love far too quickly. I mean, what am I ever going to do not knowing the love of a Montgomery?"

Mrs. Anderson chuckled from her chair, Sebastian held back a snort, and I just looked at Nick, who rolled his eyes and helped Kim out of the place.

I was tired, but it was okay. The date wasn't all bad. May was nice. But it felt like I didn't have much right then.

And then Nick sat in front of me, scowled, and I realized that I did have something. I had my friends and my family. I didn't need much more.

"So, you and May didn't work out?"

I raised a brow. "You knew her name? Did I tell you that?"

Nick shook his head. "Lake did."

That made sense, considering the two of them spoke as much as we did. "So, was it your idea to set me up on a blind date?"

"Fuck no. That was all Lake. I just do what she says. Like we all do."

I sighed and went through my appointments for the next day. "We're busy for the next month. That's good, right?" I asked.

"You're the business genius here. I just play with ink. But yes, that's good. Now, don't let your cousin set you up any more dates. Find them for yourself. You know what you're doing."

"So says the man who dates less than me."

"That's what you think. I'm more private about it. As it should be." I flipped him off as he stood up, then he gestured towards a stack of bills in the corner. "You have a few personal things that made their way here. Don't want you to miss out on them before you head home."

"Thanks, bro."

"No problem. I'm going to help Sebastian with his consult, and then I'll clean up. You should head home. Though you're doing it alone, so I feel sorry for you."

"Fuck you," I called out.

"Fuck you, too."

"Boys," Mrs. Anderson said, in that familiar English teacher refrain, and both Nick and I cringed before saying, "Sorry," simultaneously.

Sebastian snickered, then went back to work, and I headed towards the edge of the counter, picking up the stack of papers. Most were bills, some were random papers that needed to be filed or looked over. Some were just junk mail. But there was one letter, written in block print that didn't look familiar. Chills went up my spine and I opened it, wondering what the fuck this was. Maybe it was someone asking to buy my house. I got a lot of handwritten letters for that, but I didn't think this was going to be that. I swallowed hard, slid open the paper, and froze.

"I'll find you, boy. Oops. Looks like I already did. Be waiting. I know you miss me."

I let the paper hit the top of the counter and swallowed hard, trying to remain cool so I didn't worry anyone else.

I didn't know exactly who that was from, but I had a horrible feeling that they wouldn't wait long to tell me.

Read the rest in Bittersweet Promises! OUT NOW!

Also from Carrie Ann Ryan

The Montgomery Ink Legacy Series:
Book 1: Bittersweet Promises (Leif & Brooke)
Book 2: At First Meet (Nick & Lake)
Book 2.5: Happily Ever Never (May & Leo)
Book 3: Longtime Crush (Sebastian & Raven)
Book 4: Best Friend Temptation (Noah, Ford, and Greer)
Book 4.5: Happily Ever Maybe (Jennifer & Gus)
Book 5: Last First Kiss (Daisy & Hugh)
Book 6: His Second Chance (Kane & Phoebe)
Book 7: One Night with You (Kingston & Claire)
Book 8: Accidentally Forever (Crew & Aria)
Book 9: Last Chance Seduction (Lexington & Mercy)
Book 10: Kiss Me Forever (Brooklyn & Reece)
Book 11: His Guilty Pleasure (Dash & Aly)

Also from Carrie Ann Ryan

Book 12: Maybe it's You (Riley & Gage)

The Cage Family

Book 1: The Forever Rule (Aston & Blakely)
Book 2: An Unexpected Everything (Isabella & Weston)
Book 3: If You Were Mine (Dorian & Harper)
Book 4: One Quick Obsession (Hudson & Scarlett)
Book 5: Pretend it's Forever (Sophia & Carson)
Book 6: Wish it Were You (Flynn & Luna)

Ashford Creek

Book 1: Legacy (Callum & Felicity)
Book 2: Crossroads (Bodhi & Kiera)
Book 3: Westward (Atlas & Elizabeth)
Book 4: Patience (Teagan & Rush)

Clover Lake

Book 1: Always a Fake Bridesmaid (Livvy & Ewan)
Book 2: Accidental Runaway Groom (Jamie & Sharp)
Book 3: His Practically Fake Proposal (Galen & Addy)

The Wilder Brothers Series:

Book 1: One Way Back to Me (Eli & Alexis)
Book 2: Always the One for Me (Evan & Kendall)

Also from Carrie Ann Ryan

Book 3: The Path to You (Everett & Bethany)
Book 4: Coming Home for Us (Elijah & Maddie)
Book 5: Stay Here With Me (East & Lark)
Book 6: Finding the Road to Us (Elliot, Trace, and Sidney)
Book 7: Moments for You (Ridge & Aurora)
Book 7.5: A Wilder Wedding (Amos & Naomi)
Book 8: Forever For Us (Wyatt & Ava)
Book 9: Pieces of Me (Gabriel & Briar)
Book 10: Endlessly Yours (Brooks & Rory)

The Falling for the Cassidy Brothers Series:
(Formerly the First Time Series)
Book 1: Good Time Boyfriend (Heath & Devney)
Book 2: Last Minute Fiancé (Luca & Addison)
Book 3: Second Chance Husband (August & Paisley)

Montgomery Ink Denver:
Book 0.5: Ink Inspired (Shep & Shea)
Book 0.6: Ink Reunited (Sassy, Rare, and Ian)
Book 1: Delicate Ink (Austin & Sierra)
Book 1.5: Forever Ink (Callie & Morgan)
Book 2: Tempting Boundaries (Decker and Miranda)
Book 3: Harder than Words (Meghan & Luc)
Book 3.5: Finally Found You (Mason & Presley)
Book 4: Written in Ink (Griffin & Autumn)

Book 4.5: Hidden Ink (Hailey & Sloane)
Book 5: Ink Enduring (Maya, Jake, and Border)
Book 6: Ink Exposed (Alex & Tabby)
Book 6.5: Adoring Ink (Holly & Brody)
Book 6.6: Love, Honor, & Ink (Arianna & Harper)
Book 7: Inked Expressions (Storm & Everly)
Book 7.3: Dropout (Grayson & Kate)
Book 7.5: Executive Ink (Jax & Ashlynn)
Book 8: Inked Memories (Wes & Jillian)
Book 8.5: Inked Nights (Derek & Olivia)
Book 8.7: Second Chance Ink (Brandon & Lauren)
Book 8.5: Montgomery Midnight Kisses (Alex & Tabby Bonus(
Bonus: Inked Kingdom (Stone & Sarina)

Montgomery Ink: Colorado Springs
Book 1: Fallen Ink (Adrienne & Mace)
Book 2: Restless Ink (Thea & Dimitri)
Book 2.5: Ashes to Ink (Abby & Ryan)
Book 3: Jagged Ink (Roxie & Carter)
Book 3.5: Ink by Numbers (Landon & Kaylee)

The Montgomery Ink: Boulder Series:
Book 1: Wrapped in Ink (Liam & Arden)
Book 2: Sated in Ink (Ethan, Lincoln, and Holland)
Book 3: Embraced in Ink (Bristol & Marcus)
Book 3: Moments in Ink (Zia & Meredith)
Book 4: Seduced in Ink (Aaron & Madison)

Book 4.5: Captured in Ink (Julia, Ronin, & Kincaid)
Book 4.7: Inked Fantasy (Secret ??)
Book 4.8: A Very Montgomery Christmas (The Entire Boulder Family)

The Montgomery Ink: Fort Collins Series:
    Book 1: Inked Persuasion (Jacob & Annabelle)
    Book 2: Inked Obsession (Beckett & Eliza)
    Book 3: Inked Devotion (Benjamin & Brenna)
    Book 3.5: Nothing But Ink (Clay & Riggs)
    Book 4: Inked Craving (Lee & Paige)
    Book 5: Inked Temptation (Archer & Killian)

The Promise Me Series:
    Book 1: Forever Only Once (Cross & Hazel)
    Book 2: From That Moment (Prior & Paris)
    Book 3: Far From Destined (Macon & Dakota)
    Book 4: From Our First (Nate & Myra)

The Whiskey and Lies Series:
    Book 1: Whiskey Secrets (Dare & Kenzie)
    Book 2: Whiskey Reveals (Fox & Melody)
    Book 3: Whiskey Undone (Loch & Ainsley)

The Gallagher Brothers Series:
    Book 1: Love Restored (Graham & Blake)
    Book 2: Passion Restored (Owen & Liz)

Also from Carrie Ann Ryan

Book 3: Hope Restored (Murphy & Tessa)

The Carr Family Series:
(Formerly the Less Than Series)
Book 1: Breathless With Her (Devin & Erin)
Book 2: Reckless With You (Tucker & Amelia)
Book 3: Shameless With Him (Caleb & Zoey)

The Fractured Connections Series:
Book 1: Breaking Without You (Cameron & Violet)
Book 2: Shouldn't Have You (Brendon & Harmony)
Book 3: Falling With You (Aiden & Sienna)
Book 4: Taken With You (Beckham & Meadow)

The Campus Roommates Series:
(Formerly the On My Own Series)
Book 0.5: My First Glance
Book 1: My One Night (Dillon & Elise)
Book 2: My Rebound (Pacey & Mackenzie)
Book 3: My Next Play (Miles & Nessa)
Book 4: My Bad Decisions (Tanner & Natalie)

The Ravenwood Coven Series:
Book 1: Dawn Unearthed
Book 2: Dusk Unveiled
Book 3: Evernight Unleashed

Also from Carrie Ann Ryan

The Aspen Pack Series:
- Book 1: Etched in Honor
- Book 2: Hunted in Darkness
- Book 3: Mated in Chaos
- Book 4: Harbored in Silence
- Book 5: Marked in Flames

The Talon Pack:
- Book 1: Tattered Loyalties
- Book 2: An Alpha's Choice
- Book 3: Mated in Mist
- Book 4: Wolf Betrayed
- Book 5: Fractured Silence
- Book 6: Destiny Disgraced
- Book 7: Eternal Mourning
- Book 8: Strength Enduring
- Book 9: Forever Broken
- Book 10: Mated in Darkness
- Book 11: Fated in Winter

Redwood Pack Series:
- Book 0.5: An Alpha's Path
- Book 1: A Taste for a Mate
- Book 2: Trinity Bound
- Book 2.5: A Night Away
- Book 3: Enforcer's Redemption
- Book 3.5: Blurred Expectations
- Book 3.7: Forgiveness

Also from Carrie Ann Ryan

    Book 4: <u>Shattered Emotions</u>
    Book 5: <u>Hidden Destiny</u>
    Book 5.5: <u>A Beta's Haven</u>
    Book 6: <u>Fighting Fate</u>
    Book 6.5: <u>Loving the Omega</u>
    Book 6.7: <u>The Hunted Heart</u>
    Book 7: <u>Wicked Wolf</u>

The Elements of Five Series:
    Book 1: From Breath and Ruin
    Book 2: From Flame and Ash
    Book 3: From Spirit and Binding
    Book 4: From Shadow and Silence

Dante's Circle Series:
    Book 1: <u>Dust of My Wings</u>
    Book 2: <u>Her Warriors' Three Wishes</u>
    Book 3: <u>An Unlucky Moon</u>
    Book 3.5: <u>His Choice</u>
    Book 4: <u>Tangled Innocence</u>
    Book 5: <u>Fierce Enchantment</u>
    Book 6: <u>An Immortal's Song</u>
    Book 7: <u>Prowled Darkness</u>
    Book 8: Dante's Circle Reborn

Holiday, Montana Series:
    Book 1: <u>Charmed Spirits</u>
    Book 2: <u>Santa's Executive</u>

Book 3: Finding Abigail
Book 4: Her Lucky Love
Book 5: Dreams of Ivory

The Branded Pack Series:
(Written with Alexandra Ivy)
Book 1: Stolen and Forgiven
Book 2: Abandoned and Unseen
Book 3: Buried and Shadowed

About the Author

Carrie Ann Ryan is the New York Times and USA Today bestselling author of contemporary, paranormal, and young adult romance. Her works include the Montgomery Ink, Redwood Pack, Fractured Connections, and Elements of Five series, which have sold over 3.0 million books worldwide. She started writing while in graduate school for her advanced degree in chemistry and hasn't stopped since. Carrie Ann has written over seventy-five novels and novellas with more in the works. When she's not losing herself in her emotional and action-packed worlds, she's reading as much as she can while wrangling her clowder of cats who have more followers than she does.

www.CarrieAnnRyan.com

www.ingramcontent.com/pod-product-compliance
Lightning Source LLC
LaVergne TN
LVHW031535060526
838200LV00056B/4511